DOMAIN AT YAUMGAN

FIRST CENTURION KOSNETT
BOOK 6

BLAZE WARD

KNOTTED ROAD PRESS

Domain at Yaumgam
First Centurion Kosnett, Book 6
Blaze Ward
Copyright © 2022 Blaze Ward
All rights reserved
Published by Knotted Road Press
www.KnottedRoadPress.com

ISBN: 978-1-64470-317-5

Cover art:
Illustration 13886745 © Luca Oleastri | Dreamstime.com

Cover and interior design copyright © 2022 Knotted Road Press

Reviews
It's true. Reviews help. Even a short one, such as, "Loved it!" So please consider reviewing this book (and all of the ones you've read) on your favorite retailer site.

Never miss a release!
If you'd like to be notified of new releases, sign up for my newsletter.

http://www.blazeward.com/newsletter/

Buy More!
Did you know that you can buy directly from my website?

https://www.blazeward.com/shop/

ALSO BY BLAZE WARD

First Centurion Kosnett

Encounter at Vilahana

Consensus at Aditi

Hegemony at Dalou

Princes at Ewin

Empire at Gloran

Domain at Yaumgan

The Jessica Keller Chronicles

Auberon

Queen of the Pirates

Last of the Immortals

Goddess of War

Flight of the Blackbird

The Red Admiral

St. Legier

Winterhome

Petron

CS-405

Queen Anne's Revenge

Packmule

Persephone

Additional Alexandria Station Stories

The Story Road

Siren

Two Bottles of Wine With A War God

The Science Officer Series Season One

The Science Officer

The Mind Field

The Gilded Cage

The Pleasure Dome

The Doomsday Vault

The Last Flagship

The Hammerfield Gambit

The Hammerfield Payoff

The Bryce Connection

The Science Officer Series Season Two

Alien Seas

Buried Among the Stars

The Lazarus Alliance

Escape

Return

Rebellion

Revolution

Liberation

Retribution

Alliance

Shadow of the Dominion

Longshot Hypothesis

Hard Bargain

Outermost

Dominion-427

Phoenix

Princess Rualoh

The Handsome Rob Gigs

Can't Shoot Straight Gang

Can't Shoot Straight Gang Returns

Hunting Handsome Rob

Handsome Rob, Assassin

Earth Force Sky Patrol

Birth of the Star Dragon

Flight of the Star Dragon

Call of the Star Dragon

Shadow of the Star Dragon

Trial of the Star Dragon

Hunter Bureau

Mirrors

Latency

Pleasure Model

Inhuman

Phil Kosnett, Explorer Extraordinaire!!! Or something like that.

Looking at the latest reports from various departments, it felt like maybe he'd gone a little above and beyond on this one, but it simply couldn't be helped. Command Machinist Rais Hosni El-Amin, Chief Engineer in the old days, had finally gotten the time he had demanded in drydock, tearing apart *Urumchi*'s bow in order to move a few things around, reinforce a few other bits, and generally give the old lady a solid maintenance cycle.

Helped that they'd stolen a first-class drydock from that moron Baron Russand at *Jacoby*. Rais had been able to complete his list quickly. And, as threatened, he had made adjustments in case *Urumchi* needed to push a burning dreadnought away from a station.

Phil didn't figure he would ever hear the end of it from his crew, one way or the other. But that was the mark of a good team. And he had one of the best. Hell, he'd put his people up against the legends of First Expeditionary Fleet without any trepidation, after all they'd done. Battles. Exploration. Diplomacy.

He was even starting to get letters back from Casey *zu* Weigand. Hopelessly out of date, so she'd avoided talking at all about his mission, instead filling him in on news from the *Fribourg Empire* and more of her music that she'd been writing. Plus images of all the kids.

Phil found himself looking forward with a certain ill-fitting glee to the chaos that would come, one of these days. Casey and Vo had four of them now, and Casey's notes suggested that might be enough. Better, Jessica Weigand, a spitting image of her mother, blond and blue-eyed, was the oldest, followed by fraternal twins Kati and Emmerich, with the girl born first, and thus one step ahead of her own twin brother for precedence. And little Tomas, not much more than a face in swaddling clothes in the pictures, though he'd be around fifteen months old now and walking.

What would the Empire look like when their own laws caused another daughter to rise to power?

More interesting, though, would be the question if any of them demanded to train with the *RAN*, like both of their parents had, rather than the Imperial Fighting Forces that would normally be where only the two boys would go.

Not something he had to worry about today. Mother and Father were both handling the impossible tasks of rebuilding the *Fribourg Empire*, and relying on him to send home regular reports and keep them in the loop of everything he was up to out here, lest *Aquitaine* go ahead and decide to conquer the Balhee Cluster one of these days and thus nail down the only significant conglomeration of stars until you got to the next galactic arm.

Space wasn't barren and empty, even out here. Just thinner, with greater darkness between stops. All the more reason to turn Balhee into an archipelago of trade where everyone was welcome.

A rap at the hatch of his office and it opened. Markus Dunklin, his personal aide, entered with a fresh mug of coffee, followed immediately by Heather Lau, *Urumchi's* Command Centurion and Phil's right hand in more ways than most people ever understood.

He just gave orders around here. Heather made things happen.

She sat and they were alone, matching travel mugs steaming.

"I'd lost track of time," he said as an apology.

"Gosh, Phil. You?" she asked with a sarcastic grin.

"It happens," he laughed. "Killing paperwork and thinking about what happens after *Kyulle.*"

"Any change there?" Heather asked, sipping.

"Not at present," Phil said. "A formal visit to *Yaumgan,* and then we will have brought this squadron to each of the Five Nations of the Cluster. New treaties and trade agreements are spreading like weeds, every place we've been, which is almost everywhere at this point. Nations and cultures have been rocked to their cores, but I like to think that, with your help, we've left the place better than we found it."

They leaned forward and tapped mugs in toast. Or prayer. Something.

"What about *Yaumgan?*" Heather asked. "I appreciate that they are supposedly the most advanced, both technologically as well as culturally, but nobody was prepared for us."

"They've had a year to get their shit together," Phil smiled. "Not my fault if they haven't taken advantage of it."

"Are we aware of any soft spots that we might accidentally poke and disrupt things?" she pressed.

"No, and *Stunt Dude* and Sam have both had long conversations with Captain Xue Dao Zhiou off the Skycruiser *Li Jing.* That one is an ally I'm reasonably certain, and has filled in a lot of blanks for us. Presumably, under orders from her bosses, but that just means that they've seen the issues that have arisen elsewhere and want to make sure our visit goes calmly."

Heather just laughed. He couldn't fault her. *Vilahana* had

been intended as a stop to say hello to a new culture of folks and maybe start learning.

It had gone a bit beyond that before it was done.

"What about you?" Phil turned the table now. "My notes suggest that you wanted to talk about the new weapons system that Iveta and others have come up with."

"Rais got it installed and is just itching to test it, but not necessarily where we have a ton of witnesses that might spill the news to outsiders," Heather shrugged. Not uncertain. More of a commentary on the mostly-reformed pirates that now called *Meerut* home, and the Cluster's inability to not gossip. "But the theory is sound, and we have some smart folks working on it. Putting Nam Nagarkar in charge was the thing that made it work, I think. At least this quickly. We'd have gotten there, eventually. She cut a year off the work, meaning Rais could refit things now."

"What did we lose?" Phil asked.

"Just the five rooms originally marked," Heather replied. "And we could have moved a few walls around to open up space in the rooms around it. Next design can start with this equipment, probably miniaturized significantly once we've used it enough to understand."

"I remember that Iveta is no longer calling it Ghost Mode," Phil said. "Spectre now?"

"Immortality is found in history books," Heather laughed. "Keller has Ghost Mode, so Beridze wanted her own entry, rather than just being an expansion. And this is a big enough change that I agree."

"Talk to me," Phil said. "I've followed at a very high level, but we've all been so busy with *Gloran*, *Aditi*, and *Meerut* that I haven't dug in."

"So Markus *acquired* a tractor beam system," Heather grinned. Phil never asked where or how such things happened. Markus's other—unofficial—job title was *dog robber*, an ancient description. "They merged it with a Shield Projector he also *acquired*, and built a thing. Right now, every firebird and most missiles will be distracted when we turn Spectre on, because we can create a powerful doppelgänger of *Urumchi* that should fool all of them. They will turn and race towards it. That means turning around or looping back in most cases. The explosions won't do much, because we're holding a small emitter out there, and have more that we can move if they do kill the first one."

"Firebirds and most missiles?" Phil confirmed.

"*Ewin* has a few designs that rely on the launching ship providing targeting lock," she replied. "Most, however, use active terminal self-guidance, and can be fooled pretty easily."

"So *Ewin* and *Dalou* are out of luck when this design gets out?" he asked.

"Only if everyone mounts them," she shrugged. "I think capital ships will, and escorts won't. Cruisers might break into heavy and light based on have a Spectre system aboard. But yes, combined with the pulse technology everyone is starting to buy from us, all fleets are going to be redesigned. New ships will replace current ones as fast as yards can turn them out, but that will be a decade in transition. Maybe longer."

"Meanwhile, everyone is trading," Phil nodded. "Good. Maybe peace and better economics can break out around here."

"Here's hoping," she agreed.

"Does that mean *Urumchi* is ready to sail?" Phil asked.

"Just as soon as you sign the orders, so we can complete loading of supplies."

"Good," Phil said simply. "I'm not looking forward to this mission being over, but I kind of am, if you understand. It will be nice to go home for a while."

She nodded.

They'd sailed on October 5, 410. Not quite two years, but coming up on it, and he'd be closer to three by the time he returned to *Ladaux*.

He just needed to bring off this last piece of the puzzle that was the Balhee Cluster.

OGGOSAURIN

ONE

Phil watched the countdown timer at the bottom of the big projection. He had a smile on his face at how it was all going, though others were exceptionally serious around him.

Harinder was tracking everything. Her staff had the A-team up today, having cycled all the training assignments around for this moment.

Phil had always believed that you were best served as a command centurion by making sure everyone served with everyone else. That meant Bridge Crew and Flag Bridge folks trading off regularly, as well as everyone on the Emergency Bridge or any other auxiliary control space. Once you had sat some long watches with people, telling stories and dirty jokes, you had a better feel for how they would react in combat.

Every officer and bridge-qualified crew member on this ship had been in here with him at some point, learning from *The Professor*, as he was generally known. It was a good nickname to have. He'd earned it out of respect for all the things he'd done to train folks to be as good as they could manage.

And not just *Aquitaine* citizens.

He glanced over at Nam Nagarkar, sitting on his left today, ninety degrees from him and Harinder in her black and green uniform with the stripes of a Senior Centurion on her arm. She was nervous, but handling it well. She'd managed everything he'd thrown at her with aplomb beyond her years.

Across from Nam was Kohahu Kugosu. Centurion, *RAN*. At least temporarily. But he'd known another such young Centurion who'd gone on to great things. Still, Kohahu would have to fight for it, when she got ready to take her father's spot as Shogun of *Dalou*. Hegemon of the *Hegemony* itself. They had no history of women in such roles.

Anyone overlooking Kohahu, however, was setting themselves up for trouble later. He'd handed the young woman off to Heather and Iveta, with instructions to make her one of them. *RAN*. But also ready to be Shogun when her time came.

She had finally turned fifteen standard. She only sounded forty when she spoke.

Kohahu had a grimmer smile on her face than Nam, but those two had bonded as well. Outsiders attached to his force to learn. And do it in the black and green of the *RAN*.

Harinder looked up at him with a nod. Phil checked the clock. Drew a breath. Felt the ship slide out of JumpSpace as they arrived for the last leg of the Grand Promenade, as he had taken to calling it in dispatches home. And in letters to Casey.

Phil waited until all the squadron signals stabilized and locked in. This had been a relatively short hop from the last waypoint, but he still had one Survey Dreadnought, six cruisers, seven corvettes, and the *Dalou* Escort *Forktail*. And both the Clipper (ex-Raider) *Hollywood* and the Rapid Courier (ex-Picket) *Varmint*.

Everyone.

All flying *RAN* transponder codes and unwilling to miss this for everything.

"*Aquitaine* Squadron, this is Kosnett, aboard *Urumchi*. I have the flag," he said simply, something he had said so many times that it was automatic. What would he do when he finally retired? Teach, obviously, but where? Who would offer him the best adventure? "Welcome to the system that is the Gateway to the *Yaumgan Domain, Oggosaurin.* Everyone mind the standing orders. We're here by invitation, which few people get. Certainly not a fleet like this. We want to make a good enough impression that they invite everyone back later."

He got chuckles over the open line from the various command centurions and commanders around him. A damned good fleet. He would miss everyone.

"*Forktail,* you will maintain your close escort position as always," Phil continued. "*Li Jing,* you will move into the van and escort us down into the gravity well for rendezvous with the station authorities. Ladies and gentlemen, we are on the cusp of history itself, because you have all participated in a wholly new thing, and I'm looking forward to visiting *Kyulle* and completing the set. *Li Jing,* take us in."

Phil leaned back and smiled. Few had ever been invited to bring a warship to *Oggosaurin.* None had ever gone beyond that world so armed.

All of his people could take home stories of a new future that they were all, by now, engaged in building.

Phil Kosnett, Explorer Extraordinaire. He could think of no better legacy.

TWO

Heather had all her screens live. Iveta was calm in the manner of a woman prepared to leap instantly to a battle to the death, but that was Iveta. She had earned her nickname as *The Junkyard Bitch*. And proven herself far more than just the best of the Jessica Keller clones available on the open market when Heather had needed a Tactical Officer for Phil's mission.

She glanced over at Leyla. Senior Centurion Ekmekçi, Science Officer, *Urumchi*. Another one of the best, when Heather had been able to have her pick.

"Shit, boss," Leyla muttered under her breath, glancing over. "They weren't kidding."

"Talk to me," Heather said, controlling her nerves in spite or Leyla's occasional tendency to play practical jokes at inappropriate times.

"*Zhang Gualao* is here," Leyla said. "The one that was at *Aditi* and *Meerut* with us."

Heather nodded. The *Jùrén*-class, named for the Eight Immortals of ancient Chinese mythology. Enormous flying mecha that looked like bipeds in powered battle armor.

"And," Leyla continued as she read her boards. "So are *He*

13

Xiangu and *Lü Dongbin*. The latter one, according to notes from Captain Xue Dao Zhiou, is best classified as their fleet flagship."

"Three Immortals?" Heather confirmed, impressed. "Out of eight? Let Phil know, but I don't think it changes anything for us."

After all, *Dalou* had made a point to bring three of their colossal Battleships to *Ellariel* when *Urumchi* visited. Three of five in their case. Three of eight here, including the top ship.

Exactly the way to honor the outsiders, while reminding the Cluster-locals that *Yaumgan* was technologically more advanced than the rest of the Cluster.

Maybe not *Aquitaine*, at least in what they'd fielded for a fleet, but Dao Zhiou had also hinted at things experimented with, but never mounted on a ship before now.

They might be a match, until you considered how small *Yaumgan* was. Six core worlds. The Gateway. A reasonable number of colonies, but even the *Zen-Mekyo Syndicates* hadn't tried their luck in *Yaumgan* space. The *Domain* was known to shoot first, and maybe not rescue survivors.

Still…

"Same as always, Science Officer," Heather reminded the woman. And her staff. "I want a hard ping every six hours. *Viking* and *CM-507* to listen and log results. We have already fought a couple of major battles with *Zhang Gualao*, so we know what their baseline should be. Compare results and let me know if anything has changed, plus what we can expect from the other two, or any of the Skycruisers or *Zhōng*-class escorts. Is everything around here humanoid shaped?"

"So far," Leyla replied. "I presume at some point we'll run into more standard transport shapes, if only because arms and legs are way less efficient. Scares the hell out of the outsiders, though, so maybe they have a tug that looks like a guy pushing a pod through space?"

"Find out," Heather said. "All starship architecture is a reflection of the underlying culture. In our case, Yan Bedrov's upbringing in the kinds of poverty that *Corynthe* used to have before Keller. With Lady Moirrey's weapon designs, plus folks like First Centurion Whughy. If they have extended the humanoid design that far, there is a reason for it. We haven't pushed that far to find out before this, but we've had *Li Jing* handy for a while. What else does *Yaumgan* do when they are at home and not expecting visitors?"

"They were expecting us," Iveta pointed out.

"Only to *Oggosaurin*," Heather acknowledged. "They will still have trade flowing back and forth. Not even *Yaumgan* is arrogant enough to think that everyone else trading without them will be a better outcome."

"They say it's not arrogance if you can back it up," Iveta noted.

"Can they?" Heather asked. "Phil's changed everything behind us. If we just come, play tourist, and leave, how soon until *Aditi* or one of the others catches up with *Yaumgan*? How soon until some sort of super-governmental Balhee Cluster Council starts organizing things? *Yaumgan* better be on the inside when that happens, or they might be on the outside until it's too late."

She noted the nods around her. *Yaumgan* had quietly been the top dog for a long time. Would they understand that the others were no longer necessarily that far behind?

THREE

OGGOSAURIN GATEWAY CONTROL,
OGGOSAURIN

Hu Yating Kai watched the cluster of new stars appear on the scanners. Almost exactly on time, but Kosnett had struck him as the sort of commander who did that. Professional, which was the term *Aquitaine* preferred to describe themselves. To complement one another.

It was not a common term, outside *Aquitaine* ships.

Most of the nations of the Cluster were fractious and poorly organized. Previously, too much money spent on spies and pirates attacking each other under the cover of *plausible deniability*. Now, something of a lifestyle. The *Ewin Principalities* might yet come apart, in spite of Kosnett's best efforts. The *Aditi Consensus* was undergoing a generation's worth of political upheaval, possibly a century's, in a single year. *Dalou* and *Gloran* had both been subject to the crucible, and seemed to be doing better now than before.

Was it the case that they'd always been a little behind *Aditi* and now saw their chance to close the gap? Or surpass their neighbor and rival?

Yating counted those stars, recognizing most of the ships from when Kosnett had set out to capture *Meerut* and mete out justice. *Morninghawk* was no longer traveling with them, but

Omarov had been promoted to Lord and charged with creating a brand new thing in *Dalou* history. *Forktail* had taken their escort position. *Storm Petrel* anchored the cruisers. And carried the Crown Prince of *Dalou*. Two ex-Syndicate vessels even flew with Kosnett.

The Shogun's daughter flew aboard *Urumchi* these days. His spies had already managed to acquire copies of the new trade and development agreements binding elements of *Dalou* and *Gloran*, as well as understanding Lau's fingerprints on everything.

He flashed back to a conversation with Lin Na Tai, Captain of the *Jùrén Zhang Gualao*. Her question about the threat of *Aquitaine*. She had meant militarily. Yating had understood that Kosnett would disrupt the harmony of all things that had largely settled into entropy and *ennui*.

That had been good, because the other nations and Syndicates left *Yaumgan* wisely alone. This disruption threatened all things, as all disruption should.

Thus, Yating had gone to *Aditi* itself to meet with the man and take his measure. To breach all previous etiquette and protocol by inviting an armed fleet to *Kyulle* itself, that the timocrats back home could understand the man and his mission.

His implications.

Station Administrator Ko approached now, having been at a slight distance as everyone waited for the momentous sequence of events to begin. Yating noted all the officers around him were on edge. Like *Aditi* or *Aquitaine*, roughly evenly mixed for gender, but how can you build a society by ignoring half your population?

He smiled at the group.

"My friends, you are present at the dawn of a new era," Yating announced warmly to the room, just to help them frame it in their own minds. "The *Domain* has always been a private affair, for reasons we do not discuss with outsiders."

"Will that change, Ambassador?" Ko asked him.

They had been over it in private, but this was for public consumption.

"*Aquitaine* has asked for friendship with all the nations of the Cluster, Administrator," Yating replied. "Each of the others has seen the advantage of it, and now Kosnett has saved the best for last. We will welcome them and hear their words. Perhaps we will even allow more travel, as Kosnett's arrival has heralded a new order for our neighbors."

"We await your wisdom, Ambassador," Ko said with a bow.

Yes, he supposed that they did. *Oggosaurin* was usually the armed castle standing at the pass, keeping the barbarians at bay. Not always possible with Jump technology, but this was also the only *Domain* system that wouldn't immediately chase down an unwelcome guest and crush them without provocation. As such, they were both more and less prepared for the future that Yating could see dawning.

"Open a channel to *Urumchi* and broadcast it in the clear," Yating ordered one of the nearby techs, waiting for the woman to nod up at him. "*RAN Urumchi*, in the name of the *Domain* itself, I welcome you to *Oggosaurin* and *Yaumgan*. We look forward to showing you the sights and joys of our culture and learning as much from you."

He nodded at the tech and she cut the line. A lovely, brief speech. Worked out ahead of time to offer banalities and not much else, but to do it with a smile on his face.

Yating wondered how much of it wouldn't work out that way.

FOUR

SKYCRUISER LI JING

Stunt Dude watched Dao Zhiou's face. After more than a year attached to this vessel as an advisor and occasional close combat training officer, he could read her moods almost as well as he could Sam.

She caught him staring and even blushed a faint bit.

"Glad to be home?" he asked quietly, aware that the bridge of the Skycruiser was exceptionally quiet as the squadron maneuvered down into the orbital slots that had been worked out ahead of time.

"Yes and no, *Stunt Dude*," she replied with a shrug. "We have done amazing things and hopefully it will reflect well on my career. At the same time, it will all be over soon."

"Skycruisers and *Jùrén* would be a welcome sight above *Ladaux*, one of these days," he replied. "As long as you don't mind every ship in orbit drifting by to gawk at you."

That got a smile. *Yaumgan* ships were unique, as far as he'd been able to research. Everybody else build long, skinny blocks, either rounded or squared or hexagonal as they preferred. The rest of the Cluster used a *Buran*-style design, with a boom that could separate and land on a planetary surface, with the *Energiya* module containing engines, JumpSails, and most of the weapons.

Still, a *Gloran* Battlecruiser or a *Dalou* Cruiser wouldn't stand out that much.

Li Jing was different. Vastly so.

But then, Dao Zhiou's people were from farther west on a galactic map. The next arm over from *Aquitaine*, with Balhee as a pearl in this middle darkness.

Who knew what folks over there were like?

"Perhaps we will eventually travel there," Dao Zhiou said.

"But?" he asked, hearing the catch in her voice.

"*Yaumgan* is a most insular place, *Stunt Dude*," she reminded him. "We hardly talk to any of our neighbors. Only the arrival of aliens from outside the Cluster could cause the Thinkers back home to rouse and investigate."

"You thought we were someone else," he said, watching her tiny start. The others had that flinch as well whenever the topic came up.

He knew that there were deeper secrets. You couldn't live and serve aboard a ship for a year and miss them. Not if you got friendly with the crew. And led them on raiding missions to cut out enemy flagships in harbor.

Dao Zhiou nodded, but remained silent. Ahead of them, both Right Gunner and Left Gunner had looked back and inward. The Flyer and Seeker were on edge as well.

"I have not asked," *Stunt Dude* reminded them. "I have not pried. I will, however, remind you that we came to make friends of the distant strangers. You live closer to those folks, so perhaps it is time for the *Domain* to consider opening itself more to those selfsame neighbors. Everyone is afraid of you right now, for all the reasons your culture has inculcated into them, but those people are also changing. The Philosopher/Kings of *Yaumgan* should avail themselves of this opportunity."

"Else *Aditi* or one of the others grows too powerful?" Left Gunner Ying Xa-Mu asked.

He turned to study her. At one time, *Stunt Dude* had thought that she was a throwback with hair much lighter than everyone and fairer skin. Now, he suspected that she was more closely related, at least ethnically, to one of the indigenous societies that had been present when the refugees that would become *Yaumgan* arrived, quickly conquering their six core worlds and building a social and intellectual fortress in the back corner of Balhee, like a moray eel down in the rocks.

"I think that Phil ended the pirates," he said, watching her eyes. As Left Gunner, she had control of the left fist super titan bolt cluster on *Li Jing*. "I suspect without knowing that *Yaumgan* had a significant budget for funding those folks to annoy everyone else, simply because everyone else did the same. Without that, without the constant struggle against piracy and entropy, the others can make themselves more than they were. How much more remains to be seen. You should not risk them making a thing that might then threaten you. As they might, given time and those old fears."

All eyes were staring at him wider than normal, but *Stunt Dude* wasn't normally given to speeches. Or philosophical meanderings. Still, he spent a lot of time on the dojo floor thinking about these things. And training the martial forces of *Li Jing*.

He nodded to everyone and sat back. Dao Zhiou looked like she wanted to say more, but bit back her response before it emerged.

Secrets. Everyone had them. He had fewer, but he'd been a civilian for a while, and a mere Dragoon before that. Not a man who shook nations like Phil.

How bad could it be?

SENZA

FIVE

Bausse Aublahzieu looked out over the dim command space of the Assault Carrier she had been assigned to command. All her pilots were poised in their *Kuài*, the fast aeromechs that made the *Unification* such a deadly force. Her tactical crew were just waiting for the order to leap *Truhto* into battle that they could rend and savage.

After so long, the *Zerzan Unification* had finally found their ancient foe. Those damnable aristocrats who had ruled the *Zerzan Monarchy* with an iron fist, only finally falling when the people rose up and cast them down.

Scholars had argued for five hundred years whether they should have been allowed to escape in their grand caravan, fleeing into the darkness. The *Unification* still demonized them for the things they had done.

And now the *Unification* had finally located them, with the help of a new batch of refugees.

Bausse looked over at the man who had been selected to accompany her force. A pirate, no less, chased out of the Balhee Cluster with his tail between his legs and selling his soul and his story for the chance to start a new life in the *Unification*.

Had his information been any less important, they might

have all been assigned a stint in the work camps for reeducation, but had the old masters finally been located? Could vengeance be had?

The pirate had belonged to a tribe called *Nagi*. Male. Middle aged in the sense that he was old to be in command of a small Raider, but they had operated like a business, rather than a military. Apparently the entire Balhee Cluster had been one vast, mercantilistic mess, with pirates and smugglers preying on anybody and everybody.

At least until the outsiders had come. Other outsiders, supposedly from the east. Terrible warlords and brutally efficient warriors.

They had broken the pirates. Bausse welcomed that development for the improved governance, simply because bandits were a sign of a broken culture. They had driven men like Nolan Hames and his Raider *Ravenscall* out of the Cluster itself, one step ahead of the hangman's noose.

None of the pirates deserved execution, at least as far as Bausse had been able to determine. Many years at hard labor, yes, where they could contemplate the workings of a proper society and find a place to be productive citizens in it.

Hames was earning himself probation by leading *Truhto* ahead of the rest of a massive fleet, to scout out the ancient foe.

Already, Bausse knew a thrill in her soul, watching from the shadow of a gas giant as optical telescopes picked out the image of a man flying across space, pushing a cargo container ahead of him.

Except that it wasn't a man. It was a mech. Just as *Zerzan* built them. Larger than her aeromechia, but built exactly the same. And Hames had assured her and anyone who would listen that nobody else in the Cluster built such ships. Had not even considered such a design, as it was extremely complicated and required sophisticated control systems that verged on sentience.

It also made aeromechs the pinnacle of combat.

Worse, the ones who now called themselves *Yaumgan* didn't

bother building the small ones anymore, relying on much larger designs, apparently intended to engage things like Hames's *Ravenscall* or larger warships.

Had they forgotten the lessons of the *Unification*? It had only been five centuries. Their arrogance had brought them low then. Perhaps it was to be her destiny to bring them down again today.

"Optics, confirm your last readings," Bausse ordered.

Lighting was kept dimmer than normal in here, to remind everyone that *Truhto* was about to enter combat with a dangerous foe. They had to sneak up on them, because she was alone today, with only a single wing of aeromechia. Still, forty-nine of the craft should be sufficient.

"Two vessels tentatively identified as escorts, Chevalier," the man replied. "The others appear to be nothing more than cargo tugs. The station is presumably armed, but we have the pirate's records as to their expected range and efficiency."

Bausse nodded. She turned to the pirate and watched him pale a bit. That was also good. He was fearful and alone on this entire vessel, trading his soul for his mind.

"Flight Deck, stand by for final assault jump," Bausse called, looking over at the Flight Boss to get her nod.

"Transport, your jump has been laid in," Bausse said, turning to the man. "Engage."

It was a short blink. She barely had time to recover from entry when they exited again, right at the edge of the gravity well that was *Senza* orbit, surrounded by small platforms and the tugs she thought were called *Niú*. Oxen for their slow strength.

Fitting, but they were without horns today. And she had brought an entire wing of avengers to *Senza*.

"Wing Leader, launch and pursue," Bausse smiled. "Show them the mercy they deserve."

At last.

SIX

MISSION BRIEF: TRUHTO ASSAULT WING.
ENEMY WORLD: SENZA ORBITAL SPACE

Joaneus Senebach was first out of the launch tube. As Wing Leader, the forty-eight aeromechia behind him would look to him to lead. Expect him to be first into battle.

Today, they had specific mission parameters. The *Unification Elders* of the fleet wanted intelligence. Prisoners who could be interrogated. Computers that could be sucked dry of every bit of data they might hold, that the old aristocracy of *Zerzan* had indeed fled east. Or eventually turned east.

The *Unification* had been hunting them towards the galactic interior for more than a century. Only a fleeing pirate had carried the key to the *Zerzan* capital at *Kohri*.

And now they had come. *Truhto* was given pride of place for the first raid, against a minor colony well away from the world named *Kyulle*, possibly after the king of the same name, once upon a time.

Joaneus felt the acceleration drive him forward as leg and backpack thrusters engaged. He checked the Shield Buckler on his left arm, confirming that it was active, as well as the ionization torpedo he would need once he got close. For now, his pulse torpedo on his mech's right forearm would be primary.

Two escorts. Like fighting a giant from ancient legend or a

fantasy game, but he had six wings of men and women behind him. More than enough, then he could return to the thing the Chevalier had considered a tugmech.

On his scanners, the rest of the flight poured out of *Truhto's* twin flight decks, like an army racing across hot sand.

"Three and three," Joaneus called over the comm. "Odd Flights take target number one. Even Flights form diamonds on me as we go after number two."

Lights checked in as everyone confirmed.

For now, he would ignore the number one escort. Three flights should be sufficient to hold it at bay while swarms of pulse and ionization torpedoes pounded it.

He flew through space as the crew of the escort woke up to their worst nightmare finally come true.

They had been found. Betrayed by one of their own who had known their secrets because he had been taking their pay. Before they had thrown him to the wolves.

Luckily, the foolish pirate had gone west. And found people more than happy to pay him for his information.

Number two came awake. That was obvious from the way the mech spun in space to face his half-Wing approaching. Two fists came up, horizontal to the mech.

"Form defensive sphere," Joaneus ordered, cutting his thrusters to nothing so the rest could anchor on him in the center.

Twenty-four mechs formed a turtle, left arms forward and squatting, even as inertia carried them forward and down at their target. Around them the Sphere formed as each Shield Buckler merged with neighbors and came into harmonics.

The Escort fired.

Left fist was a trio of heavy torpedo weapons, fired at near light speed. Titan bolts, exactly as he had been briefed.

Right fist unleashed a pulse of ravening energy that clawed at the Sphere, impacting with such energy that the half-Wing was actually slowed as the power splashed.

A second pulse followed. A third. Even a fourth, though the pirate had not been sure. Most Balhee power taps fired three times and had to cool and recharge.

Eye beams licked out, but did little at this range. They were defensive weapons, fired in terror.

"Even numbers, fire pulse torpedoes," Joaneus ordered. "Odd numbers, ionization torpedoes."

Ionization torpedoes weren't going to be effective at this range, but it let those pilots hold a pulse torpedo ready. And they might slip some past the Shield Projector that had finally interjected between the two sides. The Escort began to fly backwards, like a swimmer moving on his back when a swarm of piranha gave chase.

Three more titan bolts emerged from the Escort, though none were aimed at him. Had they never faced a diamond before? Forgotten how such a thing worked? Or had they panicked as the ghosts of their guilty past finally caught up with them?

One of the titan bolts penetrated the Sphere, but it had served its purpose. The Escort was designed to engage other warships. Not swarms.

"Local team, break into lances and give chase," Joaneus ordered, twisting himself around again so that he could engage all thrusters and charge down the beast's throat. "Fire at will, understanding that we don't need this one intact."

Joaneus fired a pulse torpedo as his speed picked up again. Not quite matching the escort, but he had a better acceleration curve it seemed. And the Escort was suddenly beset on all sides by the first solid wave of torpedoes arriving. Many missed, as was to be expected, even at this range, but the Shield Projector wasn't wide enough to protect the whole vessel. Especially now that his twenty-four had split into six lances and could move to envelope.

Inner shields on the Escort suffered greatly. On his screens, Joaneus saw dark patches appear where deflectors had been overloaded or ionized. That would only get worse, even as titan bolts and power tap shots began impacting his own team.

One hit was not a guaranteed kill, but it would bring down a Shield Buckler and an aeromech's deflector carapace was not intended to stop things designed to kill warships.

Still, you had to hit something to hurt it, and the Escort was having problems deciding who to engage as lances spread out and began pounding him.

Vengeance felt good.

SEVEN

Bausse surveyed the results.

One escort dismembered. One disemboweled, with metal pieces flaking off and drifting away. The orbital station was firing at extreme range, but their beams lacked the coherence to be a threat to *Truhto*, and the aeromechia were too small to target. Easier to swat at midges and perhaps get lucky.

Casualties had been in the expected range, with a dozen aeromechia damaged severely, though only seven deaths. There were more pilots and mechs back with the fleet, waiting their chance.

One bulky humanoid tug ship on the same scale as a *Zhōng*. Indeed called *Niú*, or Oxen. It had wisely surrendered when overtaken and challenged by Wing Leader Senebach's team.

Bausse had the commander on a video screen. His accent was atrocious. His skin was darker than hers, as were his eyes. Black in both cases, while her hair was a much lighter brown and her eyes hazel.

"Who are you people?" he asked with fearful wonder.

"The *Zerzan Unification*," Bausse replied. "We have come for you."

"What do you want?" he pressed.

"Information," Bausse said. "You will provide it. In return, you will not be badly treated."

"Why are you attacking *Yaumgan*?" he asked, still wide-eyed.

"We are *Zerzan*," she said, as if that explained it all.

If it didn't, then these fools had forgotten their own history. Pity, in that case, because they would just be a victim of invasion and conquest, rather than deserved retribution.

Neither would stay the *Unification*'s hand, but she would derive more joy from the former.

"I do not understand," the commander exclaimed.

"It is not for you to understand," Bausse snapped at him finally. "It is for you to submit to the *Unification*, as we all do. To find your place in the harmonious totality that will be formed when all of humanity is reunited into the greater whole we once had."

"When was that?"

"Before the dark times," Bausse growled. "Before the thinking machines."

"But…"

"Enough," Bausse growled. "You have surrendered. We will come aboard and take you and your vessel prisoner. You will answer my questions. My will is law."

He gulped, perhaps finally understanding where he stood. On thin ice.

Around her, *Senza* Orbital Space lay prostrate, but she was not here as a pirate. Or a bandit.

She would return one day as a conqueror. That much was certain.

This *Yaumgan Domain* had more important worlds, but that was exactly why the *Unification* had chosen *Senza*. Intelligence value.

And surprise. The aristocrats would panic when they realized who had come for them.

Finally.

YAUMGUN

EIGHT

Phil remembered the Ambassador from *Aditi*. Hu Yating Kai, where Hu in ancient Chinese had meant something like reckless or wild, which wasn't anything at all like the man himself.

The term *man* was something of a strong term, as Ambassador Hu was strikingly androgynous at the best of the times. As well as incredibly intelligent. And a sharp operator.

They were aboard the main station above *Oggosaurin* today. The system itself was called the *Gateway to Yaumgan*, so Phil found the symbolism fitting. *Urumchi* had been the Chinese end of the fabled Silk Road, back on lost *Earth*. The ship's logo was a blocky tower next to the Great Wall itself, with an open doorway symbolizing trade and diplomacy.

Phil's bread and butter.

They had done a round of quick receptions, mostly geared towards making the locals less nervous and building up to the big event Phil had specifically requested. Cocktail parties might be dismissed derisively as diplomats standing around spying on each other and sharing gossip, but Phil had always found them one of the best ways to break down hostility and even reserve, just by standing around and talking.

Or at least being seen, in the case of Heather, but she was sharing a standing table with Captain Xue from *Li Jing* as the latter got politely lionized by other captains, officers, and diplomats for spending a year abroad with the barbarians.

Because that honestly was the look Phil got from a lot of the locals. Not that he could blame them, given a lifetime of dealing with the *Ewin Principalities*, the *Aditi Consensus*, and the *Gloran Empire* on their borders.

None of those would give most people a high opinion of the Cluster. But there was an entire galaxy out there beyond those walls. And *Aquitaine*'s wars with everyone in their galactic arm should be done and gone. *Fribourg* was calm and focusing most of its energy on keeping the former *Buran* frontier peaceful, even as new groupings and clusters of folks started to emerge over there.

Aquitaine might be growing more militant over time, though Phil still wasn't sure he believed Jež's theories. He also couldn't refute them.

So Phil was standing in the middle of the room, can of juice in one hand and Centurion Dar glowering at everyone, which served to establish a bubble around them where casual observers remained outside.

Ambassador Hu drew closer. Captain Lin Na Tai, commander of *Zhang Gualao*, accompanied him, looking young enough to be the man's daughter.

Phil nodded deeply enough to be a bow in many places. The Ambassador matched it, as did Lin.

"Welcome to *Oggosaurin*, First Centurion," Hu said with a cheerful smile. "And *Yaumgan*."

"Thank you, Ambassador," Phil smiled back. "On the one hand, I regret not being able to take you up on your original invitation sooner. As previously noted, circumstances forced my hand time and again, and I felt that it would be better if the various situations were addressed sharply, rather than left to fester."

"Interesting choice of words, First Centurion," Captain Lin joined in. "Fester. Could one make the case that much of the other nations have been festering?"

"Perhaps, Captain." Phil turned to the small woman, not all that much taller than Dar, but much wider across the shoulders. She was built like a swimmer. Or a gymnast. "If so, then perhaps my role could be seen as more of a medical professional, come to help lance such things that they might drain and heal better."

"You have greatly disturbed the harmony of the Balhee Cluster," she said. "What will you bring to *Kyulle*?"

Phil caught the faintest jolt pass through the Ambassador's frame. Perhaps they had worked it out for Captain Lin to play Bad Cop? And then she might have taken the role a bit more seriously than Hu had expected?

"Trade," Phil said. "You have an Ambassador credentialed and presumably waiting for our arrival. My hope is that we can simply be tourists here."

"Tourists, First Centurion?" Lin asked, staring up at him.

"We would like to visit *Kyulle*, Captain," Phil said. "All of my command centurions and others are part of a first, in that no outside force has ever traveled directly to *Kyulle*, just as none had previously been welcomed at *Ellariel*. I hope that you are not so fragile as a people that we send uncontrollable repercussions through your culture, as we appear to have done elsewhere."

"Indeed, Kosnett," Hu swooped in now. "Each of those nations had fragility underneath. One hopes that they will build back better when all is said and done."

"Is that *Yaumgan*'s secret then?" Phil asked, just to see the light in their eyes change. "That you do not have the fragility that caused others to waver in the face of change?"

Sure enough. Blinks. Dar was standing where the other two could not see her face, but Phil caught the ghost of a grin, gone as quickly as it appeared.

Aquitaine had been changing since before Phil had been born. It had only picked up speed when the old First Lord, Nils

Kasum, had selected a young command centurion named Jessica Keller and unleashed her first on *Fribourg* and later *Buran*.

And finally *Aquitaine* itself, but that had been after that man's time.

When you won't live up to your own standards, do not be surprised when others tried to make you. At least Jessica hadn't burned everything to the ground, though Phil personally knew several people who had been present at the meeting where that had been one of the options under discussion.

Lin looked like she'd sucked a lemon. Hu was more phlegmatic, but it was a brittle shell. Phil could see that in how his face froze in place.

"What further changes do you foresee, First Centurion?" Hu asked diplomatically.

"Trade, centered on *Vilahana*, drawing in *Gloran* and *Dalou*," he replied. "Civilian, at that, as the people involved are doing so separately from whatever military or bureaucratic rank they might hold."

"Kugosu, Zaman, and Lau?" Hu asked, confirming to Phil that the news had flown here quickly.

Possibly carried by one of *Hollywood's* people in an old Picket like *Varmint*.

"Just so," Phil bowed. "And Morninghawk at *Urwel*, drawing in *Toulouse* and *Belamel*. Or *Meerut*. In each case, letting the merchants pave a way for governments to follow, where everyone might grow richer and lead happier lives. One hopes that even *Yaumgan* might find it in themselves to engage more than has been their traditional habit."

Lin wanted to say something, but some thought stayed her tongue. Hu nodded.

"I am but an Ambassador, Kosnett," Hu said to perhaps forestall the conversation. "Those decisions will be made once you travel to *Kyulle* and the Thinkers have a chance to weigh in."

Phil took that for the dismissal it was. Or evasion.

Hu didn't look like a mere messenger. Not if he'd been sent

to *Aditi* as soon as news arrived of an unknown exploration warfleet at *Vilahana*. That spoke to deeper concerns at a cultural level, as well as a much greater governmental rank for one Hu Yating Kai.

But the man was also correct that any changes in government and culture would be driven from the top down. *Yaumgan* culture was a strongly hierarchical thing.

Phil just needed to find the handful of men and women who needed to hear what he had to say.

While there was still time to listen.

After all, Morninghawk had warned anyone that there was an avalanche coming for their souls

Not everyone had listened.

NINE

Heather kept to herself and mostly just provided a wingmate for Dao Zhiou that kept anyone else from joining them at the table when they came over to chat and wish her well.

At least here nobody was stripping her nude as they watched her.

Well, perhaps a few, but they were being much more discreet about it. None of them that she found physically interesting, but Heather had long ago learned that not every pretty boy or girl was going to be interesting in bed. And vice versa.

Still, diplomacy. Talk, as much as it required her to not grit her teeth as she stood and chatted. Smile. Answer more than monosyllabically, but not much.

Xue Dao Zhiou was the hero to these people. Heather was just the alien.

And Heather was okay with that.

The latest group wandered off with smiles and nods. Dao Zhiou sighed and relaxed.

"I'd like to say it will get better," Heather offered, hoping that the pair of them talking would cause others to sheer off. Unlikely, but anything was possible. "However, knowing Phil, these events will only get bigger and weirder as we get closer to your homeworld."

"I keep thinking that after a year, it would get easier," Dao Zhiou said. "How does it keep getting worse?"

"Partly social geography," Heather offered. "*Meerut* were all pirates, so you had to remind them to wipe the mud off their feet when they came in. *Ishiokoh* and *Ellariel* were more focused, but inward. However, Phil managed to rip apart centuries of custom and expectations accidentally, and then stand around while folks put it back together around us. Then *Jacoby* and *Ewinhome*. Not particularly good examples of anything. Except maybe bad examples. *Gloran* was angry at everyone, until we got them pointed at *Aditi*. *Aditi* is trying not to come apart while *Gloran* throws away a couple of centuries of penal fleet bullshit and tries to figure out what being a grownup looks like."

"I feel like I should sail to *Ladaux* with you when you're done here," Dao Zhiou smiled. "Just so I have some sort of palate cleanser."

"Oh, I'm sure we're just as bad," Heather laughed. "But we don't see it. Same with you. You're home, but you've spent the last year with the barbarians, so you've been exposed to all sorts of infectious ideas and now you come home and have different eyes to see things with. But I think you would like *Ladaux*. And those folks would utterly boggle at *Li Jing* or *Zhang Gualao*."

Dao Zhiou nodded and drank some juice. Heather noted that almost every commander among the squadron had largely stopped drinking any alcohol at these events, instead following Phil's trick of bringing juice from their own ships. He'd gotten that from Keller.

Heather idly wondered who had taught her the trick.

"So where would your career likely head from here?" Heather asked. "I can't imagine that they keep you on *Li Jing* forever."

"Indeed not," Dao Zhiou grinned. "I'm due for rotation, but

they might not be sure what to do with me, since I have been out in the wider Cluster for so long."

"Tell them that you need to teach squadron and small fleet tactics," Heather said. "I remember how little you understood such things when you first went out with *CB-502*. Or when *Zhang Gualao* traveled with us to *Meerut*."

"We rarely travel in squadrons," Dao Zhiou acknowledged ruefully. "Usually, we are patrolling colonies or defending core worlds. Rarely do we sweep our borders for intruders, because all of our neighbors have been taught that any incursion will be crushed mercilessly. Do you think that we will be needing more than that?"

"I think, if nothing else, that all of your neighbors will be building new warfleets over the next decade or generation," Heather replied. "And *somebody* will get a stupid idea that they have an advantage on *Yaumgan*, one that they should exploit, at least until you scare them off or annihilate them."

Dao Zhiou nodded.

"Squadrons of escorts or cruisers, then?" she asked.

"Yes. Unless the Eight Immortals are going to be rebuilt into devastating weapons that can hold a planetary orbit all by themselves," Heather said. "Pulse technology means that firebirds and missiles are no longer a threat. Shield Projectors are nice, but they were designed to detonate such tracking weapons well away from the ship. If everyone builds things Expeditionary-style as a result of us, then you will need to rethink how your humanoid ships will fight when folks get close enough, metaphorically, to punch them in the mouth."

"I fear you are correct," Dao Zhiou replied. "Hopefully, they will listen to me."

"Oh, they'll listen," Heather acknowledged. "Will they believe you is an entirely different question."

TEN

OGGOSAURIN AMBASSADOR'S QUARTERS,
OGGOSAURIN STATION

Yating had drawn Captain Lin with him when he finally retired to his suite. They were in the front room, all his servants having been waved off to leave them some privacy.

At least the illusion. All were within earshot if someone raised a voice, but he could also rely on them to remain silent about his ruminations.

"We have had a year," Lin said now quietly, sipping at a glass of water cut with lemon juice and salt. "Our spies and diplomats have watched Kosnett's fleet in action, and spoken with Command Diplomatic Centurion Sillamon on *Kyulle* at length. What terrible thing does he bring to our doorstep?"

Yating started, at both the audacity of her question and the accuracy.

He considered deflecting her, but that would just make it worse. She was one of the smartest people he had ever met. Pity that she had chosen military service over government, but she was young enough to have a full career in the one and still return for success with the second.

"He rides at the head of a barbarian army," Yating said, waving off her interruption before it could be fully formed. "Oh, I know Kosnett himself, and his people, are at least as sophisticated as we are. *Aquitaine* is an advanced society. It is the others that come with him. *Aditi* might be the best of a bad lot, but they are still a bad lot themselves. *Dalou*, whom we rarely encounter, preferred it that way, as insular as we have been. I wonder if they represent the sorts of pressures that have been building underneath the *Domain* for some terribly long time and will erupt, as Kosnett has successfully done so many other places."

"Change can be positive, Ambassador," Lin said carefully.

"Controlled change," he countered. "None of those situations were done with control, except where our spies suggest that Kosnett has worked his ass off to keep things from utterly spiraling into the ground and exploding, as they might have in more than one situation. The *Domain* is a controlled place."

"Are we too insular?" Lin asked.

"That, Captain, is one of many fears," Yating nodded. "You saw how casually Captain Xue relaxed with Heather Lau?"

Lin nodded back.

"A year ago, she would have been standing ramrod straight with pursed lips and a scowl," he said. "Here, she was smiling and chatting. Good, yes, because that means that she has learned how to be like them. Bad, because others will see that and wonder."

"Is she a vector of disease?" Lin asked. "At least socially or culturally?"

"By definition," Yating grimaced. "Hopefully, as Kosnett explains, in a good way."

"I spoke with her briefly during the reception," Lin said. "Towards the end. Lau suggested that she should teach squadron or small fleet tactics after she completes this mission, as the barbarians might yet decide to test their mettle against us. She thought that our fleet should either be built out with current technology, or rebuilt to include some of the new things that have never come out of the lab."

"And I fear she is right, Lin," Yating said. "Until now, we

have been content to remain ahead of everyone else, but it is possible that we are behind *Aquitaine* as they exist today. If Kosnett's pulse technology is to become the new standard, we will have to at least match it, if not improve on it."

"Improve?" she asked.

"Faster recharging cycles," he said. "Longer focus on beams. Things to convince even the most ferocious *Gloran* berserker to pause and perhaps bother someone else."

"Have we begun?" she asked carefully.

"That is above your pay grade, Captain," he replied tartly. Then smiled. "However, it would not be a bad assumption to consider on your part. The Eight Immortals will not be the most powerful vessels in the fleet for much longer, as I understand things. Perhaps you might be interested in a lateral transfer to something experimental?"

"That would be most pleasing, Ambassador," Lin smiled. "I have toured *Urumchi* and *CB-502*. They are impressive, but I cannot help but wonder how they could be built better."

"Remember one key piece of social history, then," he said, waiting for her to nod. "*Aquitaine* is at peace. They built this second generation of Expeditionary vessels on the lessons of the first, in which Kosnett and Lau served. However, they are not at war with anyone, so they could perhaps relax their intense militarism. *Urumchi* is, as Kosnett notes, perhaps only one third as powerful as her sister Heavy Dreadnoughts. *Viking* probably follows a similar pattern. They could ramp up quickly if they needed, so we need to build to that scale, rather than what Kosnett has with him."

She gulped. Yating found that edifying, as it meant that she understood just how dangerous *Aquitaine* could be. Could have been.

A conquering empire could have rolled over the entire Cluster fairly quickly.

Arguments among the Thinkers back home were split evenly on the topic, as *Aquitaine* could have taken Balhee, including *Yaumgan*, though that would have been the hardest nut to crack.

What did it mean that Governor Kosnett, as opposed to the First Centurion, was working so assiduously to maintain all of Balhee intact?

What did the man know?

Or fear?

ELEVEN

Iveta had gathered her combat team, which included all of the Tactical Officers off of Phil's force, including Sub-Commander Chaudhari off *Aranyani*. The rest were commanding officers, because nobody else split the role. Captain Sugawara off *Forktail*. Captain Yukimura off *Storm Petrel*. Striker Solo from *Shadowbolt*. Cruiser-Captain Khan of *Juvayni*.

Captain Xue had not been invited, but only after consultation with Phil and Harinder. Nobody wanted to talk about how to dismantle their own fleet with strangers. Outsiders.

Best not to put the woman in an awkward and compromising situation then.

Leyla was just finishing her presentation on the colossal *Jùrén* class. *Zhang Gualao. Lü Dongbin. He Xiangu.*

"Since *Meerut*, there are no visible changes," Leyla said. "We fought side by side with *Zhang Gualao* at the moorage, and in the orbital battle. Heavier weapons than everyone else in the Cluster has, with the super titan bolt cluster firing eight from the left fist and the Sunsword, that mega power tap that fires ten rapid pulses before it needs to cool. Serious ships, when you include the upgraded eyebeams over *Li Jing's* that they use as point defenses like a Type-1-Pulse. Not as fast or effective at range, but similar enough for our tactics."

"What are their shortcomings?" Iveta asked the room now, going face to face.

Gotzon Solo grimaced so hard it looked painful and nodded at her.

"Solo?"

"There aren't that many of them," he said quietly. "Even here, three of the Immortals, plus Skycruisers and smaller ships. Low hull count. If an *Ewin* force could actually be held together long enough not to devolve into duels and stupidity, they really could relentlessly swarm the mecha with missile waves and drive them off."

He shrugged as people chuckled. *Ewin* and *organized* didn't belong in the same sentence.

"He's right, you know," Iveta nodded to the grateful Striker. "They are configured to curb-stomp enemy cruisers and dreadnoughts, but would have troubles against a force of nothing but missile frigates. Or *Gloran* Type-5s with combat pods."

"Does anybody do that?" Sub-Commander Chaudhari asked.

"Not today," Auke Alma, First Officer off *Viking*, said. "No reason that they couldn't, if somebody put that problem in front of a planning committee and asked the same question. *Ewin* had a solid idea with missiles and fighters. Just couldn't ever execute on it for…other reasons."

More chuckles. Understatement of the year, right there.

"What happens when they add better pulse weapons?" Cruiser-Captain Khan asked.

He was almost a new being, after the adventures at *Carinae II*. Iveta approved. He was more like an adult these days and less like a bright, lunatic kid fresh out of the Academy and ready to take on the universe.

She remembered those days.

Around the table, faces got long and contemplative.

"Can you pulse a Four?" Captain Sugawara asked carefully.

Even Iveta blinked as the room fell utterly silent.

"Whole arm and most of both shoulders would have to be pretty much nothing but generators and batteries," Auke replied in a voice suggesting that he was doing the abstract math to solve that problem in his head on the fly.

He did that.

"However, I can't see why you couldn't," he continued. "Built from the ground up. Nobody has ever needed to. Before now."

"That doesn't solve the *Ewin* problem," Solo spoke up. "You will need a whole bunch of Pulse-Twos. Maybe more than you can mount."

"Unless you built it with four arms," Chaudhari said. "This is Balhee. They remember the ancient Hindi goddess *Kali-ma*, with a sword in each of four hands. That's a bunch of extra fists firing Twos."

Iveta shared a glance with some of her *Aquitaine* folks. Nobody here would know Keller's royal patch, with Kali on it. But some ideas had stood the test of millennia.

"If *Dalou* built gunships with waves of shrike firebirds," Senior Centurion Makana Christensen off *CB-502* began, glancing at Yukimura and Sugawara. "That might serve as an interesting interim weapon. Perhaps a viable threat to *Yaumgan*. Have you ever fought them directly?"

"We have not," Captain Yukimura replied. "No common borders and we would have had to go looking for a fight, which was not in our interests."

"Be interesting to wargame it out, though," Auke interjected. "Tabletop style. Might program something and see what it tells me. We have enough data on everybody to balance it well."

"Okay, people," Iveta stood up and rapped her knuckles on the table. "I am not about to order you to not go home and share these thoughts after *Aquitaine* leaves. That would be silly.

And I don't expect trouble with *Yaumgan* while we're here. Mostly, this meeting was because nobody really understands them today. At the same time, five years from now, I don't expect any of your fleets to look like they do presently. That includes *Yaumgan*, so most of what we come up with today won't be relevant then. If we do get into trouble and are facing an attack by *Yaumgan* mecha, I'm likely to order everybody to hold their seeker weapons for a joint launch, time-on-target, so that every damned one arrives at almost the same instant and we can overwhelm some stupid fucker. As Solo notes, they don't have the firepower to really stop a missile and firebird swarm, but nobody has ever tested that out. If we have to fight, we'll start by crushing them one mecha at a time, firing everything else just enough to keep the rest honest. Your homework assignment, if you care to, is to think about how you might take on a *Jùrén*. Or two at once. They don't use seekers, either, so it would be Fours, Threes, and Twos on our part. That means close. That means close, such that the rest of you probably have to get closer than you are usually accustomed to. Questions?"

None. Lots of pensive looks.

Yaumgan had a reputation as great and powerful sorcerers that you should leave alone lest they take your soul. Iveta wondered how much of that was really just good public relations work, and how much was them coasting on old victories.

None of those beasts looked all that impressive, kilo for kilo, but Iveta understood that they were designed to kill enemy flagships, so that poorly commanded leftovers would panic and run.

As *Ewin* would do.

Who was a threat to *Yaumgan* these days?

TWELVE

Phil had previously settled in his office, writing a letter to Casey by hand, just to try to consolidate everything into one coherent narrative. To sum it all up, as he was approaching the end of this glorious quest and the fantastic career that hadn't gone anything like he'd expected, save that Pet Naoumov had promised that she would take care of him when the lean years hit, and she had.

CS-405, at a time when a lot of ships were being mothballed and a whole decade's worth of officers put on the beach. *Cyrus* after that, when he had his fourth stripe.

Urumchi, and all the legends that would accumulate around his name after he retired.

Not a bad way to go.

He closed up the journal and wondered if he should ask her about publishing these letters as a non-scholarly tome, one of these days. Reflections in raw terms, rather than a history book someone would demand he write at some point. Maybe the First Lord of the Fleet, either Pet or perhaps Whughy if and when he followed her.

Phil wasn't sure. Didn't matter today.

The clock in his head had him standing and coming around

the desk when Markus opened the hatch to summon him. He joined the three women at his table and got Heather's projection on his right.

As was her wont.

Countdown clock said two minutes to arrival. The others were wound up. Phil was feeling phlegmatic.

He settled, confirmed his mug of coffee, and smiled at everyone.

"Almost there," he said.

Harinder would probably have a job teaching at the Academy after this, if those people had the brains the Creator gave a goose. Nam was set for a promotion that should see her commanding her own frigate, or First Officer on a cruiser.

Kohahu Kugosu had her whole life in front of her.

Emergence.

All the signals came live as Leyla got to work.

He must have made a sound, because everyone glanced over at him.

"Science Officer, this is Phil," he said simply. "This does not feel right. Give me one hard ping immediately and route any complaints to my desk for summary disposal in the round file."

He couldn't say what he saw, but something in the image rang entirely false. Like a cracked bell.

"All ships, this is Kosnett, aboard *Urumchi*," he said simply. "I have the flag. Stand by for sailing orders, but hold your current positions now. *Li Jing*, you maintain your current position in the van but we're not going anywhere."

"Phil, I'm hearing something like three times the amount of comm traffic I would normally expect for a world this size," Leyla came back a moment later.

"Chickens with their heads cut off?" he asked her.

That might explain the sound in his head.

"Maybe," she said. "Permission to summon my *pixies* from the depths of the faelands?"

"Quietly," Phil replied.

Pixies. A friendlier name for the Cryptographic Analysis team that Heather had insisted upon, in spite of the number of black marks next to Senior Chief Harman Abadjiev's name. That same sailor who had cracked *Ewin's* most sophisticated naval codes and used that knowledge to give Phil a major advantage at *Ewinhome.*

Phil understood now that the man had a compulsion. If you ignored all those specific complaints from his record, the rest was almost spotless.

And Heather had vouched for him when building this force. Phil and everybody else in the squadron would today.

Zhang Gualao was flying with the force. The other two monsters were already blasting inwards towards the main station about as fast as they could accelerate.

"Harinder, get me in touch with Captain Lin or Ambassador Hu," Phil said. "Whoever feels like talking right now, but we are willing to stand by if something terrible has happened and *Urumchi* arrived at the wrong moment. Not like that's never happened before."

"Understood," she said, typing furiously.

Both Nam and Kohahu were wide-eyed. *Kyulle* was a beautiful world. Blue with greens and browns. Two moons above the squadron's orbit that would be visible in the night sky, one almost a tenth as big as the planet and one perhaps a twentieth.

Something was very definitely wrong.

Ambassador Hu had won the coin toss. Or lost it. He appeared in the big projection. His general androgyneity had gone so pale as to almost appear Anglo today.

"There have been developments, First Centurion," he said tersely.

"Thus was my impression, Ambassador," Phil nodded to the image. "As at *Ewinhome* or *Carinae II*, we are prepared to withdraw the squadron to a neutral waypoint. Or perhaps *Oggosaurin* as needed. I will rely upon you to make the determination as to what would be best, for whatever the situation is."

Across the bottom of the projection, someone—Leyla?—suddenly injected a scrolling marquee that would wrap all the way around in a loop for all four of them to see.

Phil managed to not gasp out loud. Nam and Kohahu were not so fortunate.

****Yaumgan colony Senza attacked. Orbital defenders routed or destroyed. Suggestions that* **They've found us** *keep coming up in encrypted messages. ****

Phil focused on being calm.

"Thank you, First Centurion," Hu said. "For now, if the squadron could remain here, I will need to contact my superiors for orders."

"Understood," Phil said. "We will await your needs, sir."

The line went dead and Phil blew out a breath.

"Oh, shit," Kohahu muttered.

He looked over at her. The young woman straightened her spine and locked eyes with him.

"My formal education has also included certain elements of informality related to *RAN* intelligence briefings, First Centurion," she said, back to sounding forty years old instead of fifteen. "Most people assume that *Yaumgan* arrived from the east as refugees, some four hundred and fifty years ago, give or take."

Phil nodded. Part of the reason he was here was to build cultural and social maps that would be even more useful and important than physical ones.

"*They've found us?*" he asked.

"Refugee suggests a previously undiscussed war in their past, First Centurion," she replied. "Or escapees from someplace terrible, as the ancient Jews or the early Americans fleeing religious persecution in their homelands. It also suggests someone else, someone on the other side of a war, perhaps finally locating someone they've been seeking."

"I concur," Phil said. "At present, we have no formal treaties with *Yaumgan*, but they have been exceptionally friendly with us from the beginning, so I intend to give them the benefit of the doubt here. They might have just been pulled into a war not of their making."

"First Centurion, the timing seems suspicious," Nam observed.

"Not if somebody from the Syndicates went west to escape us and had valuable information they could sell to whoever they found when they got there," Heather said, causing the women to start. "Then it makes perfect sense. Does it lay an ethical burden upon us?"

"Ethical?" Phil asked. "Probably. Social, cultural, or military, however, remain to be seen."

THIRTEEN

JÙRÉN ZHANG GUALAO, KYULLE ORBITAL SPACE

Yating flashed back to that first moment when messengers had brought news of an unknown fleet that had arrived at *Vilahana*. The fear that the *Zerzan* had finally come for *Yaumgan*, in spite of successfully hiding for so many centuries. They had not, then.

It appeared that they had now.

He sat next to Lin Na Tai on the bridge of her Immortal, watching her crew come to battle-readiness in the last space they should have expected it. They were calm, but he could smell a hint of fear in the air.

Nobody in the Balhee Cluster had been any sort of threat to the *Domain*. *Aquitaine* had been an outside force.

"We are certain it is *Zerzan?*" he asked.

"That is the message I have, Ambassador," Lin replied, showing him the screen where it had been decrypted. "That and orders to immediately move to a defensive orbit near the station. One presumes that the Thinkers will send a shuttle to retrieve you?"

"No," Yating replied. "Let us save them the extra step and fly directly to the station itself. I will disembark there and you can move outward."

"What of *Aquitaine*?" she asked him.

"Let him know what you are doing," Yating said. "Kosnett will remain in place until someone orders him elsewhere, though I think that I need to talk the others out of such a stupid action."

"Stupid, Ambassador?" Lin asked. "This is not their battle."

"None of them have been so far, Captain," Yating said. "Not one. And yet, Kosnett has taken it upon himself, time and again, to do the right thing, when measured on generational scales that include the entirety of the Cluster. If *Zerzan* has invaded, they must feel that they are a sufficient threat to the *Domain* to succeed. Can anyone else in the Cluster resist such a thing?"

"They could not," Lin nodded. "Nor would they come to our aid."

"That argument might hold some merit, but we will need to challenge it with the Socratic Method. All the more reason I need to be at the station."

"We are already in motion," she said.

And indeed, the Flyer nodded, typing with precision as the screens adjusted. Both Gunners had transformed from laconic relaxation to feral mindfulness.

Would *Zerzan* attack *Kyulle* itself? Today might be the best possible day for such a thing, at least from his point of view, with four of the Immortals right here in orbit, plus Kosnett sitting off to one side as a rabid porcupine if bothered.

"Station confirms flight path," the Seeker said from his position. "Estimated arrival nineteen minutes."

"I will head below now, Captain," Yating said. "Thank you for a most pleasant and successful journey. May your luck continue."

"And yours, Ambassador," she replied.

Then he was headed aft, down the neck and into the belly of the great machine. The scowl on his face must have been terrible, given the way crew members scampered out of his path, but he was focused on other issues and only remembered it later.

The docking went quickly. Yating found himself met on the far side of the airlock hatch by none other than Wen Qing Jian himself, something of an emeritus these days, with his gray hair pulled back into a scholar's braid and wispy beard. He still dressed like a dock worker in heavy boots and thick pants from an affectation of his ancient youth, though, plus a blue tunic that didn't have any food spilled on it.

Yet.

"Welcome home," Qing said ironically as they fell into a rapid walk deeper into the station. "The messages arrived about eight hours ago. Just perfect for maximum chaos as the outsiders arrived. What is their status?"

"Kosnett has offered to hold or withdraw as we order," Yating said.

"You did not immediately order him to leave?" Qing asked.

"Nor will I, until we gather and speak," Yating replied. "I have my reasons."

Qing shook his head but maintained his brisk pace, especially for an old man.

But more than once Qing had explained that he was almost out of time to do things, so dawdling was unacceptable.

Even more so today.

They reached the Council chambers quickly, passing through several more layers of guards than had been the case even a week ago. Thus was everyone panicking at the news.

The First Speaker rose as they entered, the full group gathered on couches, chairs, or pacing as was their norm.

He studied her. Li Chang Ling. Scholar like himself. First Speaker, as she led this council in discussion and decisions.

Chang was a tall woman. Heavyset. She had been an athlete in her youth, focused on the hammer toss and shotput, events that did not need speed so much as raw power.

Not as bulky today, though still big. She was also in her mid-fifties, almost as gray as Qing, and almost as energetic.

"You saw the message?" she confirmed.

Yating nodded.

"We have been awaiting your arrival, as that means four of the Immortals are here, now," she said. "What of *Aquitaine?*"

"As at *Ewinhome*, Kosnett immediately parked his force on arrival," Yating said. "He offered to remain, or to depart to either a nearby waypoint or to *Oggosaurin*, at least until messages could arrive to update him."

She gawked a bit, but Yating supposed that everyone had expected him to order the strangers to depart before they learned too much.

It was already too late for that, he feared.

"Why have them remain?" Chang asked.

"They could be allies, First Speaker," Yating offered carefully, gauging the looks and body language of the other Scholars in the room. Split pretty much into three equal parts.

As normal.

"They are outsiders!" someone yelled from behind him.

Yating turned around, but couldn't tell who had spoken.

"And thus have no vested interest in conquest," he said. "If the previous year has taught us anything, they are doing quite the opposite. Indeed, they seem to be dedicated specifically to the ideal of a stronger cluster, with all five nations continuing to be independent, but closer aligned by trade and diplomacy, while advancing technologically until we represent potential partners to *Aquitaine*. Kosnett's actions resonate with his words in that case. And I will remind everyone that we are outsiders as well, though we have lived here long enough."

"Qing," the First Speaker ordered. "Bring Yating up to speed."

Yating found a spot on a couch and sat, touching legs on both sides.

"A single ship came out of Jump at *Senza*," Qing began. "There were two *Zhōng* in orbit, but they were quickly overwhelmed by a force of what the station observers classified as *Kuài*, the fast aeromechia we used to build, when we lived elsewhere. However, these were even smaller, perhaps having only a single pilot from the scale reported. And better armed than anything in our records. A combination of some sort of ionization torpedo as well as a firebird-like device even smaller than a *Dalou* shrike."

"And yet they overcame the defenders?" Yating asked.

"There were forty-nine such *Kuài*, Yating," he said.

Yating felt himself flinch. Even with a single pilot, that was a significant force. Comparable to the largest *Ewin* carriers, and likely far more sophisticated. Far more dangerous.

"Casualties on their side?" he asked.

"A dozen damaged, though we cannot be certain how badly, as they were all recovered after the battle, along with a *Niú* tug that was captured," Qing replied.

"Why *Senza*?" he asked the room.

"It suggests that they found the gap at *Loong*," Chang replied evenly.

"Which suggests in turn that someone told them about it," Qing followed up, looking knowingly at a group in one corner.

Yating remembered them as the ones who had argued to simply cut off the Syndicate ships that had worked so closely with the *Domain* for so long. They had made an exceptional argument and carried the decision.

Qing was suggesting that it had been a grave error, at least in retrospect.

But then, weren't all of them?

"Do we presume others coming shortly?" Yating asked. "Perhaps an entire fleet of carriers bearing hordes of *Kuài*?"

"That is the current assessment," Chang told the room. "We have moved the entire government to a war footing, only awaiting your force returning from *Oggosaurin*."

"Is it enough?" Yating asked.

Around the room, faces fell.

They had all lived their entire lives with that shadow over them. All grown from childhood with the stories of the great

Exodus from *Zerzan*, running across the stars for an entire generation, until they crossed the darkness and found *Kyulle*, capturing it from the natives who have lived here before. Similarly, *Angox*, *Kreniea*, *Loarfti*, *Ontan*, and *Cinnramud* had been taken, after which the *Yaumgan Domain* was proclaimed and the borders extended to a defensible wall of stars not all that dissimilar to *Dalou*, across the sphere. Colonies were few, mostly because the populations had never been allowed to boom.

Yating wondered how many people still expected to load up on starships and flee into the darkness again. *Aquitaine* next time? All of those stars were mapped and known now. Claimed, so his people would arrive as refugees, rather than an invading force, as at *Kyulle*.

"Tell me about Kosnett," Chang ordered him.

"You have read my reports from *Aditi* a year ago," Yating said. "In that time, he took *Zhang Gualao* to *Meerut*, then kept *Li Jing* and Captain Xue Dao Zhiou with him, traveling to *Dalou*, *Ewin*, *Gloran*, and *Aditi* again. Now, he comes here, following our original invite after the events at *Vilahana*. Xue speaks highly of him, as do all his actions over that year."

"Would he assist us?" Qing asked, even looking a little like Socrates these days.

"He saved the *Ewin Principalities* from themselves," Yating pointed out. "Even caused the first trade and reciprocity treaty to come into place with *Ewin* and *Dalou*, just to secure the borders so that *Ewin* internal politics did not rupture everything. *Gloran* was ready to start a war with *Aditi* over the *Carinae II* raid. Again, Kosnett stepped in and provided a different outcome."

"We're invaders here," someone called angrily.

"And the indigenous population has not suffered greatly," Yating countered. "They did for a century. Now, they are of us, just as we are of them. Any might rise to be a Scholar."

He was looking directly at Qing when he said that. The old man was not of the old *Zerzan* stock in anything greater than one-eighth. But they were all *Yaumgan* these days.

"Digging up the past will simply cause us to collapse and fail," Qing agreed. "We have many plans in place against today. How many of them should we activate?"

Yating went cold all over. The most extreme involved a set of arks stored at each of the six homeworlds, sailing in the direction that they now knew to be *Aquitaine*. At least they knew that they would receive something of a welcome, were it to come to that.

"Do we assume *Zerzan* is without mercy?" Chang asked the room.

"They attacked without provocation or notice," one of the women in the corner replied, bodies in the way preventing Yating from telling who. "Those are the actions of a pirate or a bandit, not long-lost cousins come to visit."

"They probably tell worse stories about us than we do them," Qing noted. "If they are here, and came secretly, I would presume they have already declared war on the *Domain* and someplace like *Senza* was merely a scouting mission. You note that they captured one of our ships. A tug, granted, and thus of no military value. However, it had a crew. That's likely their purpose. To confirm that *Yaumgan* represents that which once was *Zerzan*, before the revolution. Again, what stance should we take?"

Yating stirred and leaned forward, certain that he was about to gamble his name, his career, and possibly his place in this council room. Thus are all such gambles valued.

"Could we ask for help?" he challenged them.

"Who?" someone yelled derisively. "*Aquitaine?*"

"Them," Yating acknowledged. "There are also four other nations in the Cluster. We are at peace with all of them. Kosnett has been insistent that we come out of our shell and trade with them. Do you honestly think that *Zerzan* would send warfleets this far, then stop once they had captured the *Domain*? Or would that be the stepping stone to take the entire Cluster next?"

The ancient word was *bedlam.* Utter chaos as voices rose and bounced off one another. Fists and fingers shaken in faces. Socrates, reduced to the loudest voice rather than the most cogent questions.

But sometimes, that was necessary, too.

The First Speaker let it rumble for longer than Yating had expected, but eventually everybody got it out of their systems. Had she been using that as an excuse to let things boil over in a controlled circumstance?

Possibly. She was that smart. That exceptional as a First Speaker.

Her yell finally brought silence.

"What makes you think they will?" she finally asked him when everyone else had settled.

"Kosnett arrived with a dreadnought, a cruiser, and seven escorts," Yating said. "At present, every nation of the Cluster has at least one warship sailing in his squadron, going to war on his orders, whether against pirates or princes. If that is not the basis for some sort of grand fleet for defending the entirety of the Balhee Cluster, First Speaker, what is?"

She studied him for a long moment, everyone else in here deadly silent, breaths held and eyes focused.

"We might be that desperate," she finally admitted.

And Yating understood what fear really was.

FOURTEEN

Senior Chief Harman Abadjiev was occasionally teased by his staff as *King of the Fairies*, since the group was now known informally as *Pixies*. Centurion Fabre was his boss. Young enough to be his daughter. And smart enough to let him indulge himself, because she had figured out where to draw the line with him.

That was all he'd ever really needed out of life.

Today, he was using a significant portion of the navigation computer's horsepower to crunch numbers. Brute force sure, but sometimes that was what you needed. Most codes tended to be simple substitution things, so all you needed to know was the original language itself, then you could start analyzing linguistic tendencies.

He wasn't sure what language the locals spoke at home, but like everyone else, there was a hard thread of Hindi woven through everything. Made sense, since it had been one of only a handful of languages that had survived the long centuries in space in the old days.

Plus, the combination of crap he was picking up without encryption—commercial radio, for instance—would let him identify the rest. Right now, the computers were suggesting an underlying current of northwestern European sub-language of some sort, blurring ancient German and ancient French in equal parts, going back to the Early Space Age.

But then again, electronic communications tended to rupture small languages on a generational scale, even as the big ones got reinforced. You wanted to be able to speak the lingo of folks doing business, and your kids might not learn the old tongue in the process.

Hindi and Euro. Weird-ass mix. Still, he turned to Spacer Jacob, sitting next to him and monitoring things. The kid looked up expectantly from his screen. Another one young enough to be one of his literally, instead of just metaphorically.

"Science Officer turned us loose," he reminded the young man. "I'm routing you five sets of things I've identified that look interesting. I want you to write me a program that identifies the base language that they were written in, so we can work forward into crypto terms. This is your top priority for the next six hours."

He could give that order. Leyla and Cerere Fabre had *turned him loose*.

"What are specifically are you looking for, Chief?" he asked.

"Not everybody in this system is going to be encrypting things," Harman replied. "Most of it will just be packet segmentation designed to keep things from getting messy. I've located a couple of civilian channels, but we're not set up to talk on them right now. Weird sub-band stuff. Likely nothing I've seen, but Hindi is not their first language. I can guess at what is, but I need you to locate me a full linguistic breakdown sufficient to order dinner at a nice restaurant and have a conversation with someone over food."

"Gotcha," Jacob said. "Coming up."

Harman nodded and went back to his stuff.

Euro? Early Space Age? That had meant dozens of different languages, stuffed into a tiny peninsula on the western edge of the main continental cluster, if his memory served. Important mostly because the first big industrial revolution had started there, expanding their cultures and languages elsewhere as they gained technical power.

"Chief, I got something weird," Able Spacer Haug called from across the dark chamber. "Message transmitted to *Li Jing* and *Zhang Gualao*. New crypto signature, but derived from an older one we have the key to."

"Crack it?" he asked automatically.

"Need a couple of days," she nodded back. "Probably have to have Jacob hit it with a few thing firsts. Trick is, I have a new phrase that doesn't fit any other linguistic signature. Might be a code, but feels like a simple substitution in this case."

"What's the term?" he asked.

"*Zerzan Unification*," she replied. "Part of a report from *Senza*, if I'm translating semi-coded Hindi correctly. They got it from transponders, I think."

"Show me," he ordered, wondering if he should poke the Centurion. She was doing paperwork right now, leaving him to run things without having to stop to answer stupid questions on the fly. At some point, she needed to step in and take the credit for the shit he was likely causing around here.

Nobody appreciated spies, but nobody wanted to do without them, either.

Harman read the message. Washed it through a couple of things he'd been meaning to try on *Li Jing* one of these days and hadn't gotten around to. Upped the coherence nearly sixteen percent when he did, with a ninety-three percent confidence. Good enough for government work.

"Who has the flag?" he asked the room, leaning back to study the new message.

Harman had been too busy to listen on the command channel, already digging in like a tick when the First Centurion had smelled a rat on arrival.

"Heather," Haug replied.

Harman shrugged and flipped a coin in his head.

She was his guardian angel. He might be needing that shortly.

"Haug, you're in charge until I get back," he said. "Anything interesting and you can't find me, contact the Centurion and bring her up to speed before the big bosses get on the circuit."

"Got it."

Harman locked everything down and rose. Pulled his uniform a little flatter, happy that he hadn't spilled anything on himself today. Bridge wasn't that far away. Nobody bothered him as he entered.

Command Centurion Lau locked on him like a Type-4 battery as soon as he entered, eyes like a hawk.

He suppressed a natural grimace and moved towards her, stopping a respectable distance away and waiting. She finished typing something and gave him her full attention.

"Chief?" she asked quietly.

Harman stepped close and pushed the button on her console to open a privacy field around her station. And him. Wouldn't completely isolate things, but it would make people have to work to overhear him.

"The bad guys here might be called the *Zerzan Unification*, Command Centurion," he said simply. "They might be the folks that chased *Yaumgan* out of wherever they used to live in the before time. They are freaking pissed, because they only stopped blowing shit up at *Senza* after everyone who could had slipped close under the station's guns or ran like hell and made it to JumpSpace while the defense forces were getting their asses handed to them. I'm two days out from fully cracking everything, but that's the message that comes out of the hash with the most coherence. Folks around here expect *Kyulle* and the other core worlds to be hit next. Like tomorrow, though there's a serious deep sigh going around that we're here and brought three of the Immortals with us. Folks are on the edge of panic."

"How bad?" she asked.

"Somebody asked if they were going to activate a plan for the arks to flee to *Aquitaine*," Harman said. "Whatever *that* means. Again, moderate to high confidence in the translation, but I'm going to need a few days to break *Yaumgan*'s codes to the point I can be certain. I know enough to alert you right now. And more will be coming."

"Anything specifically you need from me?" she asked.

"Plot a single JumpSpace course out of here and let me have the computers after that?" he asked. "Or let *Viking* do it instead so I can unleash all that processing power?"

"You got it, Senior Chief," she nodded. "I'll let Phil know. You keep me, Iveta, Harinder, and him in the loop as things come up."

Harman nodded and backed out of the field.

After the stupid shit at *Ewinhome* the first time, everyone had given him credit for keeping the squadron out of an irrelevant fight.

"Oh," he said, stepping back in again. "Also, a lot of folks are asking each other if we're here to help *Yaumgan* or if we're some sort of *Zerzan* Trojan Horse. All civilian traffic right now, but that's likely to change."

She nodded and Harman walked away. He had a lot of things that were good enough he was willing to bet money on, but none of them he was willing bet his life on yet.

Give him and his people two days, though…

FIFTEEN

Bausse studied the image on her screens. Rather than remain with the main fleet, she had been resupplied and sent out on a new mission. More important than the last one, but also a reward for the successful raid on *Senza*.

The aristocrats had come to *Kyulle* first, of all the worlds in this Balhee Cluster where they could have settled. False trails left behind had led the *Unification* astray for centuries, tracking closer to the center of the galaxy and conquering several worlds and nations, but never locating a clue towards their ancient overlords.

That aristocratic scum had fled into the darkness instead. The galactic wastes between arms, where the stars were thin and distances great, save for a single, shining pearl in the night sky. A star-forming nebula that had bubbled out the center and created an entire cluster of worlds and stars inside.

And now, *Kyulle's* star was a brighter gem in the firmament of night. *Truhto* was hiding as far out as possible, shadowed by a ball of ice in the darkness. Watching over the rim of the world at the warm spots closer in with nothing but passive optical equipment.

She turned to the pirate. Once Captain Nolan Hames of the

Nagi vessel *Ravenscall*, now a recent member of the *Unification*, serving penance for past misdeeds and earning a spot somewhere other than a reeducation camp. Probably.

"Tell me about *Aquitaine*," she said, pointing to a cluster of ships that had arrived a day ago, the messages from their transponders only recently arriving this many light-hours out. "And the others."

Hames was average height. Muscular. Shaved bald but for a bristle of graying fur on his chin. Probably used to being in command.

He wasn't a pirate anymore. The *Unification* had no use for his kind, and only needed the man himself for what he contained in his head.

He might yet prove his worth.

"You are from the west, as seen from Balhee," Hames reminded her.

It was a stupid distinction, but he was a stupid man, prone to explaining things to her like she was a child. Or perhaps his sexism was just that overwhelming, even yet. She might need to break him. Later. For now she nodded.

"*Aquitaine* comes from the next arm east on the map," he repeated himself. "They supposedly fought several terrible wars with places called *Fribourg* and *Buran*, winning both and establishing peace."

"Without conquest?" she confirmed, still appalled at such behavior.

Why fight a war if not to expand your nation?

"Without conquest," he nodded. "They built a survey fleet and sailed to Balhee to explore. At *Vilahana*, they got on the wrong side of the Syndicates and went to war. Kosnett won at *Meerut*, and the *Zen-Mekyo Syndicates* are no more. Everyone had a price on their head, regardless of previous activities, so *Ravenscall* loaded up with supplies and fled to your territory, where we were captured and interned. You apparently knew the

Yaumgan people from before, so I have put all my knowledge at your disposal to return."

At least he had that part correct. His penance. Her decision.

"You worked with *Yaumgan* in the past," she said.

"And thus knew about the accessible gap at *Loong*," he nodded. "A few others do as well, because they used to pay us to bother *Ewin* or *Gloran* shipping, but doing so in a way that could not be traced."

"Tell me about Kosnett," Bausse said, tapping an icon called *Urumchi* on the screen between them.

"Massive warship," he said. "They call it a Survey Dreadnought. *Viking* is a Survey Cruiser. Both are heavier and more dangerous than anything around here."

"Including those four capital ships?" Bausse touched the icon for *Lü Dongbin* next.

"One on one, the *Yaumgan* Immortal might win," Hames shrugged. "I was not at *Meerut* to see it in battle myself. Kosnett also brought a fleet of escorts with him. Plus he has all those cruisers from the other nations with him, including *Yaumgan*."

"Nothing can stand before a *Zerzan* Swarm," Bausse snarled.

Hames nodded and kept his mouth shut. At least he could learn, having attempted to argue with her previously. And lost.

"Will you attack *Kyulle*?" he asked, mostly sounding curious more than anything.

"Our current mission was to scout," Bausse said. "To track down the three Immortals that had gone to *Oggosaurin* to meet *Aquitaine*. With this information, we will return to the fleet and let the Unifiers determine. Your assignment, as we return, is to fill in everything you know or suspect about all of these vessels, the ones representing the other nations of the Cluster, so we can decide how dangerous they might be."

"Will you conquer the rest after *Yaumgan*?" Hames asked.

"That is not for you to know," she snapped.

She nodded a dismissal and he bowed, backing away and leaving with the two guards who had been quietly watching him.

Aquitaine was supposedly at least the equal of this *Yaumgan Domain*, though they only had a small force here instead of sufficient tonnage and firepower to withstand the *Unification*.

It would probably be necessary to destroy them quickly, though, before they could send panicked messages home for reinforcements.

"Transport," she said, turning her attention to the woman in charge of piloting and astrogation. "I have seen enough. Plot a course to get us back to the fleet as quickly as possible, then engage."

The woman nodded and Bausse went back to her screens.

One force of warships built in the old style, rather than mecha like advanced nations did it.

How dangerous could something like that be?

SIXTEEN

Senior Centurion Aurelius "Auke" Alma sat and monitored signals. Centurion Danil Watton was watching the Sciences station for the Science Officer. He looked up now.

"First Officer, I have an anomaly," Watton said with a confused/concerned tone.

Auke's hand hovered over the alert switch that would bring the shields to full and sound alarms capable of raising the dead from their sleep.

"Details, Centurion?" Auke asked, careful not to swear at the young man. Sunan hadn't broken the kid into leading with important things instead of grunts.

Auke could fight any battle, but only when he knew what was coming.

"I have a signal anomaly, Senior Centurion," Watton repeated himself, but fell into reporting cadence. "We keep watch on every object close enough to *Kyulle*'s star to offer a measurable solar reflection. Twelve hours ago, something changed in the albedo of one of them, but we don't have sufficient astrogation records of this system to know if the object I saw was large enough to have a gravitationally bound moon orbiting it in such a way that the image changes."

Lots of rocks and iceballs out there far enough, big enough, and they tended to be stable enough to draw in smaller objects, given time. Lots of *maybe* though. That was why you watched, because a smaller moon orbiting might look just like *Viking* or some scout peeking over the top of a moon from the darkness.

Hide With Pride was more than a motto. It was a way of life.

"Keep watch to see how it changes," Auke ordered, shifting his hand over to the button that would bring Barnaby Silver out of whatever reverie the Command Centurion might be currently engaging in.

"What do you have?" Barnaby asked as soon as he came on the line.

"A bad feeling," Auke replied. "Nothing sufficient to warrant an alert, because we're looking backwards in time twelve hours, and anybody even halfway competent would be gone by now."

"Enemy ship?" Barnaby asked.

"A year ago, I would have said pirates," Auke laughed. "Or fools. Both met their match at *Meerut*, so I'll suggest Kosnett's *Pixies* might be onto something and we had a scout at the edge of the system."

"Route it here," Barnaby ordered.

Auke nodded to Watton and watched the kid press a button on his console.

When Auke was in charge doing that sort of thing, *Viking* would broach for all of about five or maybe eight minutes. Just long enough to let the sensors drink a big gulp of data, then drop down, spin in place, and run like hell into the darkness, so you had time to digest everything without worrying someone might catch you.

A cubic light-year didn't sound all that big, until you had to find an enemy warship hiding in the middle of it.

Barnaby was back a few moments later.

"I concur, Auke," he said. "Ping Kosnett and ask him to ask the locals if they want to send someone out to investigate or send us and a couple of the corvettes."

Auke cut the line and shifted over to *Urumchi.*

Leyla Ekmekçi appeared next on his screen with one eyebrow raised.

"Routing you a scan," he said simply. Leyla didn't need a big production. "Barnaby asks if the locals want to scout it or send us."

"Will let you know," she replied.

Auke cut the line and leaned back.

He was suddenly back in the *Buran* days, when ships like the legendary *RAN Ballard* set the bar high for sneaking into an enemy system and stealing all their secrets, setting the stage for Keller to come storming out of the night with her pack of wolves.

Somebody was setting up to attack *Kyulle.* While they had the heaviest part of their fleet here, or just waiting for the locals to turn their back and send Immortals elsewhere?

Auke composed an extra alert note to be routed quietly to everybody in the squadron, just in case the locals decided to go look.

He didn't think they were prepared to be on the receiving end of that sort of thing. Nobody had dared *Yaumgan*'s frontiers in decades, as far as their public relations work went.

That might work against them now.

SEVENTEEN

KYULLE STATION ONE, KYULLE ORBITAL SPACE

Yating was sitting in his personal quarters, blessedly alone, when a bell at the door announced a visitor. He rose to see who intended to interrupt his quiet time, alone for the first time in weeks, not counting time on *Zhang Gualao* where he dined with the officers every meal.

The First Speaker stood in the hallway. Alone, because they were in a secure part of the station and he didn't need to worry about people.

Yating had known Chang for nearly three decades at this point, a few years younger than him and running in different circles until she had given up on sports and focused on the mind. Still a physical presence in ways that only Kosnett really matched, and he suspected she outmassed the First Centurion as well.

Yating stepped back and gestured her to join him. He closed the hatch and returned to the warm seat with the mug of tea where he had been reading. Chang moved to the couch.

He was always surprised that a woman that big could curl her feet under her like a cat, but she was also that limber, in spite of age and size.

"There is a message from the *Aquitaine* flagship," she began as he settled. "In Kosnett's name, but transmitted quietly. Their big scout ship spotted something at the edge of the system they suspect is a *Zerzan* vessel scouting, though they didn't call it that."

Yating nodded.

"If *Viking* so classified it, I would assume that they are right," he replied. "What action will you take?"

"You assume correctness on scant evidence?" Chang asked, confusion visible in her eyes, though not her face.

"Xue Dao Zhiou has spent a year with them," Yating said. "She has learned and communicated to us the centuries-long war with *Fribourg*, then the greater war with the god of winter known as *Buran*. They are a nation forged in warfare, in this generation. In the question of military competence, I would trust them. And I ask again, what action will you take?"

"You know them better than we do, however little," Chang nodded. "What would you suggest? They offered to go scout or let us do it."

"We are none of us warriors, Chang," Yating said. "For military advice, Lin Na Tai would serve you better. But you know that, so I presume you want social and political advice."

Her wide face and big eyes smiled at him. Big woman, made of muscle and bulk, but she still reminded one of a fairy when she smiled like that. Probably why she did it.

"Kosnett, as I spoke of previously, has gone out of his way to help," Yating said. "Even when it was unnecessary. I think he would do the same here. I appreciate that we are the thralls of centuries of secrecy and guile, but I also wonder if that works against us."

"How so?" Chang asked, shifting more of her body square to him now as he had her attention.

"*Dalou* is the most like us," he said. "Was. Kosnett's arrival caused a cascade of changes that have seen the future Emperor of *Dalou* travel to war with him. The middle daughter of the Shogun has proclaimed her intent to rise to power. She serves on

Kosnett's flagship in their uniform, so I presume she is learning their ways and will cause that to transform the Hegemony in her time."

Chang nodded. Old reports, from Captain Xue and other spies.

"*Ewin* was broken, but Kosnett caused the pieces to be glued back together," Yating continued. "*Gloran* nearly came to blows with *Aditi*. Again, Kosnett intervened."

"*Zerzan* is not here to make peaceful overtures," Chang said darkly. "Not if they have raided *Senza* as they did."

Yating paused and let the moment of silence stretch as he sought the words.

"Captain Xue called the new Lord Morninghawk a herald of destruction and change," he said. "*Dalou's* words, apparently. But a herald is not the agent of change. Merely he who proclaims it. Kosnett is the progenitor. If we mean to fight *Zerzan*, and I presume we do, whatever other contingency plans are activated, we will need allies. The others might not listen to us, having been warned off time and again. In fact, two years ago, before Kosnett, I would have been willing to wager that *Ewin* and *Gloran* would have gladly aided *Zerzan* in attacking us. *Aditi* would have been more circumspect, but no less aggressive. I do not believe that *Yaumgan* will ever have a better chance to ask for help."

"You believe we need it," she said flatly.

"*Zerzan* seems to believe we need it," he countered. "They would not have attacked out of the blue but for surety on their part that they could take us. I have looked at the logs of the attack. Forty-nine small aeromechia, splitting into two teams and overwhelming the two defenders because they seemed to have built a force designed to engage big mecha. Sunswords and titan bolt clusters will be like shooting at a swarm of rats. Eyebeams work some, but this is nothing we've ever planned for."

"*Zerzan* built a fleet to destroy us?" Chang asked.

"Once upon a time, the Skycruiser was the epitome of technological sophistication," Yating reminded her. "We built the Immortals to defend our worlds. Did *Zerzan* build these swarms of smaller vessels because they knew us so well? We have better and more interesting weapons, but how quickly can those be brought to the field? Not quickly enough. We must rethink everything."

"What becomes of *Yaumgan*?" she asked.

"What becomes of it if *Zerzan* conquers us?" he volleyed back. "Do you think anything of our current culture would survive? The question, First Speaker, is not if we can afford to consider change. That choice is no longer ours. We must identify the form it will take and attempt to shape it while the hands in control are still ours. Given the choice, I would reach out to this Lord Morninghawk and ask him how and when he came to see the future. He did the most to shape what will become of *Dalou*. Perhaps the entire cluster before he is done."

She had gone still. Yating found that he was forward to the edge of his seat, so he leaned back again and reached for his tea, finding it still warm enough to drink and not taste of ashes.

She leaned forward as he retreated. Fixed him with those terrible, dark eyes.

"I need to meet Kosnett in the flesh," she said. "Take his measure. But not here, where he will be on his best behavior. I need to go aboard his flagship and meet his crew as well. If we are to trust our fate to their hands, as you suggest, I need to know how they will shape *Yaumgan*."

Yating nodded.

That which he had known was about to die, but change was the nature of all things, and a trained philosopher was better equipped to understand that than most people.

He nodded.

Yaumgan would need to transform. *That which it will become tomorrow.*

And Kosnett would hold those reins in his hands.

EIGHTEEN

Phil was surprised by the speed with which things were moving. Everyone always talked about how slowly *Yaumgan* did everything, to the extent that their sudden movement to *Aditi* when he first arrived had been the biggest thing anyone had known in their lifetime.

Now, the First Speaker of the Domain had asked for a meeting aboard *Urumchi*. As in immediately. And had set out as soon as he had cleared everything and warned Chief Bottenberg that they would have company to feed.

The Chief of the Wardroom did not answer to gender. Only to cooking as the highest form of love.

A small dinner was planned. It would still be amazing. The Chief was like that.

Urumchi had moved closer to the station, but not close. A polite hailing and sailing distance, compared to before.

Zhang Gualao still was the ship that made the journey, though considering the passenger, he could understand.

He and Heather met the party at the airlock. First Speaker Li Chang Ling. Elder Scholar Wen Qing Jian, looking like he had just worked a shift on the docks moving crates before joining them. Ambassador Hu Yating Kai. Even Captain Lin of *Zhang Gualao* was present.

The First Speaker was the dominant personality. Phil just had to watch the body language of the others to see that she was in charge. That helped, as Hu had been evasive and deflective most of the time.

And it was interesting meeting a woman his size. They were not that common, and most tended to be built more like Heather, tall volleyball players. First Speaker Chang had shoulders as wide as his, but she was not fat. Just big. Muscular.

Powerful.

Dar escorted them to a conference room and Chief Bottenberg got everyone settled with juice, coffee, or tea.

"Thank you for inviting us, First Centurion Kosnett," the First Speaker spoke immediately as everyone sat. "I appreciate that we did not transmit a meeting plan ahead of time, and thus would catch you somewhat off guard with whichever direction the conversation might lead."

Phil nodded. First Speaker was a position apparently awarded by acclaim, rather than votes in a republic, like *Aditi*, or inheritance, as the others. An odd way to govern, but he had read enough Plato in his time to understand the fundamental underpinnings of the logic.

Identify the best and the brightest according to your culture. Train them up with socialization and expectations. Watch them like hawks before awarding them supreme executive authority.

Smart people. Insular. He only had to read *Stunt Dude's* reports on Dao Zhiou to understand that they presented a closed face to the outside world. Even after a year.

"I am here at your sufferance, First Speaker," he replied. "We are the first outsiders invited to *Kyulle* in a considerable stretch, and thus it behooves us to act as polite guests. How may we assist in your current troubles?"

The quick glances around the four spoke volumes, but they

probably didn't appreciate what his *Pixies* had done. Continued to do.

Being inside somebody's decision curve was a lovely place to be. You could predict where they were going to go. And perhaps even guide them. Control outcomes.

"One of our colonies was recently attacked by an outside force," First Speaker Li said. "The perpetrators were not local, as near as we have been able to identify. There is an expectation that they may launch other attacks."

Phil nodded. About what he'd gotten from folks whose job it was to piece these things together from random tidbits.

"As I noted in conversation with Ambassador Hu, we would be happy to withdraw," Phil said, just watch their body language adjust. "I would presume that *Oggosaurin* would be a minimum in such a case. Alternatively, perhaps we should reschedule this event for later, so as to not distract?"

Phil wondered how much of the vaunted superiority of *Yaumgan* rested on the factor of how hidden they were from most of the Cluster. None of them were particularly good at hiding their emotions right now.

Or they were, and were even more scared than he had expected.

"On the contrary, First Centurion," Li spoke. "We have a different problem. Our expectation is that those seeking to destroy us believe that they command sufficient force to do so. That they will seek one of the core worlds. *Kyulle* is the best defended at present, with four of the Immortals at anchor."

"You seek allies," he said simply.

Nods.

"I hope that Captain Xue has sent home sufficient reports then, of what this squadron has been up to over the last year," Phil said. "Captain Lin, you were there at *Meerut* with us."

"Indeed, First Centurion," the woman replied. "My reports as well as Xue Dao Zhiou's form something of the basis of this request."

Phil turned back to the First Speaker.

"Who are these enemies that seek to do you harm?" he asked in a voice that even sounded innocent.

That had been the one piece *nobody* had been able to fill in.

Yet.

Li looked like she had sucked on a sour lemon. Phil wasn't surprised. If they wanted something, they were going to have to give up something.

"They call themselves the *Zerzan Unification*," the woman said.

Phil nodded and leaned back, inviting explanations and stories from his own body language.

"*Yaumgan* represents a small group of survivors, First Centurion," she began. "Exiles. Once, we were the aristocratic elite of a place known as the *Zerzan Monarchy*."

Oh? Phil continued to smile neutrally.

"A revolution that turned bloody caused our ancestors to flee, initially heading deeper toward the galactic core. After a period measured in decades, a decision was made to travel across the darkness between galactic arms, with the expectation that they would not be able to find us. We conquered *Kyulle* and the others, absorbing the native populations and forming the *Yaumgan Domain* instead. We have hidden here for centuries, unwilling to even look for our old aggressors, lest we accidentally lead them to our new Eden. They appear to have found us."

"The timing is suggestive," Heather offered, causing the other four to jolt, having probably forgotten that she was there. "Did we chase off a pirate that used to work for you, and they sold you out?"

The older male scowled.

"Thus, Command Centurion, is part of our dilemma," he said. "We cannot know at present. We might never know, at least until such time as they conquer us and round up the survivors to whatever fate awaits them on our old worlds."

"*Yaumgan* has friends," Heather opined.

"The *Domain* has neighbors who fear and respect us," the old man countered. "As they should. We have played the role of the terrible dragon guarding its horde for a long time."

Phil wasn't sure he'd heard a more evocative, and utterly accurate, description of the Philosopher/Kings."

"Did they come via *Vilahana*?" he asked, just to see how honest they felt like playing this.

Captains Xue and Lin had both been good sailors, but these were their superiors.

Phil still remembered his part in bringing down his own government, back home, for treason and other crimes.

Sometimes, following orders was the wrong thing to do. Any competent military understood that the nation itself was greater than the people who led it.

Because politicians sometimes lost sight of that point.

All power corrupts eventually, unless you wake up every morning and commit to being a better person than you were yesterday.

Three of the visitors had turned to Ambassador Hu. Telling, that.

"There is a gap called *Loong*," he spoke. "Not far from *Senza*. We suspect that they arrived thus, especially given their first target."

"Because that was the path the pirates used to take when they went raiding *Gloran* or *Ewin* for you?" Heather asked.

Slight gasps, magnified by the vast silence around them.

Ambassador Hu bowed his head.

"None of us have clean hands, Command Centurion," he offered weakly.

"That was yesterday," Phil rescued him adroitly. "Today you are in need of friends. Tomorrow, you will need allies. That is why I am here, but *Aquitaine* is too far away to help in the short term. You will need the *Aditi Consensus*. The *Gloran Empire*. The

Dalou Hegemony. And yes, Creator help us all, even the *Ewin Principalities.*"

The emotional let-down in their faces was telling, but honest. They had spent careers warning off the very people that they would need to visit, possibly hat in hand, if things were bad enough that the First Speaker had come to him like this.

Phil started to speak when the alert chimes sounded overhead.

"*Aquitaine* squadron, this is *Junkyard,* aboard *Urumchi,*" Iveta's voice overrode everything like the *Voice of Doom.* "I have the flag. Hostile ships are inbound. All crews and vessels to battle stations. Unlock and prepare to unleash hell on my orders."

Phil nodded to Heather and she was off, Captain Lin in her immediate wake. That made sense, as *Zhang Gualao* would need their commanding officer.

But what to do about the other three?

All four rose slower. The older gentleman, Scholar Wen Qing Jian, bowed.

"Perhaps, First Centurion, we might inflict ourselves on your hospitality a bit longer?" he asked.

"And not *Zhang Gualao?*" Phil countered.

"Captain Lin will fly into the center of battle, as she has trained her entire career," the man noted. "We have concerns that *Yaumgan's* fleet might not be capable of resisting *Zerzan,* even with your assistance, and we do not know if the enemy will realize that we are aboard your flagship. Plus, we can answer questions with what pitiful store of information we currently possess, if you find yourself drawn into the war, even accidentally."

Phil returned the bow.

They were stuck here. And likely expected *Zhang Gualao* to be destroyed in battle.

He'd withdrawn from *Ewinhome* the first time, rather than get engaged in a war not of his choosing.

At Second *Ewinhome*, it had been necessary to get personally involved.

Now, he stood at *Kyulle*.

Possibly already waist deep in somebody else's war.

95

NINETEEN

Iveta had the flag while Phil and Heather were entertaining guests. *Zhang Gualao* was flying alongside like a man in the water with dolphins or something. Everyone else had already stepped it up a second notch from the one they'd gone to after Auke sent around a note about uninvited visitors.

Leyla was at her station, pulling a double today because a lot of her people had been borrowed by the *Pixies* and she didn't want to slow that effort down.

"We got trouble," Leyla suddenly spoke out in a clear voice. "I have a whole block of ships that just came out of Jump at the edge of the gravity well. About where I'd drop if I meant to launch an attack."

Iveta brought her screen up. Yes. Someone had studied Keller. Or understood that there were only so many ways that you could do something like that.

"Oh, shit!" Leyla added. "I have a crash launch on all of them. Those are carriers and they are launching fighters as quickly as they can clear the tubes in front of them!"

"*Aquitaine* squadron, this is *Junkyard*, aboard *Urumchi*," Iveta said as she keyed the widest channel, including the open comm so the local mecha ships could hear her. Whether they understood and believed her was something else. "I have the flag. Hostile ships are inbound. All crews and vessels to battle stations. Unlock and prepare to unleash hell on my orders."

She switched channels now.

"*Zhang Gualao*, you come alongside immediately and dock so we can get your captain aboard."

"Understood, *Urumchi*," a male voice replied. "Same pattern as before."

Iveta nodded to Bozhidar Virág as he slid into the Pilot's station, displacing the woman who had been earning credit training. Now was not the time for anybody but the A-Team at the stations.

"Iveta, this is Phil," the boss's voice came over a comm. "Most guests are remaining aboard for now, once Captain Lin transfers."

"Roger that," Iveta replied. "Flag bridge?"

"Affirmative, you remain in command while we sort everything out. What are you facing?"

"Fleet carriers like the old days, Phil," Iveta said. "Scaled down mecha that look like single-crew snubfighters with arms and legs. A crazy number of them. Hundreds now and they keep coming."

"Assume they know who our visitors are and behave accordingly," Phil said. "I'll head forward now."

Iveta turned her attention to the two behemoths disgorging plagues of locusts like a freaking clown car.

"Leyla, scale them for our old carriers and estimate wing sizes," Iveta ordered. "Gunner, I figure the Type-4s will be wasted on something that small, so you concentrate on the carriers. Pot shots at range are acceptable, if it drives them off. Also be prepared to use the big guns to break up any concentrations that think they can gang up on someone."

Nods and assents. She had time, because everybody was already nervous so they'd been paying attention.

And launching hundreds and hundreds of those little ships,

even twelve at a time, six at the bow and six at the stern, took a while, with the squadrons forming up instead of immediately charging.

On the one hand, that was good, as it meant that they didn't think the first wave of berserkers over the wall would be sufficient. On the other hand, it meant that she might be fighting all of them at once.

"*Aquitaine* Squadron, form up in *Consensus Echelon* astern, with *Viking* just ahead of *Urumchi* on your current flank. All the cruisers take your usual wings ahead of that. *Forktail*, close escort as always. Corvettes stand by to repel boarders. *Varmint*, get gone as fast as you can and circle back in twelve hours. Phil will have a message pack for you now to haul to *Meerut* if things go really bad here. *Hollywood*, do you want to stand or withdraw?"

"Why would I run, *Junkyard?*" *Hollywood* Ward replied instantly.

"You're a civilian these days," Iveta reminded her. "And even an ex-Raider like yours isn't built to stand toe-to-toe with what's coming. Couple of extra guns would be nice, but you might be better served getting the word out to the rest of the Cluster."

"What do you expect them to do?" *Hollywood* asked.

"Be prepared to be next," Iveta said. "Dunno. Shit just got real around here."

"I'll cover your rear flank," *Hollywood* offered. "And I can drop down and slingshot out the back side of the gravity well if it gets ugly."

"*Hollywood*, this is Phil," he came on the line. "If it gets exceptionally bad, I would ask that you go directly to *Ladaux* for me and talk to the First Lord of the Fleet. As with *Varmint*, stand by for a message pack."

Iveta gulped in spite of herself. Phil had threatened to ask the First Lord for *Götterdämmerung* itself on more than one occasion. Eight Heavy Dreadnoughts in formation, with thirty-plus and more corvettes.

Given the shit in front of her, Iveta would have asked for

sixty corvettes and damn the heavy ships. Maybe one or two Expeditionary cruisers along as command hulls, but just bring along all the Pulse-Twos ever built.

Somebody hadn't gotten the message from Doysan IV and his friends.

"I have launches," Leyla called. "Left fist and right fist sort of thing, from the way they are standing in space. Tracking like small firebirds, but I'm not getting the same sort of homing signals."

"Ballistic and terminal guidance?" Iveta asked.

"Maybe," Leyla shrugged. "Or just ballistic and charge in behind them? No clue. Never seen anything like it."

"Start scan logs under a new enemy file," Iveta ordered. "*Zerzan Unification* Assault Mecha and assume advanced versions of *Yaumgan* ships for now. Are they making any threats? Calling for our surrender? Trash talking?"

"That's just it," Leyla said. "I've been monitoring everything. It's all encoded, and seems to be flyer to ships, like we used to do it. Nothing at any of us, *Yaumgan* or squadron."

Iveta nodded and found the menu item she wanted on her screen.

Harman looked up at her in surprise when he realized who had called.

"Enemy ships talking to each other in code," Iveta said simply. "I'd like to know what they're transmitting."

She cut the line immediately, certain she had just loosed a rabid fox into the hen house, since Harman and his people were already working pretty much with *carte blanche* to crack *Yaumgan*'s signals security.

Let's see what Zerzan *has to say.*

TWENTY

Bausse watched Wing Leader Senebach form up his group on the bow of *Truhto* and start to dive inwards on a Skycruiser and Escort sitting to one side of the larger orbital groups. The two Overlord Transport Carriers, *Bertev* and *Rauda*, were leading the major thrusts of this assault, *Bertev* against the defenses around the largest orbital platform and *Rauda* going after the outsider fleet that signals intelligence suggested was hosting high ambassadors of the *Yaumgan* government.

Truhto lacked the sorts of firepower to engage such a foe. Hers was an Assault Carrier, bringing a full Wing of aeromechia after she'd replaced crews lost at *Senza*. Forty-nine was a sizeable force, but *Rauda* carried nine hundred and eighty-two, all of them tuned and launching.

Nothing could stand before such a force as twenty full Wings began swooping in.

"Optics, confirm target status," Bausse ordered, looking over at the man.

"Our two targets were at a higher alert status than we expected," the man replied. "Perhaps we were noticed when scouting."

"Or the outsiders are not trusted guests and they were

prepared for some double-cross," Bausse noted. "Transport, hold this line and maintain status. We will be closest to the enemy today, so our job will be to provide a platform for damaged aeromechia needing to land. Flight Boss Beauvoie, remind your people that anybody we do end up rescuing will be damaged enough that they'll probably need to be dragged out of the landing bay by hand. Also, keep a line to your pilots so nobody lands hot on top of them."

"Understood, Chevalier," Beauvoie replied, going back to his various teams.

The *Zerzan Unification* hadn't launched an attack on this scale in almost a decade. Back before she'd risen to Chevalier of her own vessel and had been serving as a Flight Boss herself.

Today, *Yaumgan* was about to understand that they should have kept running, perhaps halfway around the galactic curve, just to keep enough space from *Zerzan*.

Bausse watched the myriad dots indicating attacking forces work their way inward.

Revenge, at last.

Phil had a bit of a crowd today. Nam's normal duty station was no longer one of the Pulse-Two batteries, as he'd moved her to his flag bridge permanently so he could pick her brain as he needed to. Exceptionally useful right now. Kohahu was there as well, rising and bowing to the First Speaker and the other two as everyone got settled around the projection table.

The image displayed was enough to take his breath away.

"Science Officer, have we confirmed those numbers?" he asked on the bridge line, trying not to sound surprised.

"Affirmative, Phil," Leyla said. "The big ones carry just shy of one thousand. The four little ones each have about fifty. Scans suggest that they are in the same mass and firepower range as those fighters that Bedrov designed, back when we still thought they could be useful against *Buran*."

Phil grunted, remembering *First Trusski* and that nightmarish encounter. Playing tag with swords in a pitch black room. Keller had won, but the costs had been nearly Pyrrhic. Star Controller *Auberon* smashed, along with a lot of the flight squadron. But *Buran* had still gotten the worse end.

He opened a line to Iveta.

"Sir?" she asked, looking up at the screen.

"One, are they acting like *Buran?*" he asked. "New and unknown technology."

"Negative," Iveta replied. "They landed almost exactly where I would have, if all I had were carriers like the old days, without significant beam firepower. *Second Thuringwell,* but I don't have d'Maine handy to surprise them."

Phil nodded. Best thing Heather had ever talked him into. Not just a Jessica Keller clone, as that had almost been a given with the mission parameters. But one with a working, encyclopedic knowledge of Keller's career, as well as several others. Always studying battles and campaigns to glean some new strategy or tactic.

Or to be instantly ready to respond.

"We're backing in echelon?" Phil asked, checking the flight path.

"Affirmative, First Centurion," Iveta said, her eyes getting cagey as she realized he was up to something.

Retrograde was the obvious response to this sort of attack. Keep them in front of you, firing and holding them off as long as you could. *Yaumgan's* fleet wouldn't be able to make as much use of it as he could because they didn't have anything heavier than eyebeams for short range against those mini-firebirds.

Phil assumed *Zerzan* was counting on that, especially the way they were starting to spread out, like a net with hardpoints. Close in and engulf you, where *Yaumgan,* like everyone else in the Cluster, had shitty point shields and too great a reliance on the Shield Projector.

Tough, but only on one part. The rest of you was open to envelopment.

"I want prisoners, *Junkyard,*" Phil said now. "Fighters don't count, because the pilots will be low-ranking officers who are never in the room when policy is being made. I need a Command Centurion or something."

He watched her eyes grow distant. The thousand-light-year-stare that she got when she was reaching deep into the tactical files.

"Can we count on drydock facilities here, Phil?" she asked, obliquely letting him know that she had a plan, but it would likely be a mess.

He turned to the First Speaker and her two cohorts, only one of whom he had spent any significant time around.

They looked inward and came to consensus quickly.

"Anything you need, First Centurion," the older man said. "Obviously, you've been drawn unhappily into our mess. Your help today might be the difference in our survival, so our resources will be at your disposal."

"Got that, Iveta?" he asked.

"Affirmative," she said. "Stand by."

He drew a breath as she changed over to the squadron channel.

"*Aquitaine* force, this is *Junkyard*," she said in that distant, deadly voice. "All ships come to rest immediately, relative to enemy Supercarrier designated *Alpha*. I am transmitting a new course. On my orders, come about to this new heading and go for maximum acceleration. Escorts, you will sideslip in place to cover my right flank, engaging defensively. Heavy units, hold offensive fire until we get into range of target *Gamma*, then we'll hammer them into the mud as we go by. Phil wants that ship too broken to flee. Execute deceleration and stand by for battle."

Phil nodded.

That was the one he'd expected she'd go after. On a flank and possibly looking the wrong way. Plus, they'd gotten down into the gravity well much deeper than the big *Alpha* and *Beta*.

Now, to find out if they could make it work.

TWENTY-TWO

I veta didn't have that ninth sense like Auke on *Viking* did. She didn't do the complex math in her head that let her know how any enemy would flow. At the same time, they had talked about it privately over wine and he didn't have that sense that told her what the enemy commander was thinking at any given moment.

He saw vectors. She saw souls.

The Command Centurion of *Gamma* was paying attention to the wing he had launched. Plus, if she had to guess, they were setting up as a lily pad platform. Someplace for damaged fighters to get rescued.

Aquitaine didn't have snubfighters anymore, but those had only started being phased out after she had gotten commissioned, so she'd studied them closely. Keller had made her name in a Strike Carrier, after all. Launch the wing then surge in behind them firing the big guns and forcing the defender to pick who he engaged.

Gamma was going after a Skycruiser like *Li Jing*, trailing in orbit. If they'd gotten better organized, Iveta might have sent them a note to charge madly down and away, drawing eyes and minds after them. As it was, *Urumchi* and *Viking* were likely to surge out ahead of the cruisers because they had a better thrust to mass ratio. The Corvettes would hold a defensive line, leaving her out on the tip.

No, *Forktail* would be there with her to the death. Wild horses and rabid dogs couldn't keep Captain Sugawara from doing his job. *Morninghawk* had infected an entire culture. At least one. Maybe all of them.

Time to put that to use.

"Pilot, plot the next course," Iveta ordered. "I would appreciate outrunning *Viking* if you can, so do everything you can to get me speed. Leyla, *Gamma* still ignoring us?"

"So far," the woman replied. "Standard sensor pings on a different frequency than we use, but nothing aimed at us right now. The mob from the supercarrier is starting to tighten up, though. I think they smell a rat."

"Good," Iveta said. "Gunner, stand by with the Spectre. I will want it high and even with us, so that anything seeking with terminal guidance doesn't accidentally lock on a friendly instead and flies over the squadron."

"Understood, Tactical," Hào Boyadjiev replied. "Fours have a soft, optical lock on *Gamma* until we get closer and they start to maneuver."

"Excellent," Iveta pronounced, looking over at Heather and smiling.

Heather just nodded, keeping watch on damage control parties and engineering, so Iveta didn't have to worry about the ship.

Iveta took a deep breath and felt herself flow into that higher plane of existence that *Ground Control* talked about occasionally.

"*Aquitaine* squadron, execute maximum individual acceleration regardless of formation," Iveta said grimly. "All ships *charge.*"

TWENTY-THREE

Phil saw the maneuver for what it was. Something of a gamble, but he'd hired the best gamblers he could, given more than a year to sort personnel files into stacks. *Ground Control* and the *Junkyard Bitch* would save his ass, if anybody could.

"What is happening?" Ambassador Hu asked delicately. "None of us have any direct naval experience."

"The gravity well determines how well JumpDrives and JumpSails work," Phil replied. "You can only get so close to the planet before your matrix breaks down and you have to rebuild it. That takes time. As a result, most people forget that you can just blindly jump up and out. Space is empty enough that the risk of hitting something is low. *Urumchi* and the squadron are going to come about and charge after this smaller carrier, over on one corner of their formation. Most of the heavy weapons on local ships face forward, with only *Aditi* and *Yaumgan* able to easily engage a target behind them. And yours only because you can fly through space with your arms backwards."

He paused and waited for them to digest it, back to teaching Advanced Piracy to Third Year students at the Academy.

"The small ships will be chasing us as we suddenly go after

one of their carriers," Phil said. "I have not seen anything that convinces me that they understand the actual effective range on the Type-4 beams on *Urumchi* and *Viking*, so they might think they can outrun us."

"Aren't they pointed somewhat down?" Scholar Wen, the old man in the heavy boots, asked. "Will they have to rotate in place if they wish to escape the gravity well and your wrath?"

"Indeed, sir," Phil nodded. "Assuming they don't panic jump, we can bash them heavily as we approach, and the cruisers around us can start taking potshots themselves. The Sunsword on *Zhang Gualao* has more pulses than other nations build, but no greater range. Similarly, *Storm Petrel's* Condor is terrifying to watch, but falls off in effectiveness, the farther it travels. Still, if that is a simple fleet carrier like we used to build, they will not have the defensive ability to withstand us."

"Used to build, First Centurion?" the First Speaker asked. "Why did you stop?"

"Lady Moirrey *zu* Kermode helped invent the Type-1-Pulse beam," he said. "Later, she figured out how to pulse a 3. *Viking* has those."

"What does *Urumchi* have?" she asked, curious rather than diplomatic.

"First Centurion Whughy, whom many expect to be the next First Lord of the Fleet, invented the Pulse-Two when we were engaging with pirates and the sharks of *Buran*," Phil smiled. "Shortly, you will see them engage, as my corvettes mix Twos and Threes. Ah, there we go. Outer range on those mini-firebirds that *Zerzan* uses."

He stopped talking at that point and watched as the corvettes cut loose with everything they had. All of them. All at once. *Forktail* would stay on the bow facing forward. The cruisers started to engage, but they were not designed to handle massive missile fire.

Nobody was.

Nobody *else* was. Yan Bedrov had angrily and profanely

proclaimed the end of missiles and snubfighters when he imprinted *Aquitaine,* and later *Fribourg,* with *Expeditionary* logic. No more consumables than minimally necessary. No Primary beams anymore. No missiles a t all. The Pulse-Two ended snubfighters as anything more than missile platforms, so they went away next.

"Squadron, this is *Junkyard,*" Iveta came over the line. "That caught them off guard and a lot of the incoming crap is going to miss. Update your tracking and ignore anything that isn't aimed at you. Hold your cooling elements for when this turns into a stern chase and we have to start zig-zagging to make them miss."

Phil nodded. That first salvo seemed to be ballistic. Fired at a point, with an extremely narrow cone that the bird could see into to achieve a lock. Hundreds of them were sailing wide, even as the mechs that launched them had to shift their acceleration and turn sideways. Even then, they would end up hooking around his stern before they could make adjustments.

Phil wondered if Iveta intended to sit above them in the gravity well so she could go after their carriers. If they chased off those capital ships, the fighters would be forced to surrender, as they weren't big enough to mount any sort of Jump device.

Not unless *Zerzan* had leapt ahead of *Aquitaine,* and he didn't think so. Different, but that didn't mean better or worse until you started punching each other in the mouth.

He'd put his money on the *Junkyard Bitch* in that case.

TWENTY-FOUR

Bausse watched the screen as her Wing chased the two ships that were their target.

They were running, but every maneuver that made bolts miss meant that the aeromechia could get that much closer. It wouldn't be long now until her force could spread out again and hit them from a wide enough frontage that their Shield Projectors couldn't save them.

"Chevalier, I have an incoming weapons lock," the Optics Officer suddenly called over the nearly silent bridge. "It appears to be from the primary force that *Rauda*'s team is engaging."

A moment later, the entire hull rang with thunder and Bausse was nearly thrown to the deck by an earthquake.

"What was that?" she yelled.

"Two of the enemy vessels, *Urumchi* and *Viking*, have opened fire on us with beams that should only be mounted on stations, Chevalier," the man replied.

"Get the Shield Projector around to protect us," Bausse ordered, even as lighter pings sounded like hail on the hull.

As deep as she was in the center of *Truhto*, something was absolutely hammering the hull. Not the shields. Raw metal.

Systems around her were already failing. Hull plates seemed to be buckling. *Truhto* itself screamed in pain.

"Damage report?" she asked, turning to one of the engineers.

The woman's face had gone white in the last second, then another earthquake tossed her bodily from her station. Bausse found herself floating in the air.

"We've lost gravity," someone bawled, just in case nobody else had noticed.

Most of them were seated. About half had buckled themselves in. Bausse had been standing as usual, and not strong enough to hold on when the entire ship had flexed around her.

She could smell smoke in the air as something shorted.

A panel exploded in a roostertail of sparks in front of her until someone grabbed an extinguisher and hosed it down.

Bausse reached the ceiling and pushed off to the engineering console. The woman manning that station was still swimming in space, then someone managed to grab one of Bausse's ankles and pull her in.

"This is the Chevalier," Bausse called as she grabbed a headphone and jammed the mic to her mouth. "What's our status?"

"One engine is ruptured, Chevalier," the man on the other end of the line said. "We might need to replace it entirely. I have generators going off-line in a cascade as things short out. Gravity is gone. Most of the gyroscopes are spinning down and we'll start tumbling soon. Jump has been ruptured as I barely have the power to keep the shields and life support intact right now. We're a sitting duck."

"Keep at it," Bausse ordered.

There wasn't much more she could say or do. Something had gone desperately wrong. How had *Aquitaine* been able to so suddenly savage her ship? And from that far away? Nothing mobile should have that range at all. Let alone the power to do that to her.

She looked at the readout and noticed how many things had

changed from green to red in the last twenty seconds. The pounding hadn't gotten any better, either. Someone was trying to see if it was possible to literally destroy her ship with beam fire.

Or worse, simply keep stomping on it like an empty can until it was crushed.

"Can we do anything?" Bausse asked the room.

Hangdog faces looked back at her.

The *Zerzan Unification* had been so dominant for so long that she couldn't remember the last time they had lost a major battle. Raids were intended to frighten and intimidate. Attacking the *Yaumgan* Capital was supposed to fall into that category.

Something had definitely gone wrong.

"I have a call that identifies itself as being from *Urumchi*, Chevalier," the Optics Officer looked up. "In Hindi. They call on us to surrender immediately, or be utterly destroyed."

"Is there a visual signal?" she asked.

"Yes, ma'am."

"Bring it up," Bausse decided. "I want to see my foe."

TWENTY-FIVE

DATE OF THE REPUBLIC AUGUST 13, 412 RAN
URUMCHI, KYULLE ORBIT

Iveta smiled as the background became clear behind the woman. No solid bridge hits, but the ship had taken one hell of a wallop when three of the Type-4s had connected at once. *Zhang Gualao* had hit them with the Sunsword and even managed to stitch a good chunk of the aft hull, in spite of the incredible range.

Everyone else who could was pounding away, even as every defensive beam in the squadron that could be brought to bear was picking off the firebirds giving chase. It only took one hit to mash them. Sometimes, if several were close enough together, the small explosion would even cascade sideways.

There were still a metric shit-ton of launchers back there. The Spectre had done its job, though, drawing off a lot of those torpedoes as she moved it in behind everybody to distract missiles.

Might even be enough.

But for right now, she had the enemy command centurion on the line. Didn't look like a junior officer promoted when something bad had happened. This woman looked like she was used to being in charge.

"This is Tactical Officer Iveta Maria Beridze," Iveta said

sternly. "You can surrender to me, or I'll make sure you crash into the planet below eventually. I am feeling benevolent right now. That will change shortly."

She studied the image. Brown hair much lighter than Iveta's. Eyes that might have been hazel. Almost a triangular face with wide cheekbones and a narrow chin. Late thirties, give or take, depending on whether her hair was naturally still that dark or had been dyed.

Iveta let the woman study her for a long moment as well, knowing she would see the Mongolian heritage that had caused Iveta to be teased during the *Buran* era. Black hair. Siberian features. Dark eyes.

Yeah, my ancestors were born about ten thousand kilometers east of yours, lady.

"Do you even understand me?" Iveta asked when the woman remained silent.

"I understand you," the stranger replied instantly.

"Good, because the First Centurion would like you alive," Iveta said. "But he didn't specify that your ship had to remain so. I can pick up survivors after you all get into escape pods because I will not hold my wrath much longer. You can surrender and honor it, or die. Which will it be?"

"Honor it?" the woman snapped. "*Yaumgan* has no honor."

"We're the *Republic of Aquitaine*, lady," Iveta growled. "When I make you a promise, I'll keep it. You pick which one it is. **Right now.**"

Something got through to the woman. Maybe another explosion in the background, because Iveta hadn't told anybody to stop shooting that dead fish. The Type-4s might even be able to break it into pieces, if she could stay far enough ahead of the swarm of angry locusts behind her. Might be fun.

Woman consulted with somebody off screen. Iveta could see that they'd lost gravity because folks were flying through the smoke. Couple more good hits and Iveta might break the entire ass end of that ship off. And all their generators.

She'd told her folks where to aim, after all.

"We will surrender, *Urumchi*," the woman said. "What is your ransom?"

"Hold things together as well as you can," Iveta replied. "We'll have to deal with the rest of your attacking force before I trust sending engineers and damage repair crews over to help you, but I will send an order to everyone in orbit to leave you alone. Eventually, we'll find a way to trade you home, once we figure out who to talk to and where. On my honor."

The woman studied her for another long moment, then nodded and cut the line.

"*Kyulle* orbital forces, this is Tactical Officer Iveta Beridze, aboard *Urumchi*," she said, switching lines. "Target *Gamma* has surrendered on honorable terms and they are my prisoners. I will expect them to be treated as such. All ships that can will render aid when it does not threaten your own safety. Otherwise, leave them alone."

She cut the line and studied the two mobs of mechs still wanting to bother her. The smaller one in front and below had just found themselves caught between the two *Yaumgan* ships they had been attacking and her. Hammer and anvil, so they were in the process of splitting and running. Teams of four, so she presumed some sort of old-style mounted lance arrangement.

Behind her, the thousand little shits were losing ground, because she could maintain a higher acceleration, and had caught them with the wrong vector with that first sudden maneuver.

Getting out of a gravity well was a lot harder than diving into one.

"Leyla, where are *Alpha* and *Beta*?" Iveta asked, dialing back her screens to show ninety degrees of orbital arc.

"Here," Leyla replied, plotting a big red star.

Out a ways. Top of the gravity well where they could escape

easily. Assuming they didn't mind leaving behind their entire force of thousands of little mecha.

"Phil, I'd like to pull the greatest bluff in history," she said, switching her comm to the flag bridge. "Permission to risk serious damage unnecessarily?"

"Who's next on your list?" he asked.

"*Alpha* **and** *Beta*," Iveta grinned. "I'm sure they just scanned what the Fours can do. I'd like to go after them. Their mecha will be able to broadside us, but only briefly because I'll go up and over. If they're smart, they can cut the corner on us and possibly engage us before we can get to their carriers. But it will be close. And if they try it, they risk blowing by me again at high speed before they can decelerate and board their carriers."

"Mind games, *Junkyard*?" he asked with a grin.

"We've got them on the back foot, First Centurion," Iveta turned serious. "No better time to push."

"Understood," he replied. "Walk a thin line on this one."

Iveta nodded and went to the team line. Then she switched to the wider line that everyone might be able to pick up, friendly and otherwise.

"*Aquitaine* squadron, prepare to go straight up and clear the gravity well," she said. "We will come over the top ballistically and offer battle to the two supercarriers. All *Yaumgan* forces, stand by to assist however you can."

She had no idea what any of them might be able to do, but just the thought would cause somebody to look over their shoulder as she got close.

That was all she needed.

TWENTY-SIX

MISSION BRIEF: ASSAULT CARRIER TRUHTO.
ENEMY WORLD: KYULLE

Bausse watched the outsider force turn away from her as simply as that. Every single weapon that had been raining death on *Truhto* cut off at the same instant, leaving silence.

How tight did this Beridze control such a force that she could issue that order and not even the two *Yaumgan* ships would take a moment to get the final word in?

*What was **Aquitaine**?*

"Someone get me the specs on those heavy beams," she ordered.

Half the people she could see were literally fighting fires or handing out breathing masks. The other half were only doing it metaphorically, trying to keep her ship from exploding or coming apart.

Gravity was still out. Probably the last thing that would be fixed, if they only had so much power to route around. Gyroscopes and shields first. Engines to insert *Truhto* into a stable orbit above the planet so that someone could salvage what could be salvaged.

She was trapped here at *Kyulle.*

"Flight Boss," she called, drawing Verrais Beauvoie's head around. "Order the wing to return to *Rauda* or *Bertev* immediately. There is no reason they should be captured when we are."

Gasps around her as the certainty of their situation hit. She'd lost track of the other target, focused on her own and certain that nothing could hurt *Truhto* from the range at which *Aquitaine* would pass.

How had she guessed so wrong?

"Optics, what are they doing now?" Bausse followed up.

"Going straight up, Chevalier," came the response.

Straight up? That made no sense at all. They would only need to do that if they intended to flee entirely, and the woman on *Urumchi* didn't give that impression. She looked more like a wild mutt growling.

Who was there to growl at?

Shit.

"Optics, contact *Rauda* and *Bertev* immediately," Bausse ordered.

Only a few seconds passed and Chevalier Fortier appeared on her screens. She'd never liked the man, but she respected him. And he was in charge of this operation.

"Status?" he demanded.

"Broken and captured," Bausse replied evenly. "They have taken my ransom to remain behind. My wing has been ordered to rendezvous with your force. More importantly, I believe the entire *Aquitaine* force is about to turn your direction and attempt to do to you what they just did to me, namely, engage at extreme range with station-class beam weapons."

Bausse watched him turn to someone on his own bridge. Probably his Optics Officer. The line was muted because his mouth moved but no sound emerged.

She was rewarded when he turned back to her, eyes large.

"How is that possible?" he demanded.

"I am not sure," Bausse said. "*Yaumgan* appears to have allies that are more sophisticated and dangerous than the pirate led us to believe. However, I intend to keep him with me as well, so perhaps they will welcome him home and punish him for us."

"Serve your ransom well," Fortier ordered.

"*Aquitaine* said that they would trade me home, once they knew who to speak with, so perhaps they are honorable, Chevalier," Bausse said. "We shall find out."

He nodded and the line went dead.

"Optics, what is *Bertev* doing?" she asked, still hanging in the air as more of a witness to history than a participant.

Or a shaper.

"Stand by," he said. "I have red-shift detected, Chevalier."

"Good," she said aloud. "Watch the aeromechia as well. I expect Fortier to either order them to intercept *Aquitaine*, or perhaps the entire assault force will withdraw at this point. Something went wrong and it might be better to live to fight another day than to die gloriously to no purpose. All of you keep that in mind."

Nods. The *Unification* demanded much of a person, but returned it as well.

Bausse wondered if they had grown so arrogant, conquering worlds and civilizations, that they had forgotten how to answer someone with greater strength. There had been none in centuries.

What would *Aquitaine* want?

TWENTY-SEVEN

AQUITAINE FLAGSHIP URUMCHI, KYULLE ORBITAL SPACE

Yating had even reviewed the logs of the twin battles at *Meerut*, yet he was flabbergasted. Gobsmacked.

The Sunsword had been the most powerful weapon ever mounted on a *Yaumgan* Immortal. And the experience could be described as a flute playing in the background while the percussion section pounded on the big, kettle drums, watching *Urumchi* and *Viking* mangle the enemy carrier.

Worse, Kosnett took it all in stride, even ordering Beridze to continue the attack on the other two ships.

How badly had everyone underestimated the man?

"Questions, Ambassador Hu?" Kosnett asked now, smiling genially as the one known as Dunklin delivered a fresh carafe of coffee to the table.

"*Truhto*, First Centurion," Yating managed. "That name was the same as attacked *Senza.*"

Kosnett nodded sagely.

"Carriers tend to be fragile craft, Ambassador," Kosnett replied. "The need for large internal spaces for fighters means that they cannot be as effectively braced as a cruiser. Another reason we stopped using them for the most part, as we were at the time engaged with a foe who could suddenly jump to point-blank range before firing.”

“And now you intend to attack the others?” Chang asked, seated next to him. “What of their impossible number of little ships?”

“*Truhto* is trapped here,” Kosnett replied. “They have surrendered to me, so eventually we will load them on a ship for transport to wherever home is for them. The others now have to make the same calculations. Hopefully, we can chase them off for today. Capturing or seriously damaging even one of those two ships might break the back of their invasion.”

“But *Urumchi* risks being damaged?” Wen asked now.

“Worse than we have been,” Kosnett nodded. “None of this is bad at present. Bolts that got through gaps and overloads in the shielding. The outer layers of *Urumchi* were designed to absorb such damage cosmetically, without affecting our ability to fight or sail. What Iveta is about to attempt might allow *Zerzan* the ability to really hurt us, thus the earlier request for repair facilities, so we don’t have to sail back to *Meerut*.”

“Oh, no, First Centurion,” the First Speaker said firmly. “You have already done us a great favor, just capturing someone who might be able to provide answers. Up until now, all of us have been operating in the dark.”

Kosnett nodded, but Yating had the impression that the man knew more than he had been letting on.

The two younger women had been quiet. Kohahu Kugosu spoke now.

“*Can* they be reasoned with?” she asked Kosnett.

“*Truhto* surrendered rather than face certain destruction,” he replied. “And Iveta would have hit them with several more salvos as the squadron passed. Perhaps even changed course to allow everyone close range shots to finish them off.”

“As at *Ewinhome*,” she nodded.

It took Yating a moment. His confusion must have shown.

“At *Ewinhome*, Iveta had already defeated the Prince who

was Kosnett's enemy," the young woman continued. "They had detached their boom section, which is the traditional signal for the end of combat. Iveta did not recognize that and continued to fire into both sections. She would have destroyed him entirely had he not come to understand that death was coming for him. *Truhto* did not need to be made an example of, but the others might."

Yating nodded at that. Again, he had seen those reports, but lacked the context into which to understand what was happening around them.

Had the *Domain* grown so insular behind the stout walls of reputation and intimidation that they risked being left behind? Technologically, *Yaumgan* was ahead of everyone except *Aquitaine*, and could bring forward weapons and systems that had remained theoretical until now.

Culturally, they lacked.

"Will it be enough, First Centurion?" Yating asked finally.

"That is entirely up to them," Kosnett replied.

Yating could not help the shudder that passed through his system.

TWENTY-EIGHT

I veta watched all the vectors shift and roll as various formations adjusted to one another. *Urumchi* had led her force straight up, blasting past the edge of the gravity well to a spot where they could have even risked a short, sideways hop like the sharks of *Buran* used to do it, landing right on top of the two supercarriers over there.

She didn't think that *Urumchi* could survive the wild fracas that would break out as everybody let loose with everything they had at knife-fighting range. Her Balhee ships would probably just melt under the furious onslaught.

Good thing that it wasn't required today. Khan and Solo were probably saddened, though.

Such a *Beau Geste* was always a possibility. The *Grand Gesture*. Sometimes, you had to charge into a battle that would be your death, to protect those behind you, either to give them time to escape, or to break up an enemy formation in such a way that they could mop it up.

Yaumgan might be polite people, but Iveta had no reason to sacrifice everything for them.

Not if this worked.

"Gunner, can we hit them from here?" she asked.

The question sounded idle, but it was anything but.

Below them, the mob of mechs had turned, finally decelerating to the point that they could effectively return to their bases. If she hadn't turned *Urumchi* towards the carriers, the mechs might have even just kept it up and raced madly around the rim of orbit, but that would be two hours that would turn the battle.

"Both are turning away from us," Gunner Boyadjiev replied. "Presenting minimal cross-section targets at this range. I can try, but odds are against us connecting."

"I just need them scared," Iveta replied. "*Viking*, turn your big guns on the mechs. Hit any big concentration you can target at this range until they spread out. Everyone with power taps and titan bolts do the same. *Storm Petrel*, hold everything in case they get frisky and suddenly decide to come about. Lots of targets, but they are fragile, and you are likely to hit something, just because they are packed so closely together."

Iveta paused and considered. Now was when the *Zerzan* commander might get his shit together and realize that she would be committing suicide if she charged in there. All he had to do was interpose his waves of locusts and he could force her back.

The other plague of mechs had wrought a terrible toll on the defending forces. Iveta could see Skycruisers hanging limp. Escorts missing limbs. *Zhang Gualao* had drawn more fire than *Urumchi*, but the Spectre had evened those scales significantly. As had all those Pulse weapons on her side of the ledger.

Nobody was permanently crippled, though *Zhang Gualao* and *Li Jing* were hurt. She'd kept *Shadowbolt* and *Juvayni* over on that flank for a reason. Striker Solo's missiles weren't all that much, but they'd forced the mechs to attack them defensively. More fire not coming after her. And Cruiser-Captain Khan had conducted an absolute masterclass in missile salvoing today, timing things and aiming in such a way that he complemented *Shadowbolt*'s massive waves of arrows.

They had mostly held their own. Stalemate across the battlefield.

That was about to change.

Urumchi fired the two Fours. As Boyadjiev had said, nearly impossible at this range to score a hit, but Iveta had seen the smaller carrier take a shot in the ass. Massive damage. All she needed now was one hit on either of those monsters.

He missed, but both suddenly began to maneuver.

"*Alpha* and *Beta* are starting to accelerate away," Leyla called. "We should have the higher top speed, since they need to pick up fighters eventually."

Iveta nodded. The rest of the squadron started after the mechs like a woodpecker. Tap tap tap.

Casualties, but not enough to alter the equation all that much. The range was extreme.

"Hey, that's interesting," Leyla said. "They just started forming into teams of sixteen. I'm detecting a new kind of deflection shield coming into place around each group. It's like each of them contributes to a larger whole when they're like this."

"They still firing?" Iveta asked.

"Negative," Leyla said with a smile in her voice. "Maybe they have to take all the recharge energy and put it into shields to do this?"

"That would be nice," Iveta said. "Pilot, slide us out a little more, away from the mechs but still on track to chase down the carriers. I want to see what he does."

"Roger that," Pilot Virág replied.

Iveta settled in and tried to out-guess her unknown enemy.

Things were going to get ugly.

TWENTY-NINE

Heather was keeping watch on Damage Control. Less things broken than there should be in a battle this big, but the outer hull was pockmarked with damage. Those bolts hit like nails, which was good and bad, as they might locally overload a shield array and a few slip through. But *Urumchi* had been designed by the pirate for the sharks, and nothing *Zerzan* had was a match.

On two of her side screens, she was tracking the carriers and the cloud of mechs that were racing parallel to the squadron to get back and defend the carriers.

That gave her an idea.

"Iveta," she said, drawing the woman back down to earth from where she'd gone. "They're running from us right now, correct?"

"Yup," Iveta nodded. "My fear is that they let the mechs keep sliding in until they can cut us off and force us to stay at a distance."

"So why not let them?" Heather asked.

"What do you see?" Iveta asked.

All eyes had turned Heather's way.

"There are four of the eight Immortals in system," Heather

said. "What happens if *Zhang Gualao* suddenly goes into turnover and decelerates, then crosses over to join up with the other three? They've all taken up some level of safety around stations that have big enough guns to hold the other groups at bay. At least until *Zerzan* all forms back up into a single massive ball that can probably roll over anybody."

"So what do four Immortals do to change that equation?" Iveta asked.

"Orbital space is round," Heather smiled.

"Oh, that's ruthless," Iveta laughed. "I like it. Phil, can you convince the locals to form up an Immortals squadron here?"

"Stand by, *Junkyard*," he replied. "I have the right people handy to ask."

Heather nodded. She was no longer in charge of Tactical around here, but she still had a few tricks up her sleeve to teach the youngsters.

THIRTY

Phil turned to the First Speaker, noting the confusion in her eyes.

"Iveta and Heather have an idea that putting the Four Immortals here pinches the attacking forces, at least psychologically," he said. "If you were to gather up every ship that can still fight, we might convince our friends to finally depart."

"Or to swarm in and utterly destroy the forces protecting *Kyulle*," she replied crisply.

"I intend to defend this planet," Phil said with a bit of a growl in his voice. "My message to my own commander back home, First Lord of the Fleet Naoumov, was that she needs to send a major warfleet here to help, if I don't rescind that request before *Hollywood* departs. *Urumchi* is a small exploration squadron, First Speaker. I mean to have my boss bring enough force to annihilate *Zerzan* as a threat if they can't be dealt with diplomatically."

"Would she do that?" the First Speaker asked. "For *Yaumgan*?"

"She would," Phil replied. "A stable, productive, peaceful Balhee Cluster were her orders to me before I left to visit you. I can't do that if *Zerzan* is a threat to everyone else. If I have to go hunt them down and crush them to make my point, nothing they've brought here today changes anything except the loadout of forces I would request be put under my command."

"Can we win?" the older man, Scholar Wen, asked now.

"Victory, like surprise, occurs in the enemy mind, Scholar," Phil said. "If we can surprise them again, we can force them to make bad decisions in the heat of battle. Such things have already cost them significantly. I would like to up the bill of lading before they have to pay it. Iveta has them in a bad tactical position. Heather's suggestion compounds that. Eventually, either we make a mistake, or the enemy commander has to fight from extremely bad terrain. The costs will likely be high if your fleet launches an attack. I will not deny that. Or if your forces form the anvil against which *Urumchi* is the hammer. However, we are on defense, so every ship of theirs we can hurt has to be repaired somewhere else. Every pilot they lose has to be replaced from home. You do not have long lines of logistics here. They do. And I don't believe that they were prepared for the *RAN* today. Eventually, they will figure out our capabilities and adjust. However, not today. We can push, but you have to give that order."

He sat back and watched.

"Would you prefer to retire to a private room to discuss things?" he asked. "I can have one put at your disposal."

"That will not be necessary," the First Speaker said. "All of what you have said makes perfectly logical sense. The failing is ours, as we have fashioned ourselves into a nation of philosophers, rather than warriors such as *Aquitaine*. I will not apologize for that, as it was to everyone's benefit that *Yaumgan* was not aggressive. At least until now. *Zerzan* has changed almost all equations."

"I agree with the latter," Phil nodded. "*Zerzan* must eventually be dealt with as a people. Today, however, they are a threat to the fleets protecting *Kyulle*, and that takes precedence."

"Could you put me on an open line that our ships can hear?" she said.

Harinder nodded, but she was always at least one step ahead when it came to things like that. Nam was pale. Kohahu might have been carved from granite. But then, *Dalou* had brought three of their five battleships to *Ellariel* against the dreaded barbarians doing something.

Against the small force he'd brought that day, that might even have been sufficient. Right up until Phil came back with *Viking* and everyone at the *Meerut* moorage that might have a bone to pick with *Dalou*. That would have gotten ugly, and Kohahu had a much better understanding of it today.

"You're on," Harinder informed everyone.

"Domain military forces, this is First Speaker Li Chang Ling," she said in a firm, calm, commanding voice. "I am aboard the *Aquitaine* flagship, consulting with First Centurion Kosnett, who has come to our aid in our time of greatest need. Now, it is our turn to assist. *Zhang Gualao*, you will depart and rendezvous with *Lü Dongbin*, *He Xiangu*, and *Lan Caihe*. *Urumchi* will place your attack ahead of the invaders and between all of our efforts they will be defeated."

Phil nodded, watching how much just that little had taken out of the woman, in spite of her mental and physical strength. Committing to kill someone for no reason at all was one of the hardest lessons you learned in command. And why so few made it to the rank of Command Centurion.

"Iveta, you and Heather work it out," Phil said on the private line to the bridge. "In fact, Heather, you might take over tactical flag for that force while Iveta handles this end of things."

"Understood, Phil," Heather replied.

Phil nodded and poured himself some more coffee, then offered to do the same for the others.

All battles went through phases of manic and quiet. This one was ramping down as everyone selected their death ground.

Then they would dance.

THIRTY-ONE

Heather got a direct line to Captain Lin on *Zhang Gualao*. They'd worked well together at *Meerut*, and the young woman was a capable officer.

Today, Heather was acting like she had her fourth stripe. Auditioning, perhaps, though she had no idea if the folks back home would be thrilled or appalled to consider her as a Fleet Centurion.

"*Zhang Gualao*, I need you to slingshot down and around hard," Heather said as she got the woman on the line. The other three captains were there as well, but none of them were folks that Heather knew that well. Normally, she might have even sent Dao Zhiou, but she suspected that she needed that little bit extra here with *Urumchi*.

Captain Lin nodded.

"I am plotting a course vector and a location," Heather continued. "I need the other three of you—*Lü Dongbin*, *He Xiangu*, and *Lan Caihe*—to come about and rendezvous with *Zhang Gualao* on this vector about here. Every other *Yaumgan* ship that can should attach themselves to your force. I want you coming around the planet and forming up here as if blocking them."

"We can't withstand that force, Command Centurion," Captain Lin pointed out.

"I'm aware of that, Lin," Heather said. "You don't have to hold long. I need you drawing their minds forward while *Urumchi* continues to hound them from the rear. At some point, they have to decide if they want to attack you or me. Either option forces them to leave the other an opening that causes the potential for serious damage to the carriers, because those ships aren't built as sturdy. And if we take one of those out, their entire invasion is in trouble."

"Are we going to charge right through them on the far side if they move to attack the Immortals?" Captain Yung Chui-Qui of *Lü Dongbin* asked. It was the fleet flagship, as much as they had such a thing, so she was probably the senior-most captain in the fleet. Kind of like how Heather was with the *Aquitaine* force.

"We'll see when we get there, Captain," Heather replied. "The amount of damage you would sustain might be terminal, but it would also open the carriers to their own destruction, and *Zerzan* hasn't struck me as berserkers intending to die in battle unless they have to. The more likely expectation is that somebody over there figures out what I'm trying to do to them and they decide discretion is the better part of valor and leave."

"They'll come back," he warned.

"And we'll stop them when they do," Heather growled. "They didn't count on the *Republic of Aquitaine* Navy being here to kick their asses."

That silenced them. Hard faces, but they were willing to listen. And Phil and the First Speaker had put her in charge.

Heather flipped a switch to broadcast on a frequency that *Yaumgan* would hear. And hopefully not *Zerzan*.

"All *Yaumgan* forces who can hear me," Heather called to the entire system. "If you can, move to this point to assist the Immortals and the *Aquitaine* squadron in repelling the invaders. This will be the battle that determines your freedom when all is said and done, so today is the day for extraordinary measures."

She left it at that and cut the line. There were Skycruisers and Escorts that had gotten away from the locusts, just as there were a frightening number of *Yaumgan* vessels that had lost limbs in the few hours of battle she had witnessed. *Yaumgan* would be working overtime to replace them, she was sure, so Heather and Iveta just needed to buy the *Domain* the time to do it.

And maybe ask the First Lord to send help.

This was going to be a mess.

THIRTY-TWO

Chevalier Donatien Fortier stood at the center of his bridge and listened as his Optics Officer laid out the maneuvers that the *Yaumgan* forces were initiating. His ship and *Rauda* were not fleeing the *Aquitaine* force, but moving rapidly away from them while the combined aeromechia force slowly closed the gap, able to sail a shorter distance from lower in the orbital space of *Kyulle*.

Weapons fire from his forces had forced *Aquitaine* to maintain a higher line. Combined with their maneuvering to avoid massed pulse torpedo fire, they had only hit *Rauda* once with those impossible beam weapons, and missed *Bertev* entirely.

Still, that one hit had taken down *Rauda's* Shield Projector and nearly overloaded the ship's inner shields as well. Even leakage from the blow had caused significant systems overloads.

"Where will they come out?" Donatien asked, watching the four largest vessels moving away from him at high speed.

It was obvious that they were going to use a gravity slingshot to get in front of him somewhere. Did they think that nearly two thousand aeromechia couldn't completely savage them? Even with the smaller ships sailing to assist, he could annihilate

Yaumgan's defenders, including four of the so-called Immortals that were their heaviest vessels.

And in doing so, he would probably have to sacrifice his own squadron, because something quietly whispered in the back of his mind that *Aquitaine* was controlling those maneuvers. He would send the aeromechia forward, and *Aquitaine* would suddenly pounce somehow, though he wasn't sure. Close to short distance and destroy *Bertev* and *Rauda* just as surely as they had *Truhto?* His force would be stranded and captured.

And the invasion would have failed.

This attack had been a gamble. Even Donatien Fortier was willing to admit it had miscarried. Not badly, as he had indeed inflicted terrible losses on his enemies. At the same time, he could see how thin a line he walked, where one misstep would cost him everything and gave *Yaumgan* perhaps a year or more to prepare as *Zerzan* would have to rebuild their forces to try again.

Plus, the *Unification* needed to know that *Aquitaine* existed. And that they were far more dangerous than anyone could have imagined. Donatien would need to study the logs to understand these exotic warships, built like blades instead of bipeds, and he did not have that luxury today.

Only a fool fights in a burning house, and he had already lost *Truhto*. Plus his Assault Carrier *Gosa* had been badly damaged.

Donatien nodded to the Optics officer. Then the rest of his bridge crew, all obviously waiting on pins and needles to see what his orders would be. Death or Glory, charge or retreat.

"Attention *Unification* Forces," he said slowly, his voice stern enough to override even the hotheads who might argue with him. They could choose to be left behind today, and by the *Unification* itself. They would obey him, or pay. "All aeromechia begin to withdraw to the nearest carrier that can provide transport, regardless of your usual duty assignment. Flight Bosses, begin organizing to retrieve the maximum number of aeromechia you can for a short period as we will withdraw from battle and return directly to our forward base. We cannot win the war today, but we can lose it right here, and the *Unification* needs to know what we have learned. All vessels execute an orderly withdrawal immediately."

He held a heavy sigh inside as mouths around him fell open. The *Zerzan Unification* had always been triumphant.

Before today.

Aquitaine had saved *Yaumgan* from being dismembered in space, and he was not sure how they had done that, other than they flew impossible ships with impossible weapons.

Normally, he would have asked Bausse for her thoughts, as the best of his Assault Carrier Chevaliers, but today had cost him her as well.

At least for now.

He would see just how honorable *Aquitaine* felt, after she told them the truth about *Yaumgan*.

THIRTY-THREE

"You're certain?" Iveta asked automatically.

Harman's scowl could have been used to grind and refinish bulkheads.

"You asked, Tactical," he replied darkly.

She had.

Iveta nodded.

"Thank you," she said.

Harman nodded back and cut the line.

Iveta took a deep breath and read the message that had provoked that conversation again.

Normally, she would go all in at this moment.

For the throat.

This was probably what growing up felt like.

"Phil, I have a message from the *Pixies*," Iveta said to the flag bridge, aware of the number of folks on the other end listening. "I assigned them a mission and they just earned extra kibble in their rations for me."

She waited.

He came back faster than she expected, so he must still be sitting at the table instead of moving to the privacy of his office nearby where the *Yaumgan* politicians wouldn't hear what was happening.

"Go ahead and speak in the clear, Iveta," he said. "We're past secrets today."

Oh, we are, are we?

But she didn't say that. Just nodded.

"The main *Zerzan* supercarrier, named *Bertev*, just issued an order to all of those damned mechs to find the nearest friendly carrier and board so that the force can withdraw," Iveta said, not saying that the message had been encrypted when it was sent out.

Harman didn't approve of enemy codes. **Really** didn't approve. So he'd done something about it.

Like she knew he would.

"Heather, gold star next to your name," Phil replied ambiguously. "Two in fact. Maybe three. Iveta, excellent work across the board. What was your next step planned?"

"We can continue harrying them from here, to little effect but a lot of headaches," Iveta said. "Or we can close and get into the scrum with a lot of panicked rats that I've managed to corner."

"I'd rather not," Phil said. "The toll today has been high, but not nearly as high as it could have been. Can you snipe at the mechs instead? Every one of those we damage or destroy has to come from home, wherever that is."

"Understood, First Centurion," Iveta said. She switched lines to the local one. "Squadron, this is *Junkyard*, I still have the flag. Start firing at the mechs with everything that can reach, while retaining range. *Storm Petrel*, a condor up their asses would be nice. *Forktail*, you hold for escort. Everybody else cut loose and try to inflict as much damage as you can on the little ones. They'd gotten the order to withdraw and won't be coming after us unless we decide to go into the corner after them to chase down a loose puck."

Iveta cut the line and watched the situation unfold. The

mechs were below her and ahead, cutting in such a way that they could have fallen on a flank or rear had she chased down the carriers. That would have been utterly ugly. As it was, they were getting bounced around by all the Fours and Threes, plus titan bolts fired with proximity fuses.

Nothing that would really hurt another cruiser, but these were tin cans with shields. Any hit threatened a kill.

Every kill today was one less asshole she'd have to deal with later.

And Iveta knew she'd be facing these folks again. When they were better prepared.

She would need to dig deeper into her bag of tricks next time.

BAUSSE

THIRTY-FOUR

MISSION BRIEF: ASSAULT CARRIER TRUHTO. ENEMY WORLD: KYULLE

Bausse kept her emotions compact and on the shortest leash possible as the enemy shuttle nosed into her ship's flight bay and came to rest on the empty deck that should have been crowded with her wing of aeromechia.

Most of them had escaped with *Bertev* and *Rauda*. A few were going to be prisoners, and she was the senior *Unification* officer left in the system with the rest fled ahead of *Urumchi's* vengeance.

Shit.

Still, calm.

She was suited up and standing out in the empty bay, counting empty docking cradles with terrible longing as the shuttle's hatch opened and a small group emerged in gear more than simple bodysuits and less than full armor.

Each of them was armed.

Her suit was a basic one, not intended for heavy duties so it lacked armor plating beyond the basics of knees and elbows one needed when operating without air or gravity, though *Truhto's* engineers had gotten that fixed. And enough engine power to at least hold their orbit for now.

She would need massive repairs if the vessel was ever going to leave *Kyulle* orbit again.

Bausse suspected that to be a moot point as the two in front walked closer, with four others behind them acting more like security troopers protecting a pair of officers.

The taller one stayed back a step, but had an air of command about him, as though he was the senior of the two. He looked male but it was hard to tell in his suit and if so he was somewhat short for a man. The other one was undoubtedly female, from the way the armor framed her curves and chest.

All six wore black pants with tops that were primarily a dark green, with white on the sides and gray for the upper arms, plus a band across the chest with various stripes and color dots Bausse took to indicate rank and division.

The small woman had a single white stripe on her right upper arm. The male had nothing.

Still, the two she took to be officers were armed with pistols. The other four had something more in the carbine range.

Bausse had gone out to meet them alone. Bringing bodyguards would make the wrong statement, and the rest of her crew were furiously working to keep the ship from coming apart around them anyway.

"I am Centurion Xochitl Dar," the small woman said over a local comm frequency they had agreed to use earlier. "I understand that you can speak Hindi, though both of us have horrible accents, relative to the other. Are you Chevalier Aublahzieu?"

"I am," Bausse replied, nodding enough to make it less hostile around her.

Urumchi had withheld the blade at the moment they could have broken *Truhto*. Killed everyone without mercy. Now, they had sent aboard this group to take her formal surrender. Bausse had noted several other shuttles floating nearby before she left her bridge, each supposedly loaded with supplies, engineers, and medical crew to help her own.

Truhto had gotten right up to the edge of the cliff and looked over.

A strong wind might still tip it.

"First Centurion Kosnett has ordered me to come aboard and take formal possession of the vessel, but you will remain in command of your crew," Dar said. "If you are still willing to abide by the previous agreements, I have technical help that can land and get to work under your authority. Is this acceptable?"

Bausse turned to the other officer. The short male. Shorter than her. Outweighed her from the way he stood and the width of his shoulders.

"What do you intend?" she asked both, though she stared at him.

"My name is Trinidad Mildon, Captain," he said. "I am technically a civilian, but have served in a role similar to Dar's. I also have the most experience in dealing with alien cultures of just about anybody in Kosnett's fleet. Additionally, I have been his representative aboard a *Yaumgan* Skycruiser for the last year or so, so I am something of our resident expert there. Given that we are strangers to one another, Kosnett felt that attaching me as something of an ambassador for now would help everyone smooth out misunderstandings as they arise. As to what we intend, once your ship is stabilized and safe, I believe that most of the crew will be transferred to a camp on the ground, or aboard one of the stations, while the First Centurion works with you to answer some questions and eventually arranges to return you to your own people."

Bausse couldn't help the way she rocked back on her heels at that. Might have stumbled, but for the magnets in her boots that had just enough hold to keep her standing.

The man Mildon nodded.

"In a previous war, I was part of a team, with the First Centurion and a few others, who liberated an entire prison planet and rescued all the men who had been condemned to live out their lives and die there by a *Sentient* system who thought it was a god," he said in a dark tone that seemed to penetrate clear to her bones. "Those men would never have gone home. The First Centurion has extremely strong opinions on that topic, and I am certain will be arguing your case with the local political structure. Iveta promised you that she would get you home. We will see it done. I don't know how long that will take, or what hurdles we will have to overcome first, but it will be done."

Shit.

And these people couldn't know anything about who *Yaumgan* really was. Not if they were willing to make her such a promise.

This was who they were at home, as the old saying went.

Bausse found that she had much to learn. The *Unification* had prepared her for *Yaumgan*, once their ancient foe—the dark overlords—had finally been discovered.

Nobody had prepared her for *Aquitaine*.

THIRTY-FIVE

Heather sat on the bridge and watched her screen as the shuttles all landed on *Truhto* and quickly departed. One good thing about a carrier like that, you could enter from one end and sail straight down the flight bay and out the back. It helped that there were no mechs aboard.

Nothing but crew. Casualties had apparently been horrendous, but that was what happened when the Fours started hitting the bare hull of a hollow cube. Already, medical evacuations were hauling folks to the corvettes.

They would save all of them that they could. Iveta had put their honor on the line with this one.

And probably won the battle because of it, once Chevalier Aublahzieu had spoken about that with her superiors.

"Heather, could you join us on the flag bridge?" Phil's voice came out of nowhere, rousing her from wherever she'd gone.

"Be right there," she said, unbuckling and standing. Iveta was taking a nap, so she turned to her Pilot. "Bozhidar, you have the bridge. Yell immediately if anything comes up."

He nodded and Heather headed aft.

Flag Bridge. The heart and soul of the squadron, with Phil and Heather. Plus Nam and Kohahu had pretty much taken up duty assignments here as advisors. *Stunt Dude* was aboard *Truhto* hammering things out there, but everyone seemed to be behaving.

"Sit," Phil ordered, so she did, between Nam and the older scholar who had come with Hu. Wen Qing Jian. Family Wen. Personal Qing. Jian for the innermost ring of friends and family who could tease you with the old stories and dirtiest jokes. *Yaumgan* did it weird, but who was she to argue, however many thousands of light-years from home herself?

"I wanted to thank you, Command Centurion Lau," the First Speaker said as Markus delivered a fresh mug of coffee.

"Heather," she corrected the woman automatically.

Command Centurion was a title. As was *Ground Control*. She was both, and neither. And this conversation didn't look formal.

"Heather," the woman nodded.

Heather studied her. Li Chang Ling. Big woman. Taller than Phil. Heavier, but she wasn't fat. Just built like an oak tree with a youth of training for athletics. Oh, and leader of an entire culture and society of philosophers.

"The First Centurion is of the opinion that your inspiration to send the Immortals into combat long ways around broke the will of *Zerzan*'s forces," the First Speaker said.

Heather shrugged. Lots of options on that board as everyone moved around, jockeying for position. She'd seen the one that would do the most psychological damage, but Iveta or Phil would have too at some point.

"We cannot know without asking their Chevalier in charge," Heather answered.

Chevalier? What a weird title for a Command Centurion. Suggested a Western Euro culture, but according to her *Pixies*, that didn't seem to be far off. She wondered if they spoke English or Hindi as anything more than trade languages. French and German had once been languages that were pretty broadly used. Just hadn't survived millennia in deep space as anything more than local dialects on a few planets.

"You might not be aware, Heather, but *Yaumgan* does not really have a rank equivalent to First Centurion," First Speaker Chang continued, nodding back to Phil. "Our Captains command their own vessel, but rarely do we have large formations like this squadron operating formally."

Heather nodded. She'd had this conversation over wine with Dao Zhiou. And suggested that they put that woman in charge of a new training program, since she had the most experience. At least in *Yaumgan.* Hardly any, compared to the Command Centurions with Phil.

Oh, shit.

She glanced over at Phil and caught his subtle nod.

"I have been speaking with the First Centurion," First Speaker Chang continued, apparently not noticing the unspoken conversation passing by. "In order to survive what might be a full invasion by the so-called *Zerzan Unification, Yaumgan* will need to make drastic changes. And do so in short order. Days, not even weeks, to say nothing of months or years."

Heather nodded warily, already not liking where this conversation seemed to be going. At least Phil was smiling. Petitely, sure, but smiling.

"What changes did you envision, First Speaker?" Heather asked, going ahead and playing the straight man here. Better to get it over with quickly.

"As I understand it, during your war against *Buran,* when the scout ship *CS-405* was trapped behind enemy lines, then-Command Centurion Kosnett took it upon himself to execute the rank of Fleet Centurion as you and your crews began capturing enemy vessels and turning them into a small fleet," Chang said. "And I correct?"

"You are," Heather said. "For a time, I executed as Command Centurion of the supply vessel *Packmule.*"

Heather managed to keep the scowl off her face, but it took

work. This was going to be necessary. Even she could see it. At the same time, it would be around strangers. Worse, people other than *Gloran* or *Ewin* viewing her as some sort of war goddess, wasn't it?

Pallas Athena, reborn?

"We would like to offer you the position of Fleet Centurion over *Yaumgan* forces that will be attached to First Centurion Kosnett's forces," the First Speaker said. "Which will be as many as we can spare. You have impressed both Captains Xue and Lin with your abilities, and myself and my close advisors in the most recent battle. First Centurion Kosnett has assented to my asking, but would not order it."

Because he knew how little she would appreciate being forced into the position, as opposed to volunteering in her own right, which she might have done, given a week to weigh her options.

They didn't have a week. Eighteen hundred or so enemy mechs had escaped. Granted, that meant four hundred had been damaged, destroyed, or the pilots killed in the battle, along with more than half of the *Yaumgan* Skycruisers and Escorts handy.

Not quite apocalyptic, but you could see it from here.

She turned to Phil now, filling in all the subtext with body language. They'd served together long enough that entire conversations could be had silently.

"We can't defend six worlds and however many colonies," she told him flat out. "Not against that kind of concentration of force. They would pick off each one and eventually roll up the entire fleet and toss it in the waste incinerator."

Phil nodded.

"Yes," he said simply, acknowledging all of that, which somehow just made it worse. "I need to talk to the Chevalier on *Truhto*. Understand the woman. That won't take long, because either she'll feel like being helpful, or she won't. Either way, the call will go out and as many *Yaumgan* ships as can be spared over the short term will be assembled here. And placed under your command."

Shit shit shit shit shit.

Heather kept her face neutral.

War Goddess of the Balhee Cluster.

How long until they deified her?

"We're going to go after them?" she asked/said. "At the place called *Loong*?"

She had turned to the First Speaker for that last part, spearing the woman with her eyes.

If you've just promoted me to supreme warlord of your entire culture, you better learn to come clean and use your words clearly.

But she didn't say that. Conveyed it with pheromones, perhaps.

First Speaker Li nodded.

"We cannot be sure, but that is the most likely spot," Li said. "It is the gap in the outer wall through which we came originally, our ancestors, and more recently was used by our agents in the *Nagi Syndicate*. Small and secret, unlike the mouth of the amphora at *Vilahana* where you entered."

Heather nodded. Gaps existed. Markus had lead a team that had actually come up with entirely new mathematics to predict such gaps by the way nebulae and stars overlapped. The whole cluster had come about a long time ago when some mega-supernova, or perhaps several of them close together, had exploded, bubbling outwards in ripples that triggered the remaining nebular gases to coalesce and form star systems.

But the outer surface was still mostly solid. *Vilahana. Meerut.* And now *Loong.*

"What percentage of the entire *Yaumgan* fleet was present today?" Heather asked. "By weight and by numbers."

Ambassador Hu got a calculating look on his face and everyone turned to watch him.

"Four of the Immortals, as noted," he mused aloud. "All in reasonable shape in terms of repairs that can be completed in a few days. Roughly twenty percent of the fleet by numbers, I think, as we had pulled in many ships against possible *Aquitaine* betrayals."

He said that with a pained look on his face, but Heather let it slide.

They didn't comprehend *Aquitaine*. And certainly didn't understand the *RAN*. He was projecting himself, and in a telling way.

"In terms of weight, I think we're much higher," he continued through an embarrassed blush. "Possibly thirty percent, but I'd have to ask an expert to refine that."

"Sufficient for my needs," Heather said, turning back to both Phil and the First Speaker.

"It's not enough," she continued flatly. "If we stretched, they could probably form a squadron about twice or maybe three times the size of *Urumchi's* for numbers but not effectiveness against those snubfighter mechs. And then only by stripping systems bare against anything *Zerzan* wanted to do to the surface. Would they bomb if nobody was there to stop them? Or destroy any and all stations, including armed ones? They have the firepower to do it."

"We don't know," Li had the grace to admit. "We know hardly anything about them."

"Perhaps," Heather said pointedly, "you need to tell us why the *Zerzan Unification* hates you so much then, before we start planning how we might react to such an invasion. Because I have the impression they came for you specifically."

At least they had the courtesy to grimace. All three of them. That alone told Heather how much information had not been shared yet, and she and Phil were the people *Yaumgan* might be counting on to save their asses.

Not until she got answers.

As Phil had threatened others previously, *Aquitaine* could always go home for a generation and try again later.

With whoever had survived.

THIRTY-SIX

AQUITAINE FLAGSHIP URUMCHI, KYULLE ORBITAL SPACE

Yating turned to Chang and Qing for their approval before he spoke. She had sent him as ambassador to the barbarians originally, so they had had extensive conversations about things that could and could not be discussed.

Command Centurion Lao was even harder than the First Centurion. Or Kosnett had understood how Heather Lao would approach the situation and let Yating and the others walk into a bear trap that was even now grinding against the bones in his ankle.

Chang nodded first. Qing shrugged. He had been First Speaker in his time, but that was a job for younger people, so he had gratefully passed it to Chang and somewhat retired.

Still a gadfly in the best—or worst—ways, and having far too much fun at it.

Yating took a deep breath.

"There was a time when we were known as the *Zerzan Monarchy*," he said, watching the many heads around the room lean in to listen. *Yaumgan* would likely have no secrets left after today. And possibly no mystique, if the *Unification* had just undone them in a single afternoon.

Everything might come to rest on Heather Lau's shoulders.

She nodded for him to continue, not impatient, but not impressed either.

"Some five centuries ago, there was a revolution against the Crown," Yating did continue now. "I will not say that they were wrong to do so, based on the kind of historical studies one is required to undertake to become a scholar. Our ancestors were brutal aristocrats, utterly wedded to the concept of the divine right of kings, and their treatment of the lower classes might best be described as bordering on crimes against humanity itself."

He paused, uncertain if he had heard a growl emerge from Heather Lao's soul or just imagined it. Her eyes promised that she might go for his throat with her bare teeth.

Yating drew a breath to gain a moment.

"The last king of *Zerzan* was executed by the rebels, along with his entire extended family," he said. "Much of the rest of the ruling class was taken into custody as well. About half joined their king quickly. The other half were deposed and stripped of titles and wealth as the revolution, the *Unification*, was a social leveling tool with a bayonet attached. A handful of former lords managed to secretly assemble loyal retainers. Together, they fled into the galactic interior."

"Interior?" she asked sharply.

"Almost directly up that galactic arm along the spiral, rather than a straight line hopping arms and gaps," he nodded. "We sought to hide socially instead of just physically, passing through various star nations that were rebuilding from the Great Darkness. Mind you, thiswas after Doyle Iwakuma, who I understand to be an *Aquitaine* hero, helped rediscover the JumpDrives that let people originally colonize most of the galaxy. Later, another *Aquitaine* hero in Baudin invented the JumpSails that almost everyone uses now. Thus, we were aware that such a place existed, but the gap across darkness was too great to explore it. At that point, my ancestors were fleeing for their lives."

"What caused you to come to Balhee?" Command Centurion Lao asked.

"Stories talk about a merchant who had come from there," Yating said. "Possibly from your neighbor that would become the *Fribourg Empire* in time. He had a map and a story of a hollow pearl. The refugee fleet decided to cut across and down, back closer to the galactic rim and more or less between *Zerzan* and *Aquitaine*, but hidden. We found the gap at *Loong*, conquered the natives on *Kyulle* and then the five other core worlds. Eventually, we claimed *Yaumgan* space and forced all three of our neighbors to withdraw beyond our borders."

"Until *Zerzan* found you," she said.

Yating nodded.

"*Nagi* pirate who sold the information after they fled the Cluster rather than go straight?" she asked.

Yating shrugged.

"It could be any of a number of things," he said. "The information and the attack on *Senza* were so recent that we have not had a chance to determine probable causes, let alone ask anyone who might know."

"So they might have a reason to come all this distance and destroy you?" Lao asked now, getting to the heart of the matter.

"No," Kosnett said abruptly. Firmly. Decisively. "They do not."

"First Centurion?" Chang asked, surprised.

"Five centuries?" Kosnett asked.

Yating nodded. Everyone used the standard years that had been inherited from ancient Earth, as well as local calendars. The math got interesting over time.

"Nobody alive today remembers those crimes," Kosnett said. "Nobody alive today is responsible for them. They are, I suspect, guilty of the Sins of the Fathers fallacy. What I don't know is if they will listen to reason on the topic."

"Reason, First Centurion?" Yating managed, though his voice broke in the middle.

"Are the sons guilty of the crimes of their fathers, Scholar Hu?" Kosnett asked. "Is an entire culture, five centuries removed, guilty of the acts that their ancestors undertook? If that is the case, then everyone would be at war with everyone else for blood feuds that would never end. It is a conversation I look forward to having with Chevalier Bausse Aublahzieu, once she has her situation under control."

"All well and good, Phil," Heather Lao replied. "It doesn't solve my immediate problem. *Yaumgan* cannot resist *Zerzan*."

"No," the young woman from *Dalou*, Lady Kugosu spoke up, breaking the tension. "They cannot. Not alone. They will need friends."

Yating wondered if someone had bashed him over the head with a sandbag or something from the way gravity itself seemed to wobble in the room. And the sudden ringing and pounding in his head.

"Friends?" he managed to sputter, somehow recovering faster than Chang or Qing could. Or the others. "*Yaumgan* has no friends. We have always kept the Cluster at a distance, willing to leave you alone in return for the same consideration."

She nodded serenely. It took him a moment to remember that Kohahu Kugosu was barely fifteen years old, because those eyes spoke of long decades of deadly intrigue and danger.

Heather. That was who she reminded him of. The daughter of the Dalou Shogun was turning into Heather Lau.

Was anywhere in the galaxy safe when that happened?

"I understand, Ambassador," Lady Kugosu replied with a firm nod. "But that time has passed. Do you think that *Zerzan* would be satisfied to just conquer the *Yaumgan Domain*? To ignore the rest of us? I find that highly unlikely, especially as they are at least your match for power, and thus superior to anyone else in the Cluster. But not *everyone* in the Cluster, unified into a greater whole. Is that not Kosnett's mission? Has that not been what he has been working assiduously towards since he first emerged about *Vilahana*? One Balhee, joined in trade and friendship? It must begin today. Here. Now. Else we all will fall beneath their heel eventually."

Yating felt his mouth fall open, but nothing came out. That condition seemed infectious, too, as both Chang and Qing were similarly stricken. And the rest of the table. With one exception.

Heather Lau.

Of course.

"Would they answer?" Heather asked the young woman, in a voice suggestive of a private conversation between the two of them. Perhaps over tea. The rest of them merely ghosts watching invisibly from nearby.

"If Kosnett asked?" Kugosu replied. "Perhaps. I have something better in mind. A message that will resonate with *Ewin* and *Gloran* even more than *Dalou*. Only *Aditi* might hesitate, but I think that they will quickly see the writing on the wall, because Phil has broken them of their arrogance as well."

"What did you have in mind, then, Kohahu?" First Centurion Kosnett finally managed to ask.

"*Morninghawk.*"

Yating was lost, but the warm, sudden smiles on the faces of the folks in *Aquitaine* uniforms brought him solace.

Whatever it was, they believed.

THIRTY-SEVEN

S *tunt Dude* was mostly in charge because he knew the various players better than anybody else Phil could send. Heather or Phil himself would be better, but they had other things that were more important.

Xochitl was in charge of security because that was the job for someone like her, on her way to being a Dragoon somewhere for her next assignment. Might as well gain experience thus.

Trinidad had been more places. Done more things. Escaped more deadly situations than he was willing to admit while sober.

Right now, he was in a small conference room with the Chevalier of *Truhto*, Bausse Aublahzieu. At least the set designer had earned their pay with the verisimilitude. Gray walls that had a seam in the middle suggesting you were in the middle of a hexagon. Raised table without chairs, because a lot of the time they seemed to stand. Smoke in a few places where the life support had blown it rather than taking a hit. This was one of the few places on the ship that hadn't buckled, but it still felt like a space battle vid. Maybe that one piracy flick he'd done.

The woman representing *Zerzan* spoke a Franco-German dialect *Stunt Dude* had learned along the way. Trinidad had always had an ear for languages. It had helped him in the movie business, because he could walk in, deliver one or two lines and nail the accent perfectly before leaving to put on his disguise and go be a stunt guy for the star.

Back in the old days.

"You can understand me?" the Chevalier asked.

"Well enough," *Stunt Dude* replied. "Given time, I will get better and pick up more of your language. Hindi is fine, as is Mandarin or Mongolian. Any of those are my strongest, but I learn."

"What happens next?" she asked.

"Dar is off supervising our folks and keeping them in line," he replied. "They will mostly be fine, but this is your ship and they might forget to ask before tearing into some system to fix it. We're guests, and Dar will remind them of that."

"You captured this vessel and this crew," she said in a disbelieving voice.

He shrugged.

"Not the first enemy vessel I've done that to," he replied. "With Phil, we took *Queen Anne's Revenge*, *Packmule*, *Persephone*, and *Forgotten Mercy*. Couple of those we boarded and stormed under fire, as a matter of fact."

"And here?"

"I don't know what you people had intended from this attack," he replied. "Didn't work, but I got the impression from the experts that it could have gone either way. Right now, we need to fix things here so you can stay in orbit. Get your people medical assistance. Figure out where to go and who to talk to about repatriating everyone at some point."

"You honestly believe that will happen?" she scoffed. "We are *Yaumgan* prisoners."

"You are my prisoner," he snapped back at her like an angry Second Unit Director laying down the law. "I'm *Aquitaine*. *Yaumgan* can ask me nicely, or they can go pound sand."

That got through to her. Her eyes got a little big for a moment and she almost gasped.

"Are you folks the reason *Yaumgan* fled from their original homelands?" he asked now. Heather and Leyla had suggested as much, but didn't want to say how or why they knew to ask.

Pixies, most likely. Everybody knew they existed.

Everybody in black and green, that was.

"What have they told you?" she asked harshly.

"Nothing at all," *Stunt Dude* replied. "They are known to be outsiders to the Cluster, and didn't come from the east because we did. That generally leaves the west. Since you came from somewhere else and went after them with a broken bottle neck, I presume old, bad blood there. Feel like sharing?"

"And if I didn't?" she countered.

"Then we find something else to talk about," he shrugged. "Mostly curiosity on my part. I walked into *Buran* as it was in the process of falling apart, in order to find the woman I had fallen in love with across the battlefield. Took a couple of years, but I found her. She was born in *Buran*, but is Phil's Chief Medical Officer now."

"Phil?"

Blank face. Blank eyes.

"First Centurion Phil Kosnett," he said, reminding himself that they were complete and utter strangers around here. "The commander in charge of the *Aquitaine* force that nearly killed *Truhto* in the battle. My eventual boss, though I'm technically a civilian here. I volunteer to help a lot. It mostly doesn't get me in trouble."

"Mostly?" she asked, intrigued now.

But then, he'd learned to use his career and life story offensively to distract and defuse people. The shit he'd seen and done.

Sam was probably correct that he needed to write a book one of these days. Maybe some action adventure piece, because most people would scoff if it was supposedly autobiographical. Even after he left out some of the more outrageous parts that had really happened.

"Mostly," he agreed. "Hoping that we can get everything stabilized here. Get your people sorted out and taken care of, with some of them transferred to local hospitals that might be better equipped than my ships. Then eventually introduce you to Phil. Not sure which deck it should take place on at the moment."

"He would come here?" she asked, astonished.

Again, he shrugged, playing this all by ear. Lots of time around cameras, watching actors and directors grab the writer and edit or freelance a scene based on an esoteric emotional flow that only the director and maybe the editor really saw.

Still, he'd done enough improv in his acting classes to understand.

"He might," *Stunt Dude* said. "And he might invite you to come aboard *Urumchi* instead. I personally lean towards the latter, because all the setup that would be necessary for him to come would distract your people when they should be fixing shit, including themselves."

"But he might not order it?" she pressed. "I am your prisoner."

"Honorably surrendered," he replied. "Honorable ransom. That means we act like adults here, instead of punks. He'll ask. Would your crew be able to keep working without you giving orders for a few hours?"

She blinked. Too many times.

He'd seen it. Information overload as wrong assumptions cascaded, knocking over bunches of other ones. And he might be pushing her buttons as he came to understand which ones would move the woman.

There was always that.

He leaned back and watched the woman have some sort of mental and emotional crisis. Best to let them walk themselves through the stages of death without anyone pushing. Any more than he had.

She drew a breath after about sixty seconds. Looked at him with fresh eyes.

"I think I would like to go meet your Kosnett," she said in a voice still looking for firm ground, but no longer wondering about quicksand.

"Works for me," he nodded. "I'll give him a call and see when he's available."

THIRTY-EIGHT

Donatien Fortier stood on his bridge and studied the after-action reports as *Bertev* cut through JumpSpace. He was not pleased.

Two Overlords and four Assault Carriers. Two thousand, one hundred, and sixty aeromechia, minus a lower-than-possibly-expected seven that had suffered system failures immediately prior to launch, sufficient to withhold them from the battle.

Three hundred and eight-seven more had been damaged, destroyed, or captured attacking *Kyulle*, along with the Assault Carrier *Truhto* and his best Chevalier, Bausse.

Yaumgan's forces had suffered grievously, but *Aquitaine* had managed to keep their own damage to a minimum, using some sort of new weapon that distracted pulse and ionization torpedoes at the moment they began scanning for a target at short range.

How dangerous was *Aquitaine*? And what other forces did they have that had not been present, but available to be called up?

Yaumgan was doomed. They had built the wrong fleet to fight aeromechia, instead concentrating on large platforms and heavy weapons that were wasted trying to damage waves of little craft. Certainly, they had been effective, but *Aquitaine* had done most of the damage, when it came time to count empty cradles on his various ships.

As it was, he would need to recalibrate everything. Most of *Truhto*'s Wing had escaped to safety, and had no home. *Rauda* had suffered serious enough damage that they had to drop out of Jump regularly on the way home as things overheated or shorted.

Again, *Aquitaine* and those impossibly heavy beams.

The woman controlling Navigation got his attention now.

"Estimated arrival in five minutes, Chevalier," she said.

Donatien nodded and closed the report. Then he looked over his bridge crew, among the finest in the *Unification* as far as he allowed himself an opinion.

He was troubled by what he saw. Never before had he seen dread or concern writ so clearly on their faces. Or so widely.

Fear that *Aquitaine* had somehow found their base and was even now attacking it? Or hiding in wait for *Bertev* and the damaged *Rauda* to arrive?

Even Donatien did not believe that *Rauda* had made this last Jump cleanly. Hopefully, but not a given. Not with the damage they had absorbed. Still, he knew their flight path, and could send ships looking for them if they didn't arrive within an hour.

At the same time, he did not relish the meeting to come. What *Unification* Commissioner Murielle Abaroa would have to say about his failure. And it was his. Donatien had been the one to argue for a massive assault on *Kyulle*, designed to savage their homeworld fleet where they could see it, rather than one of the lesser worlds, like *Ontan* or *Cinnramud*.

Calculated risks. Calculated rewards.

He had gambled. And lost badly enough to force a rethink of this campaign.

Fortunately, he had damaged *Yaumgan* sufficiently that they would not come looking for him. Not yet.

He had time to gather his strength. Regain the momentum that might have broken like a wave against *Aquitaine* at *Kyulle*.

To crush those scum and finally settle the ancient war, once and for all.

Soon.

THIRTY-NINE

MISSION BRIEF: AQUITAINE SHUTTLE. ENEMY WORLD: KYULLE

Bausse still wasn't used to the concept, but he had insisted that he would answer to it better than any other name, so she called him *Stunt Dude*. It sounded radically different in Franco-German, but meant the same thing.

Still, to any outsider, it would be a name. Good enough.

They were on a shuttle from *Urumchi*, the monstrous warship that had been the bane of *Truhto* and *Zerzan*. Her. *Stunt Dude*. A navigator forward. Nobody else.

Had she any thoughts of doing something stupid, he had mentioned his background in training security troops in close combat, so Bausse understood that a thirty-eight-year-old naval officer offered him no serious physical threat, even if he was older than her. That actually made it easier, because it allowed her to not get distracted with insane visions out of some terrible action vid, where she captured the shuttle, stole something with a JumpSail, and escaped.

Even if she wanted to, she had an expert on the topic at hand, no doubt planning ahead of her.

Better to learn. If this Kosnett was intent on dealing with her equitably, she might even make it home. Bausse was still questioning that outcome, but less than she had a day ago.

"Stand by for landing," the navigator spoke from the cockpit forward.

Bausse nodded to herself and watched on a screen from a forward camera as the side of *Urumchi* turned into a cliff face with a cave entrance. They entered, rotated delicately as the pilot shifted around to put the hatch facing a nearby airlock, and landed with the clamp of gear magnets.

"Bay sealed and pressurizing," the woman navigating continued. "Two minutes to secure environment."

Stunt Dude rose now, so Bausse joined him. Towered over him some, but that was the luck of the draw, as she'd always been a tall woman, even as a child. Still, he smiled up at her, not the least bit intimidated. Again, reassuring, as he wasn't one of those men who got a chip on his shoulder from being short, and thus got aggressive around tall women.

No, *Stunt Dude* was casualness itself.

The hatch opened. He went first, then waited at the bottom of the steps for her, walking side by side into the nearby airlock. It closed behind them and opened ahead, and Bausse had her first look at the terrible man Kosnett.

Unification Commissioner Murielle Abaroa would be his equivalent, she thought, as *Stunt Dude* had explained that the First Centurion of the *Aquitaine* force had plenipotentiary powers in the Cluster, in addition to supreme military rank.

Thus, a dangerous man.

Tall. A handspan taller than her. Broad-shouldered, but not heavy. Just big. Massive was the burly younger man standing like a bodyguard to one side and scowling intently at her.

Intelligent face. Darker skin than Bausse, though more red than the *Yaumgan* or other peoples of the Cluster, she had come to understand. The *Unification* was dominated by Euros like herself, pale with brown or blond hair, rather than the darker hues of other places.

Kosnett's uniform had five stripes on one arm. The woman next to him had three, so she was a Command Centurion, according to *Stunt Dude*. Bizarre, but effective. Longish, straight black hair back in a tie. Taller than Bausse. Midway between her and Kosnett.

The dozen others were less interesting. Junior officers and security troops, to look at them.

"Chevalier, welcome to *Urumchi*," Kosnett said now, stepping forward and bowing his head.

"Thank you," Bausse managed, still a little off-keel.

Kosnett had none of the abrasive arrogance she would have expected from a *Unification* Commissioner. Or their equivalent.

He turned and indicated the tall woman next to him. "Command Centurion Heather Lau, commander of Urumchi."

Stunt Dude had explained that, as well. Worse, there was another women named Iveta Beridze who had actually been in charge during the fighting, while Lau handled the ship and Kosnett commanded the entire force.

Completely insane, on the surface of things. Mercilessly effective, when you were on the wrong side.

"I've arranged a casual meal," Kosnett continued. "The four of us alone in the officer's wardroom for now. Later there are some *Yaumgan* officials that would like a chance to talk to you. Again casual circumstances."

"I do not understand," she said simply.

Stunt Dude had warned her, hadn't he?

She had simply made the mistake of not believing him.

"I would prefer not to be your enemy, Chevalier Aublahzieu," Kosnett nodded as he spoke. "This is not an interrogation. It is four people sitting down and talking. I find that more and better things can be accomplished in such situations than by giving long-winded, stem-winding speeches that serve very little purpose beyond blowhards who like to hear their own voices."

Bausse nodded blankly, helped by the smiles around her. Welcoming smiles, in spite of her being part of a military force that had just launched a surprise attack against *Kyulle* intended to destroy the defending forces entirely and open the way for *Zerzan* to fully and completely end *Yaumgan* as a thing.

Again, *Stunt Dude* stepped close.

"I would like to take your elbow to guide you," he said. "Is that acceptable?"

She nodded again, not remotely used to such behavior.

The *Unification* had a place for everyone. And everyone in their place. As conquerors, Kosnett was entitled to put her in a small chamber and ignore her until the solitude possibly drove her mad. It would everyone, eventually.

Instead, *Stunt Dude* guided her politely into the bulk of the ship and down corridors at the center of a small cluster of people, all wearing the same uniform, though many paused to stare openly at her as she went past.

Wardroom. Long trestle tables in four rows with benches. A table with food available from troughs and containers, with sailors doling things out, often laughing.

Laughing? The *Unification* was serious business, executed by serious people.

They did not do mirth.

When was the last time she had laughed?

Kosnett went first, followed by *Stunt Dude*. Command Centurion Lau followed, and the others either peeled off or hovered nearby. Guards, obviously, but polite about it.

"What are your food allergies and dislikes?" *Stunt Dude* asked her as they both got trays and plates.

What?

He repeated himself, so she must have said it out loud. Or mouthed the word.

Bausse blinked, then processed that she would be eating the same food as everyone else in here. They weren't about to poison her or do anything else.

"That smells lovely," she managed, pointing to something brown that she thought was beef in some sort of brown sauce. "No allergies I am aware of."

He nodded and turned to the…person standing on the other side.

Bausse was unable to assign a gender to the sailor across the table. Short enough to be considered female, but without breasts or secondary sexual characteristics that were obvious. Lean to the point of skinny, with wide eyes and a chin that almost came to a point, balancing ears that seemed almost elfin.

The person smiled.

"Centurion Rei Bottenberg," they said with a smile and a nod. "Chief of the Wardroom. We will take care of you for dinner."

They spoke with such warm certainty that Bausse was taken aback. She nodded and got a cut of meat in a brown sauce. *Stunt Dude* did the same, matching things.

For her?

Insane.

And yet…

Every single thing that ended up on her tray was matched by him doing the same, plus a few things she had skipped.

Kosnett had moved to the end of a distant table, well away from the others in here, but still close enough that their conversation could not be private.

Was he a man with no secrets from his crew?

Was that possible?

What rabbit hole had she fallen into?

Kosnett was eating pasta with red sauce and meatballs. Lau a salad with all manner of things added for color and texture.

Bausse got water from a common pitcher and ate.

Somehow, she was not surprised that Kosnett's kitchen was better than hers. The *Unification* was all about socially leveling the galaxy. No more aristocracy or kings.

And yet…

He ate the same fare as any officer in here. Joked with sailors in line serving him. Treated her like a visiting dignitary instead of a prisoner of war.

What the hell was going on?

They ate in a companionable silence, broken by small talk of almost no social value at all, save that it lubricated interaction.

Friendliness.

When *was* the last time she had laughed?

The food vanished quickly. Excellent meal. Bottenberg had not been wrong in their intent.

Bausse put her napkin down and studied the man across from her. Then Lau, seated next to him. Finally, *Stunt Dude*, immediately on her right.

"I have had several interesting conversations with the leaders of *Yaumgan*," Kosnett began in a calm, quiet voice, pitched to carry not much beyond her ears and force Bausse to lean in and pay attention. "They are of the opinion that the *Zerzan Unification* represents a political descendant of the *Zerzan Monarchy*, of which they were a part, several centuries ago."

"So they admit it?" she asked, bristling some.

Bausse had expected them to lead with the lies for which their kind were so famous.

"They do," Kosnett nodded. "However, having spoken with them, and gotten their side of things, I had to remind them that you were my prisoner, and not theirs."

Bausse blinked at the sudden intensity that had come into his eyes.

He was watching her.

"Okay?" Bausse offered, mostly as a placeholder.

"The *Unification* occupies the place that they escaped from?" he asked.

"It does," Bausse acknowledged. "Plus several others that were captured and absorbed in our long quest to find them, that they could be punished for what they had done."

"I will not allow that," Kosnett replied simply.

"You will not—?" she began, only to be cut off.

"Nobody who was alive during the revolution that saw them

overthrown and cast down remains alive today, Chevalier," Kosnett said sharply. "*Nobody.*"

"So?"

"So you seem intent on punishing the present generation for the sins of people dead for at least four hundred years," he noted. "Who of *Yaumgan* has committed any sins—any crimes —against the *Zerzan Unification?*"

Bausse blinked at the words. At the implications.

He was right, of course. The war had ended in the utter defeat of the aristocracy. Of the destruction of so many of them that few traced any lineage down to the present.

The entire point of the *Unification* had been to level society. No more kings. No more dukes.

No more inherited authority. You were born in common, raised to the same standards, and rose to the level of your competence.

"Just so you understand my position, Chevalier," Kosnett continued. "What you did then was probably a righteous act, and I would have helped, given what I have learned from the *Yaumgan* Scholars currently resting forward in my Ambassadorial lounge. *However.*"

Bausse closed her mouth again, words unspoken.

"However," he continued in a softer voice. "Today, you are invading a nation that has no connection to the *Zerzan Monarchy* save ancient ties of blood. You are attacking planets and killing people because you don't like who their ancestors were. That's something *Aquitaine* would classify as racism of the worst kind. An act that borders on evil itself. You have conquered and absorbed—your words—other nations guilty of only briefly harboring your ancient enemies. Or perhaps having some memory of their passage. *Yaumgan* was clear to me that they fled for more than a century in their caravan of ships before they eventually arrived at *Kyulle*. Since they have been here, they have been a quiet neighbor to the rest of the Cluster, remaining as isolationist as possible in the face of adventurous and expansive nations on three sides. *Zerzan* threatens all of that, because I do not believe you can look me in the eye and tell me that destroying *Yaumgan* would cause you to suddenly come to your senses as a culture and call it *good enough*."

He paused to take a breath. And a sip of water. Bausse would have liked to dispute him in this moment. Argue that he was wrong.

She could not. She would be lying to try.

"Empires have two states, Chevalier Aublahzieu," he said, shifting gears verbally until he suddenly reminded her of a scholar she had studied under as a young officer candidate. "They are either expanding, or contracting. I am unaware of any empire in the history of Humanity that has successfully achieved a steady state, except when natural boundaries were so perfect as to cause their expansion to come to rest. And even then, that usually signaled the turning inward that saw power consolidated for a time, before the edges grew weak and restive and the whole fell apart again. Can the *Unification* stop, having conquered the small bubble of stars known as the *Yaumgan Domain*? Or would they immediately eye the stars of the *Ewin Principalities*, the *Aditi Consensus*, the *Dalou Hegemony*, and the *Gloran Empire* as their next victims?"

It was Bausse's turn to pause and sip water from her glass. To find some point of equilibrium against which she could brace her feet and push Kosnett's logic back.

There was none. Nothing she could wrap her arms around and present as a thing. The *Unification* had been expanding for centuries, searching for the thing they would eventually understand as *Yaumgan*.

Even in her darkest soul, Bausse was not about to lie and suggest that they would be satisfied with taking such a small bite.

Nobody had ever been able to resist them. Before yesterday, she amended herself. Thus, the *Unification* had expanded, as Kosnett suggested.

Could it stop expanding?

She was not aware of what that might take.

No, Bausse had one certainty there. *Aquitaine* could make them stop. Could draw that metaphorical line in the sand and say, "No more."

That might engulf the *Unification* into the greatest war in their history.

To what end?

Bausse found herself blinking too rapidly as she surveyed all the rabbit holes suddenly obvious before her. All the places where she could break an ankle, or lose her mind.

Kosnett and the other two merely watched her silently. Absorbing her thoughts, perhaps, if she was broadcasting them too loudly to the room.

He was not wrong. And the scowl on his face told her that he knew that. Had come to a reasonable understanding of *Zerzan* in just a few days, perhaps as a reaction to *Yaumgan* and the fact that they had been hunting the aristocrats for centuries.

And still he was sitting in the officer's wardroom, eating a meal with her. Talking to her. Or perhaps at her, as she'd had precious few words to counter his accusations.

She found them now, weak and pitiful as they were.

"I am not a scholar of history, First Centurion," Bausse offered, finding something of her mental footing. "I am, however, willing to accept most of what you have said on the face of things. That does not change the fact that *Zerzan* as a society, as a culture, seeks to destroy *Yaumgan*. They will bend every effort to such a task, until it is completed. This was only the beginning. More ships, more aeromechia will come, until the chore is finished."

"Then what?" Command Centurion Lau asked simply, having been silent for so long that Bausse had almost forgotten about her. "After you destroy *Yaumgan*. Phil mentioned the rest of the Cluster. I do not hear you denying that your imperial tendencies would push to the inner edges. The walls of stars themselves. Then what? You look across the darkness and see *Aquitaine* and the others on that far shore? You gather up your fleets like plagues of locusts and descend on more worlds, simply because you do not believe that anybody can stand before your assembled military might? At what point are you as bad or worse than the aristocrats you threw down five centuries ago, Bausse Aublahzieu?"

Bausse goggled at the woman. It might have been less painful if Lau had simply reached across the table and punched her in the mouth.

Had they become evil, in the quest of overthrowing it?

If none could resist *Unification*, they were unified. That had been the promise for how long?

Centuries?

When had the *Zerzan Unification* declared war against the entire rest of the galaxy? Or the rest of Humanity itself? She wasn't sure.

The purpose of the *Unification* had been just that. To create a single Humanity that spanned the galaxy. At some point, *Zerzan* had stopped asking if the others wished to join, conquering them instead and forcing them to be *unified*.

Steady states were not the natural resting position of the *Unification*. They had spent those centuries expanding, chasing after the *Monarchy* they had already destroyed, like a will'o'th'wisp.

Unifying all.

Regardless of innocence or guilt?

She had no words.

Kosnett rescued her.

Kosnett?

"I can see that this has been emotionally trying," he said, rising and bussing his own tray like a common sailor. "Let's get you settled in a suite and give you some time to recover. I would still like you to meet the First Speaker of *Yaumgan* later tonight, if you are up to it."

Bausse rose automatically, joined the other three. Even carried her own tray to a station and sorted things out. *Stunt Dude* took her elbow again and Bausse mutely followed Kosnett.

The walk was much longer this time. Forward, if the markings translated as she thought, Arabic numbers having been one of the things that were still universal.

Kosnett stopped at a hatch and opened it.

"I've assigned you this space, and a small staff," he said, gesturing. "*Stunt Dude* will help you check in with your crew and we'll talk again in a few hours."

He bowed his head and withdrew, Lau doing the same.

Bausse turned to *Stunt Dude*. He was still casualness. That helped. As did his wry smile.

"I did warn you," he said with a grin.

"You did, *Stunt Dude*," Bausse managed to reply. "I simply didn't believe."

FORTY

P hil had drawn Heather back to his office off the flag bridge. Markus had left them coffee and was guarding the door outside like a cave troll or angry dragon.

They were alone.

"You never did answer the original question," he said, studying one of his best-ever students.

"You are correct," Heather replied tartly. "I needed to meet the Chevalier first."

"And?"

"And I can see a way to do it, Phil," Heather finally said. "It will be hard, painful, and cost a lot of lives if the rest of *Zerzan* is as hardheaded as she is, but I will accept *Yaumgan*'s offer to become their dread warlord. For the time being. They will need it, and nobody else is prepared to step into that role. What about you? Are you ready to lead the combined forces of the entire Cluster in some grand fleet event for the ages?"

He grimaced.

"I'm not entirely sure they'll do it," he began, only to be shut down by her eruption of laughter.

"Phil, you've just spent a year and change bashing heads together to get these people to get over themselves," she said when she recovered. "You could have easily overthrown everybody but *Gloran* had you set your mind to it. Literally held it in your hands. You even caused *Aditi* to have elections centered entirely on governmental corruption."

"Because I asked?" he replied.

"Because you will ask *Morninghawk* to raise the banner," she replied, sobering sharply. "Kohahu calls him the herald of a new era. She's not limiting herself to only *Dalou* when she says that. Striker Solo has had painful conversations with his people. Cruiser-Captain Khan has been part of a revolution at *Gloran*, along with Kira Zaman, based on what he learned from *Morninghawk*. Even Kaur Singh has managed to get through to the right people, assuming there are any honest folks in that cesspool."

"Honest enough for my needs today," he nodded.

About as good as he could get, when the changes *Aditi* needed would be measured in decades, or perhaps even a few generations.

It was his responsibility to provide them those generations. To hold the wall, as First Lord Kasum had once famously said, against the darkness that sought to overwhelm them all.

He keyed his comm. She was there instantly. Because of course she was.

"Harinder, could you join us?" Phil asked.

"Be right in."

Phil leaned back and drew a breath, considering the shelf over Heather's left shoulder. The brass telescope that had been a birthday present from none other than Vo *zu* Arlo, Imperial Consort and all-around badass.

To see farther than the rest.

That was his charge today. And tomorrow.

All tomorrows.

Harinder came through quickly and he gestured her to the other open chair.

"Heather has agreed to negotiate with *Yaumgan* about

details," he told her. "I'm not feeling particularly benevolent, so they'll take what she offers and keep their mouths shut about it if they have any sense at all. I need you to review the message Kohahu drafted and make sure that Legal is on board."

"Already done, Phil," she said.

But then, Harinder Abbatelli was usually a step ahead of him when it came to that sort of thing. She'd been trained by the best Flag Centurion the *RAN* had ever known in Enej Zivkovic.

And maybe she had surpassed her mentor, too.

"Thoughts?" he asked.

"I tweaked a few things," Harinder said carefully. "And assumed it wouldn't be sent without Heather agreeing to the rest, so that's already in place. It's ready whenever you are."

Phil grunted and called up the file on his tablet, scanning the language quickly. Not a lot of changes from the first draft he remembered, but Kohahu Kugosu was the warrior daughter of a Shogun, so she understood how to rouse the spirits and call the warriors to battle.

He was really looking forward to visiting *Dalou* in a few decades, after she'd had her chance to show these fools how it *should* be done.

He found the comm line he wanted and opened it.

"*RAN Hollywood*," a woman answered quickly.

Phil suppressed a grin. They were allowed to fly his flag while they were with his squadron, but her people had taken entirely too much joy in the prospect of being deputized around here.

"This is Phil Kosnett," he said. "I need to talk to *Hollywood* herself."

"Stand by, First Centurion," she said.

"What's up, Phil?" *Hollywood* Ward asked a moment later.

"I have a priority run for you," Phil said. "*Varmint*, too, but his run will be longer and I'll let you sort all that out. I am transmitting a file to you now. I need you to carry that to *Urwel* and personally deliver it to Makara Omarov, *Lord Morninghawk*."

He caught the gasp as she opened it and read.

"Holy shit," *Hollywood* said in a quiet voice. "Seriously?"

"Seriously, *Hollywood*," Phil agreed. "It has come down to this. *Varmint* will carry that same message directly to *Derragon*, but that will take longer both directions. From *Urwel*, I need you sending your ships to *Ewinhome*, *Aditi*, *Ellariel*, and *Meerut*. Whoever you can find there or along the way. You work out how everything happens, because time is utterly critical here and I need everyone who will come. How soon can you depart?"

"Immediately," she said in a breathless tone, still coming to grips with his message. "We've stayed topped up for supplies on the assumption that you would need us going somewhere."

"Then go," Phil said. "The faster you call the minutemen, the faster we can stop the redcoats at the bridge."

"On it," *Hollywood* said. "Oh, and Phil? Thank you for believing in me."

She was gone before he could reply, but that was acceptable. Her and her people had proven themselves in the hardest arena there was.

Being on the right side of history.

"Now what?" Heather asked.

"Now, we need to talk to the First Speaker," Phil said. "I've got a lot of balls in the air right now, and can't allow any of them to hit the ground."

FORTY-ONE

Heather led. Phil and Harinder were mostly here as her witnesses. And maybe to keep her from saying something ruder than appropriate if emotions got a little high in what was coming.

Yaumgan was the last place she expected to venerate her as a war goddess. Or whatever. *Ewin* she could see. Or *Gloran*.

Yaumgan???

She opened the hatch to the suite where the First Speaker was resting, waving off the various folks assigned to take care of the three of them while she and Phil had been busy sorting out the Chevalier.

Ambassador Hu was facing the hatch and bounced to his feet. The other two were slower, but still rose as she entered. They had hopeful smiles, so Heather forced her usual resting seriousness into something friendlier.

Stewards and folks drifted into the background or shifted back into the kitchen area as she led Phil and Harinder in. Because the other three had been sitting in two of the chairs, she ended up on the couch next to Scholar Wen, the old man who reminded her of a stevedore dockside somewhere. At least until he opened his mouth.

Sometimes then, too.

Phil and Harinder took the couch across the square, with everyone turned to face her.

Wen had a mirthful grin on his face. Probably her own damned fault.

"To answer your original question, yes," she began. Better to get it out of the way off the top. "I have an interest in taking command of your forces for the purposes of leading them into battle with *Zerzan*."

"But?" Scholar Wen asked, catching the tone in her voice.

"None of you will be in a position to question my orders," Heather said simply, turning to the man and scowling. "Whether or not Phil even allows you to travel aboard *Urumchi* or with this force, you will remain out of my hair while I'm doing things. I will command. Or you can remain here at *Kyulle* when we depart."

"Depart, Heather?" First Speaker Li asked.

"When we assemble the forces Phil believes he needs, we will take them to where *Viking* spots the enemy base," Heather said. "That ship will be departing as quickly as they can finish any major repairs they still need to undertake. Barnaby Silver and his crew will locate *Zerzan* for us. Then we will go have a chat with them."

"Your tone suggests something other than a battle to the death," Ambassador Hu spoke up now.

"It might also be that," Heather retorted. "Phil?"

He nodded and squared his shoulders, looking exactly like a First Centurion was supposed to when he did that.

"We have been talking with Chevalier Aublahzieu, command centurion of the Assault Carrier *Truhto*," he began. "She largely agrees with you on historical points, but obviously sees *Yaumgan* through the lens of your ancestors in the *Zerzan Monarchy*, who they originally overthrew."

"Vengeance, then?" Li asked.

"Something of it, yes," Phil agreed. "We also talked about

the arcs of empires. Or rather, Heather and I talked—perhaps lectured would be a better term—and she, I think, listened. At least absorbed. Might be having a crisis of conscience right now, which was really my goal."

"Conscience, First Centurion?" Li asked.

"The *Unification* is expansionary," he nodded. "Sharks must swim or drown. They cannot simply stop. Empires must expand or they risk collapse. In this case, nobody in the Balhee Cluster can make them stop, so they must want to do it themselves. Or be forced back."

"Can you force them back?" Scholar Wen asked, suddenly reminding her of images of ancient Socrates, the Hellenic scholar so effective at his craft that he was still spoken of **fourteen millennia** later.

"It depends on many things," Heather spoke. "How much of *Yaumgan* we commit to this act. How well the rest of the Cluster rallies to Phil's flag in his time of need. Most of the folks we have interacted with have struck me as honorable enough to acknowledge the debt. Hopefully, they will rouse themselves now. I might still suggest that you activate some of your plans to place certain folks on arks that could escape, were we to fail and *Yaumgan* to fall to the *Zerzan Unification*."

"You know of such things?" Li gasped. As did the other two.

"We do," Heather replied without explaining Harman and all the things he'd done for her since she'd hired the man. *Why* she'd hired him. "Contingency planning should be ramped up, because we won't know until it might be too late to act. If *Yaumgan* as a culture is to survive, you should probably move immediately. Meanwhile, you need to assemble the force you think will leave you with sufficient defenses in place."

"We could assemble all eight of the Immortals," Li offered.

"Honestly, I'd rather have as many of the smallest escorts as you can spare," Heather countered. "No offense to the big ships, but they are badly outclassed against what Aublahzieu calls aeromechia. The more eyebeams I can bring to the table, the more likely we'll succeed. As you saw, *Urumchi* has the ability to pound those carriers to their destruction if we aren't dodging those small firebirds. We almost got the one called *Rauda* before they escaped me. I'm hoping that they have to return that ship to drydock. If they do, that's a significant chunk of the next battle covered, because that potentially traps that ship's aeromechia somewhere and I can avoid them or drive off the carriers. At that point, they surrender or starve and that solves a larger chunk of my problems, without *Götterdämmerung* first."

"Will we be allowed to speak with your prisoner, First Centurion?" Hu asked.

"She's resting now," he replied. "I'll check with *Stunt Dude* after a bit and see, but that's up to her."

"I do not understand," Hu replied.

"You catch more flies with honey than vinegar," Phil smiled. "I would like to bring her thinking around to a place where war between *Yaumgan* and *Zerzan* is not *necessary*. She is on that track. She might be able and willing to communicate it to her superiors. Thus, the crisis might be averted for now, while *Yaumgan* and friends repair and rebuild in such a way that *Unification* is not on the menu."

"Are you certain you are not a Scholar, First Centurion?" the old man asked, smiling at both her and Phil. "Your thinking is remarkably different from any naval officer I have ever known."

Heather smiled back.

"At home, Phil is generally known as *The Professor*," she informed everyone. "Prior to this mission, he was teaching both Command Ethics and Advanced Piracy at our navy's Academy on *Ladaux*. Plus, he is fulfilling his mission from the First Lord of the Fleet, namely to bring peace, trade, and development to the Balhee Cluster. We cannot do that if *Zerzan* is an ongoing invasion threat."

"Will *Aquitaine* be drawn into a longer, larger war in that case?" First Speaker Li asked, having obviously hopped several steps ahead.

Heather turned to Phil to answer this one. It was his responsibility.

"Heather made an interesting point earlier," he nodded. "Speaking with Chevalier Aublahzieu, she noted that the *Unification* could likely conquer all of the Cluster given time. And not even that much time, all things considered. After that, their next target would likely be *Aquitaine*, either as a future threat, or because their nature means they must keep attacking, keep expanding their borders and unifying more and more planets. Thus, *Aquitaine* is best served by holding the line here. Forcing the *Unification* to stop, else they become an even greater threat to the rest of the galaxy. That I will not countenance. I am compiling a package for my boss, laying out the current situation and prognosticating on the future. At the very minimum, I will be suggesting to her that a reinforced *Aquitaine* sector fleet be deployed to *Meerut* as a defensive measure, while she and her civilian bosses work with the Five Nations on joint defensive treaties designed to keep *Zerzan* from *Unifying* the Cluster at gunpoint. If you five choose to create a new thing in the process, that is up to you. My job is buying you the time to do it."

Heather nodded. He'd threatened to ask Petia Naoumov for enough force to destroy every navy in the Cluster if enough people pissed him off. She planned to suggest every Type-400 Expeditionary corvette in service, along with a few bigger ships to serve as flags. Plus the Spectre that had been so singularly effective saving *Urumchi's* ass from those damned miniature firebirds.

It could be done. Better to fight the war here than wait for them to consolidate conquest of the Balhee Cluster and appear on *Aquitaine's* shores.

"Your thoughts, Commander?" the First Speaker turned to Heather, acknowledging that Heather Lau would be *Warlord of Yaumgan,* at least until she could train up some folks to handle it themselves.

"Phil and I owe the entire Cluster a debt," Heather replied. "In breaking the *Zen-Mekyo Syndicates*, we caused *Zerzan* to find you, after you had been hidden from them for so long. In attacking *Yaumgan*, they threaten everyone else with *Unification*. Thus, this is our moral responsibility, *Aquitaine*'s, and we need to do something about it. Letting you be conquered is not an ethical outcome, even if you will bear a significant weight of the costs rather than us. *Aquitaine* must stand beside you. My hope is that the other four understand that and join us."

"And if they do not?" Old Man Wen asked her.

"Then we probably cannot win," Heather said. "*Yaumgan* cannot endure, and might be extinguished entirely, save for what few Scholars you load into a new caravan and send elsewhere. But we must fight this war here. Now. *Zerzan* must be stopped. It really is as simple as that."

"And you will lead us?" the First Speaker asked finally, voice formal.

"I will," Heather nodded.

She was committed.

OVERLORD

FORTY-TWO

MISSION BRIEF: OPERATIONS BASE LOONG

Donatien fixed his dress uniform, the dark gray one that almost appeared black in dim lighting, save for the gold threads in the fabric and seams that seemed to glow at times. His jacket bore no medals today. Nothing save for his rank as Chevalier and *Bertev*'s insignia over his heart.

What more needed to be said?

The shuttle had delivered him to the station, itself nothing more than a slow carrier design that moved like the ancient monitors, creeping along through JumpSpace like a tortoise while carrying a wing of aeromechia like *Truhto* had.

Truhto's loss was his fault. Donatien grimaced as he followed his escorts through the last set of hallways to the *Unification* Chambers where *Unification* Commissioner Abaroa was awaiting him.

They arrived. The door opened and the escorts stepped to one side.

Donatien entered.

Commissioner Abaroa was something of a throw-back genetically. Skin so pale that at times she appeared to be an albino, but that was just near-porcelain paleness, accentuated by hair so fine and blond as to appear as spun gold. Eyes bluer than most skies, though they appeared storm-tossed gray today.

She sat alone at a small conference table, rather than behind a desk, so at least the event would be more of a meeting and less of a star chamber. Small favors.

"Sit," she gestured.

Donatien did.

Seated, she seemed small, but that was how much of the woman's height was in her legs. Standing, they could nearly see eye-to-eye.

The hatch slid shut behind him. They were alone. Not even aides or guards in the room.

Whatever questions he answered would go no further, unless she chose to share them.

His doom rested entirely in her hands.

"What happened?" she asked simply. "I have read the reports. Seen the damage to *Rauda* once they limped in. Counted the empty cradles. Noticed the loss of *Truhto*. All of this speaks of a terrible failure somewhere."

"*Aquitaine* are not our equals for technology, Commissioner," he said. "Or rather, we are not theirs. Their two large ships mount beams I have never seen anywhere but on a station. Their entire force has something like the eyebeams *Yaumgan* uses, but many more of them, both bigger as well as capable of a sustained rate of fire that allowed them to savage our pulse torpedoes. Then they used some new something to create a scanner ghost that caused most of our torpedoes to go astray and detonate where they were useless. In short, we were utterly outclassed. *Yaumgan* got thrashed. *Rauda's* force of aeromechia tore through *Yaumgan's* smaller ships like packs of wild wolves attacking a bison. It was not enough."

"Can *Rauda* be repaired in the field, or should they immediately return to *Kohri*?" she pressed.

"I have not met with Chevalier Michelle to see what she thinks," Donatien replied. "Given their slow limp here, I suspect that they will need whatever significant repairs as they can perform now, while things are safe, and then to be sent home."

"How does that impact *Unification?*" Abaroa scowled at him, her face turning darker.

As *Unification* Commissioner for this invasion, his failures reflected poorly on her, for not choosing a better commander. That there might not be a better chevalier in the fleet right now would not mitigate much.

"The great risk at this moment is that *Aquitaine* somehow learns where we are," he said. "And follows. With *Rauda* present, we could hold them off. If I send *Rauda* away, I lose nearly half my striking power. If I send one of the Assault Carriers, *Salgui* or perhaps *Gosa* because they were already badly damaged, I could get a message home and request a replacement for *Rauda*. I cannot currently make a best guess as to which scenario the enemy will pursue, because my previous ones made demonstrably bad assumptions and are thus worthless."

"Send *Gosa* then," she ordered. "Keep *Rauda* present in case *Yaumgan* does pursue us. Prepare to defend this base until you have sufficient reinforcements. The *Unification* can pause while we gather strength. This is not the first time we have encountered a foe stronger than initially supposed. All were overcome given time."

Donatien nodded. That much would belong to her, if the rest of the *Unification* judged them to be mistakes. For whatever small amount that might shield him.

How had he guessed so wrong?

But Donatien knew that answer. He had listened to that fool pirate who had been lost with *Truhto*, may he rot in whichever most painful hell was an option for that kind.

Hames had spoken of *Yaumgan* in terms of being the most powerful force in the Cluster. And he was probably right.

"You are pensive," Abaroa said.

"Contemplating my mistakes, Commissioner," Donatien shrugged. "We listened to the pirate. He told us *Yaumgan* was the only dangerous foe. In that, he was probably correct, because he saw only the Cluster itself, and discounted the other outsiders who had come. *Aquitaine* likely outclasses *Yaumgan* as much as those fools did everyone else, and we did not take that into account when attacking them."

"Should you have gone after the other five worlds individually to destroy their defenses?" she asked.

"Water under the bridge," Donatien said. "Not worth pursuing the might-have-beens of this operation. At least not while we are in it. I will leave that to planners back home to test, once we know better what each class of *Yaumgan* or *Aquitaine* vessel can do. Again, we know far less than we might have, but chose to strike with surprise and what should have been overwhelming power."

"Should we withdraw from the Cluster and gather a larger force to overwhelm them?"

He grimaced.

"I have been gaming out all manner of scenarios in my head on the flight back," Donatien replied. "If we take time to rebuild, we give *Yaumgan* time as well. They will not be able to take advantage of it, but we cannot know what *Aquitaine* might do. Like us, they would have time to send home for forces, though our journey is somewhat shorter, assuming that they do not have major naval forces staged outside the Cluster where they might be quickly accessible. If we remain in place here, and send *Gire* or *Salgui* on raids, we can at least keep *Yaumgan* off balance while we wait for a new Overlord carrier and perhaps more forces."

"All bad choices?"

"Perhaps," Donatien noted. "We cannot be easily dislodged from this place. Not with what even *Aquitaine* has, so we can hold our beachhead. That would be my recommendation for now, if *Gosa* were to retire as quickly as they could to draw in help."

"Will they find us?"

The Commissioner seemed most concerned with that, but he understood. Politicians like her rarely went this far forward with the *Unification* forces. It had been necessary because *Yaumgan* had indeed been their old foes, finally brought to heel. The *Unification* needed to be present to see it happen.

Aquitaine had been the unwelcome surprise.

"They might find us," Donatien replied. "*Yaumgan* knew about *Loong*. It is, as I understand it, the only tunnel through the outer wall of the cluster that can be traveled entirely in JumpSpace. Not counting the main entrance at *Vilahana*, nearly opposite us. Even we would have never found it, save for the pirate buying his life with the information. Thus, we can withdraw if we need to. If we are hard pressed in battle. There is no star system here for us to navigate a gravity well. Just the gap in JumpSpace caused by nebular gases and stars too close together."

That seemed to placate her for now. Donatien didn't mention the other side of the risk, though.

The carriers could all retreat easily enough if attacked by overwhelming force. None of the aeromechia would be able to join them if they were deployed at that moment.

Would their sacrifice be worth it?

FORTY-THREE

MISSION BRIEF: RAN URUMCHI, PRISONER

Bausse sat on a comfortable couch and sipped hot chocolate from an oversized mug, boggling that the First Centurion had assigned her a staff. *Stunt Dude* sat in the same general space, but across the square from her in a single chair. Tea, or something. She'd been too surprised earlier at the offer of hot chocolate to pay attention.

One of the sailors emerged from the kitchen and came to rest nearby.

"Chevalier, there is a message from *Truhto*," he said. "I've routed it to the office for you to take."

"Not on general?" she asked.

"If you wish, sir," he said simply.

"No," *Stunt Dude* spoke up. "Go take it in the office. It will be monitored, obviously, but you should at least have the appearance of secrets. Plus, it was almost time for you to check in with your crew anyway."

Bausse rose, carefully holding her mug of warm wonderfulness as the sailor led her to a small side chamber with a desk and chair for working, rather like the office she had on *Truhto*.

Physics was physics, so the comm unit was understandable.

A handset you lifted, with one piece to the ear and the other end to the mouth. The sailor nodded and closed the hatch, leaving her alone to speak with her crew.

"This is Chevalier Aublahzieu," she said.

"There is an update from medical, Chevalier." She recognized the voice of her Optics Officer. "The guest who traveled with us succumbed to his wounds a few minutes ago. He had stayed aboard rather than allowing himself to be transferred, so we can't know if that was a terminal decision."

Bausse allowed herself a moment of grief. She'd worked Hames's ass off, once the choices were clear, but the man had lived in terror of falling into Kosnett's hands.

How much of that was a personal failing, now that she'd met the man in person?

"Understood," she replied. "How are repairs going?"

"Dar's people have piled in wherever asked and worked harder than we have, sir," he said, awestruck. "Gravity is stable. Life support now extends to all sections of the ship that are not open to space and we continue to close up damaged rooms well enough to get crews inside. We have sufficient generators back on line to hold everything in place, and they are taking apart one of the engines now to see if it can be repaired. Dar has offered to bring in parts from *Urumchi* or ask *Yaumgan* to provide something from one of their damaged ships. I do not understand it, sir."

Bausse did, but didn't bother to communicate it to her subordinate. He was not emotionally prepared for *Aquitaine*. She hadn't been, but the last few days had been eye-opening in a variety of ways.

"It is their honor," she temporized. That much he could understand. "Continue with operations. If you can get things repaired enough, you may have to move to a different orbit. That is acceptable, once we are no longer a threat to fall out of their skies."

"Then what, Chevalier?"

"I am negotiating with Kosnett," she replied vaguely. "At present, we are determining how soon the rest of you might be sent home."

"Home, sir?" he gasped.

Like her, he had assumed that he was a prisoner until *Kyulle* was captured and he could be liberated. That, or a casualty of war if *Yaumgan* demanded all of them be put to death later.

Neither had been out of the question when she surrendered, but possible death at a future date had still been better than certain, immediate death at *Urumchi's* bloody hands.

"Home," Bausse replied. "I shall keep you posted."

She hung up the line and drew a breath. Yes, all that would be monitored, but it was still better than she would have given prisoners of a captured *Aquitaine* ship, to say nothing of *Yaumgan*.

Kosnett was behaving in ways she never imagined she would see, and wouldn't have done were the situation reversed.

When had the *Unification* gone wrong?

Bausse rose and exited the office, mug in hand. *Stunt Dude* was still seated, one eyebrow asking a multitude of questions as she returned to her warm spot on the couch.

"There was a man," she said after a moment of contemplation. "His name was Nolan Hames, and he had formerly been a Chevalier of a *Nagi Syndicate* Raider named *Ravenscall*."

Stunt Dude nodded but remained silent.

"My crew informs me that he just died of wounds and burns suffered in our battle," Bausse continued.

"Was he a good man?" *Stunt Dude* asked. As if that was the only thing that mattered.

"He was a pirate," she replied. "Fled ahead of Kosnett's justice and got captured when he blundered into *Unification* space, expecting to be able to continue his criminal ways. His parole was telling us everything he knew about the Cluster, which in turn led us to *Yaumgan*. In that, I suppose he was somewhat redeemed. But he still chose piracy twice. Once when it was considered an honorable way of life around here, and once when it was not. The galaxy is probably a better place without him."

"I have known a few men and women like that in my time," he replied sagely. "Bad examples can still be something to learn from, if nothing else."

Bausse found that concept comforting. Hames had been a bad example. He had excelled at that, as a matter of fact.

"And your ship?" *Stunt Dude* pressed.

Her ship? She supposed so, until such time as it was repaired enough and her people removed.

"Repairs are well ahead of schedule," she said. "Mostly because the First Centurion supplied so many engineers to assist."

"Our honor was at stake," he repeated simply, as if that explained it all.

And it might. Good example contrasted so sharply with Hames as a bad one.

"What happens next?" Bausse asked.

"At some point, I am given to understand that *Yaumgan* wants to talk to you, but I've been waiting for you to reach a point in your meditation where good things might come of it."

It took her several seconds to parse that. Had he been meditating as he sat there?

Had she?

Something.

Thinking entirely new thoughts. Exploring new concerns she had never envisioned.

"I think I might be," she said. "Could you contact them?"

When had the *Unification* gone wrong?

FORTY-FOUR

Stunt Dude had sent one of the stewards to find Phil while he enjoyed his chai. Bausse seemed to have hit another one of those emotional breakthroughs that people do when their minds suddenly open to new pathways.

Like quitting the movies and becoming a sailor. Or resigning your commission and striking out into the middle of a warzone to find a specific woman more than a thousand light-years away.

Bausse seemed calm, but *Stunt Dude* suspected it was a fragile shell over a roiling magma interior. He'd been there. Standing in front of Sam's door with nothing but roses and hope.

Phil and the others arrived quickly, but *Stunt Dude* presumed that everyone had been forward in another one of the Ambassadorial suites prior to this, poised and waiting with bated breath. Someplace where the First Unit Director could handle all those good framing shots and conversations.

Phil and Heather. The First Speaker of *Yaumgan* and an older guy, plus Ambassador Hu who had been around them since *Urumchi* arrived at *Aditi* that first time.

The stewards had been sandbagging, obviously, because they produced enough hot chocolate for everyone to enjoy, though a dribble of dark rum would have been nice, even in his chai. Right now, however, they needed everyone sharp, rather than calm.

Stunt Dude and Bausse had risen to greet folks. They sat now, but he moved over to sit next to her, in the middle of a couch where the older man had to sit beyond him and the others took the two chairs and the far couch.

Metaphorically protecting her, because she was, at the end of the day, Iveta's prisoner. Then Phil's.

Stunt Dude just happened to be the best suited to talk to everyone at the same time, having lived aboard *Li Jing* for more than a year at this point.

"Bausse and I have been chatting," he began, feeling her flinch in the couch beneath them as he used her first name.

Personalizing things. Softening rough edges, like the hot chocolate was starting to do as people relaxed.

"Have we come to interesting conclusions?" the old man, Wen, asked, speaking just like a guy Trinidad had trained under, in the way back.

"I believe so," *Stunt Dude* replied. "Phil intends to find a way to get her and her people home. That will take time, so we need to arrange to house them hospitably for now. Safely, when the general opinions of the locals might not be favorable."

"What about *Meerut?*" Heather asked, causing all heads to snap around.

Stunt Dude turned to Bausse instead, noting the paleness that had crept into her face.

"*Meerut* is a colony world about one hundred and forty degrees clockwise from here," he explained. "Beyond *Ewin*, on the corner of their border with *Dalou*. Currently, it is neutral, enforced by Kosnett and *Aquitaine*. Most of the inhabitants are former pirates who have accepted Phil's probation to go straight."

Her mouth opened. Closed. Opened again and just hung there.

"Hames could have accepted the new rules of behavior, had he chosen," he told her. "As you said, he chose piracy twice, and it cost him."

"Hames?" Heather asked, apparently willing to speak while the others watched rapt.

"*Nagi Syndicate*," *Stunt Dude* said. "He was aboard *Truhto*, but badly injured in the battle. He died about an hour ago from his wounds. The rest of his crew, if I understand correctly, are currently interred on the planet *Kohri*, capital of the *Unification*."

Bausse nodded.

"So they are using the *Loong* Passage to invade the Cluster," the big woman who as First Speaker noted. "That was *Nagi's* secret."

"Did *Nagi* have bases outside?" Phil asked everyone.

Bausse didn't know from the look on her face. Wen spoke up instead.

"There is a vessel at *Meerut* I believe named *Aggregator?*" he asked.

"Milose Dexter," Heather replied. "*Yarmouth Syndicate.*"

"Yes," Wen nodded. "*Nagi* had something similar outside the walls. The ship's name was *Tannerhall*, I think. I do not know what became of it, but I do not remember from Captain Xue's reports if it ever went to *Meerut*."

"No ship of that name ever arrived," Phil spoke. "But our estimates are that eighty percent of the ships that had been involved in Syndicate work were abandoned or quickly sold to new owners, with most of their crews disappearing. Presumably into assumed identities. Or returning to the ones they had been born with, hoping that the law never came for them. And I won't if they did. Piracy and banditry are the crimes I care about. If they get arrested later, the locals wherever can deal with them."

"You would not punish them?" Bausse finally seemed to find her voice.

Phil smiled instead.

"My order was that they had to behave, or I would crush them," he said. "Many chose to accept that and flew to *Meerut* to take up new lives, where at least old enemies might not come for them with fleets. Others just vanished, though apparently some fled to the west and tried to stay in the life. Good riddance and I hope the *Unification* annihilates them as a result."

"Annihilates?" she pressed.

"Predators, Chevalier," Phil nodded. "They must be destroyed for civilization to advance."

"Is that is how you see the *Unification*?" Bausse asked.

Stunt Dude watched the rest of the blood drain out of her face, turning her so white he would have thought she was dead, except that she was already so pale normally.

"Unfortunately, yes I do," Phil nodded a second time. "They have not chosen to invite people to join their culture and society, even by your own words. They are conquered and *unified*. At gunpoint. I find that unacceptable, unethical, but my mission is not to go and throw the *Unification* itself down. At least not today. I have been tasked to see that the nations of the Cluster develop into positive neighbors to each other and *Aquitaine*, so that we can trade ideas, people, and merchandise back and forth. I do not believe that the *Unification* would allow that, so they must be stopped."

"Then what?" she asked.

Stunt Dude could hear the next emotional crisis in her voice. Hopefully, Phil could as well.

"That's up to them, Chevalier," Phil stated unequivocally. "They could choose to be better neighbors to *Yaumgan*, though I highly doubt that given the history involved. If they cannot conquer the *Domain* or the Cluster, would they bash their heads repeatedly against that wall, or turn to conquer other nations that currently border them?"

Okay, that was painful, but *Stunt Dude* wasn't here as her confessor. Merely her guide to understanding *Aquitaine*. And *Yaumgan* to a lesser degree.

"Another type of pirate?" she asked.

"Your words, Chevalier," Phil said. "But essentially correct as I see it. The stronger preying on the weaker because nobody can stop you. I believe that *Aquitaine* could stop you. We might be required to, given my ideas of ethical behavior. My hope is that you can return to your people and communicate this to them. Whether or not they believe you is not my problem. I will have drawn a line in the sand, made it clear to everyone involved, and allowed them to make their own choices. But you and I both agree that piracy on a national level is the outcome most likely."

"And still you intend to send me home?"

Phil started to speak, but *Stunt Dude* waved a hand and everyone paused, emotions still in check.

All eyes turned his way.

"Jessica Keller, in her war with *Buran*, did a thing," he told Bausse. And probably the other three, because he doubted that they had gone so deep into the *Buran* war. *Stunt Dude* had been there that day, watching and listening. "It harks back to the ancient Roman Republic that is at the core of who the *Republic of Aquitaine* wants to be on their best days."

"What did she do?" Scholar Wen asked, intrigued, so perhaps he had studied more than the others.

"Before the ancient Republic declared war, they would send a priest," *Stunt Dude* replied. "A *fetial*, as they were called, who would go to the enemy border with Rome's demands, speaking them to the first person he met, as well as going to the magistrates in their city. If nothing was done, that *fetial* would return to the border in a month with a ceremonial javelin, supposedly dipped in blood, that he would ritually cast across the border as part of a formal declaration of war. It was a legalistic thing, rather than militaristic, because they invoked Jupiter the Law-Giver rather than Mars the Destroyer."

"And Keller did this?" Wen asked, astonished and intrigued, all at once.

"She caused a special landing probe to be built, Scholar,"

Stunt Dude replied, smiling. "Dropped from orbit, it fell to a certain elevation, where it deployed a glider that would carry it forward. The javelin she had made was then subsequently dropped in the back yard of the governor of the planet, a man who later defected to the *Fribourg Empire* when he had his own ethical breakthrough. Thus, we know his stories firsthand from a book he wrote. Supposedly, the glider itself carried on and landed in a paddock full of sheep, though none were hurt."

Trinidad rather enjoyed the shocked looks on four of the faces around him. The other four of them, including Markus, had been there, orbiting *Trusski* with Keller's *First Expeditionary Fleet*.

"And I am to be your *fetial*, First Centurion?" Bausse asked, pain etched in her voice.

"No, Chevalier," Phil said simply. "You are my javelin. *Zerzan* can have peace. Or they can have war. The decision is theirs."

Stunt Dude nodded.

He would have liked a better outcome, but he doubted that it would be settled with anything less than bloodshed.

DONATIEN

FORTY-FIVE

Barnaby Silver was Command Centurion of *RAN Viking*. As such, he did not consider himself the inheritor of the legacy of Keller. No, that was Phil and *Urumchi*. His ancestors, at least in the metaphorical sense, had been *RAN Ballard*, the Galactic Survey Cruiser that had served Keller with such distinction in her various wars. Command Centurion Kanda Cosmina Lungu and her famous Science Officer, Elzbet Aukley.

The ship that had flown alone into danger more times that any sensible command centurion would, but scouts were never sensible folk. Just look at him and his people.

And Markus, seated off to one side because Barnaby had insisted. After all, Dunklin had led the group that had first proposed, then refined the abstruse mathematics necessary to predict gaps in the outer wall. Anybody could deadsail these thin nebulae, but JumpSpace required clear aether, undeformed by gravity. Even the negligible weight of clouds formed of hydrogen and helium and supernovae.

Barnaby intended that Dunklin's name was going to be at the top of this report, when it came time to file it. Man might refuse to be made a centurion, but he couldn't escape whatever awards the First Lord or the Senate would bestow on him later.

Barnaby smiled. Dunklin knew something was up from the scowl he returned.

They'd worked together enough, rebuilding the forward array, that words were unnecessary.

Sailing into danger.

"Pilot, what's the call?" Barnaby said.

Riny—Centurion van Akkeren—looked up and scowled. In many ways, she was the perfect foil for Auke. Tall and a little blocky, like Barnaby's First Officer, and almost as smart. Or as close as mere mortals would get to a man like Auke Alma. Fingers like a concert pianist.

"We're not coming in hot or close," she replied. "Still dropping into the middle of nowhere and hoping nobody else had the same idea. Four minutes."

Barnaby nodded. The new sensors didn't work in JumpSpace. *Yaumgan* had provided maps, but Barnaby had no way of knowing if *Zerzan* had chosen to settle near the supposed mouth of the *Loong* Passage, farther out, or near one of the three stars within a light-year.

This far out was a—hopefully—safe compromise. Out a ways, so they could check their own math against older maps. Close enough that they might see the theoretical mouth, but not so close that someone might be able to get to them.

No system, so no moons or things to hide behind.

Luck, daring, and bullshit. The recipe for the Scouts.

"Auke, you have tactical," Barnaby called. "Sunan, start with enemy ships first, then work out to Dunklin's new toys."

Nods. Walking into danger, with nobody backing them up, facing a fleet that could have probably destroyed everything in harbor at *Kyulle* if *Zerzan* hadn't screwed up in a few places and let *Junkyard* sink her teeth into them.

Viking was on point.

<h1 style="text-align:center">FORTY-SIX</h1>

DATE OF THE REPUBLIC AUGUST 21, 412 RAN
VIKING, FORWARD OBSERVATION POINT
LOONG

Auke had studied the results of dumping everything into a bucket and letting the nav computers churn on it. He'd even written around thirty percent of the code involved in what Markus had done, so he knew it would be sound.

Viking and *Urumchi* had sailed the outer wall of the Cluster back at the beginning, but didn't have things tuned to be able to pick up the gap. Nor the math to tell them where to look. Auke had argued for calling them the *Dunklin Equations*, but Barnaby had put his foot down and said no. And to keep Markus from throwing a fit.

So the coding system was called *The Viking Equation* instead.

Right now, they predicted a gap about eight light-seconds across, canted roughly thirty degrees off perpendicular to the inner edge of the Cluster wall, were it a smooth sphere.

No, what it was, was a lumpy dough of gravity wells in various states of decay and motion, stars and gas packed up on top of each other and frequently given enough electrical charge from overlapping heliospheres as to kill a JumpSail matrix.

The idea that suddenly rippled through his mind was insane. Auke started so hard he might have fallen out of his chair if he wasn't already buckled in and wearing an emergency suit against surprises.

"Talk to me, Auke," Barnaby growled.

Instead, Auke turned to Markus. Locked eyes with the man. Markus was street smart, but there was a brain in there that he didn't like to talk about.

"*CS-405*," Auke said to frame the conversation.

Said that way, it referred to *Kosnett's Campaign*, trapped and alone behind enemy lines, willing to go for their throat instead of merely limping home.

"Go on," Markus replied, like they were the only two beings in the universe right now.

"The Cluster walls induce a bizarre charge in JumpSpace," Auke continued. "Not just the gravity, but the electrical state of the gases we have to sail through."

Markus nodded warily, aware that Auke was smarter than everyone else, demonstrably so if you wanted to compare personnel records. Auke shrugged at those things, but sometimes he had to put his foot down. Or open his mouth and establish baselines.

"Can the JumpSails be insulated against that charge?" Auke asked.

Markus saw it immediately, but he had more experience repairing and tuning such devices than anybody Auke knew. Because those sails had broken on *CS-405* and he'd been one of the engineers tasked with repairing them as best anyone could, then holding the matrix together as everything slowly overheated.

"Fuck."

Rude, but an indication that Markus understood the implications.

Markus keyed a comm on his armrest.

"Nogueira," replied *Viking's* Chief Engineer from aft.

"Kealoha," Markus said, "how hard would it be to install an

insulating layer around the JumpSail designed for a specific radiation spectrum to be nullified?"

Long pause. But then, Kealoha Nogueira knew things. And understood both Markus and Auke and how crazy they could get.

"Drydock," she replied. "I'll assume a passive layer, rather than a field you intend to generate like shields, so we'd have to pull the sail generators themselves out and probably add something to the nearest frames. Maybe two layers on two frames, just for leakage. What are you blocking?"

"The Balhee Cluster walls," Markus said.

"Shit," Nogueira replied. "Can we do that?"

Markus turned to Auke with a question on his face.

"I think so, Kealoha," Auke said. "That will be our homework assignment tonight after we sort out *Zerzan*."

"Roger that," the engineer said. "You're buying the beer."

Auke laughed and cut the line. Best way to build something exotic was to hand a team of engineers beer and pizza and tell them it was impossible. Then watch them move Heaven and Earth to prove you wrong. Him included.

"Pilot?" Auke said, resetting his brain to the present tense.

"Thirty seconds, Tactical," Riny replied.

"Gunner, unlock everything and stand by," Auke said, shifting his voice into combat mode. "There will be no friendlies present, so fire on detection."

Centurion Rasmussen nodded. Not the first time he'd gotten that order. Often, you had seconds. If you knew you couldn't be shooting an ally, and they didn't know, you had that much of an advantage. Best to use it.

"Science Officer, stand by for passive operations in hostile territory," Auke turned to Sunan.

She nodded then went back to her screens.

Auke drew a breath and let it out slowly as the clock counted down.

Emergence.

Empty darkness. Good.

Auke had an echo of Sunan's main screen on one of his. No emitters anywhere close. Nobody suddenly triggering an alarm or challenging them.

"Pilot, plot a Jump course straight down and back just enough that we don't risk touching the walls in flight," Auke ordered.

Riny nodded, hands poised to do something. Anything.

Normally, they would be hiding behind a moon, surfacing just enough to see over the horizon before ducking again, then spinning in place and running like mad until she could jump.

Nothing to hide behind today.

Auke checked the screen. Markus had suggested coming out roughly one light-hour from the mouth. Close enough that they could rely on optics and passive, but far enough that nobody would be handy. *Mansi-D*, as he'd said, again reverting to those successful raids as part of *Kosnett's Campaign*.

If it worked, and the other guy didn't know about it, keep trying, and always prepared to do something else.

"I have enemy scans present at the mouth," Sunan called to the room. "Roughly five light-seconds out and a little higher. Up maybe fifteen degrees deadsailing. Counting now."

Auke held his breath. Was this the whole fleet that had attacked *Kyulle*, minus only *Truhto*? Less? More?

"Those two supercarriers are present," she continued. "Parked close to a new signal that was not at First *Kyulle*. Transponder identifies as *Hrafsto*. Albedo suggests roughly the same size as *Truhto* or one of the other Assault Carriers we faced. Two of those are here. We kept one. One is missing."

"One of the sound ones, or the other one that was damaged?" Auke asked.

"Damaged one," she replied. "Run home for help?"

"That's my guess," Auke said, turning his attention to

Barnaby. "The one supercarrier was banged pretty badly. Do we pull a Kigali?"

Barnaby's scowl might be useful to etch steel, but he understood the logic. Technically, it was Keller's signature move, back when the Expeditionary Classes had been brand new and nobody was prepared for Type-4 beams on a mobile platform.

Run as hard and fast as you could in realspace. Race right down to the edge of the gravity well but not emerge gracefully. Instead, you waited for the Jump matrix to collapse and force you out. Then accelerated down and in, blasting someone with the big guns as you went by, pulling a slingshot down and around, rebuilding your matrix until you emerged on the far side and leapt to safety.

Or inserted into orbit and came around for another pass if you'd hammered them hard enough the first time.

Keller had become famous for it, with *Vanguard* and her two cruisers, *VI Ferrata* and *VI Victrix*. But Tomas Kigali had always led the charge, first in *CR-264*, and later in *CA-264*.

Viking had steel-toed boots, if you needed to knock somebody down and kick them. Folks tended to forget that, since they didn't have the Bubble Gun forward. Still had all the rest of the guns of an Expeditionary Cruiser.

"No," Barnaby decided. "Kosnett might want to do that when we have enough help to do it right. No reason to let them know how open they've left their moorage for folks like us. Will they spot us is the real question."

"We're as quiet as a ship this big can get," Auke replied. "No emissions unless we kick the shields up a notch or open fire. Couldn't plot a course that wouldn't occlude any stars behind us, since we didn't know where they were, but we're also not facing paranoid computer ships. I give us good odds, but we're still only remaining in place another forty minutes at most before we bounce out and return to *Kyulle*."

"Very well, Tactical," Barnaby nodded. "As you bear."

Auke nodded in response and went back to his screens. And his math. And everything else.

He had a potential battle if anybody over there was paying attention. A certain battle later when the First Centurion came to say hello.

And maybe yet another revolution in navigation. At least around here.

FORTY-SEVEN

Phil had asked Sam to come to his office, rather than heading down to Medical. This would be a political discussion, at the end of the day.

"Current status?" he asked as she settled.

"Twenty-one dead, either in the battle itself or afterwards," she said sadly. "One hundred and fourteen that have been treated for various things. Forty-six of them are still in a hospital bed on one of the corvettes, but I expect to be able to discharge roughly half of those in another week, and probably lose a third because there's not much we can do for some of them beyond palliative care at this point."

"Is *Truhto* able to take over as a hospice?" he asked. "If they are going to die, better that they do it among friends than strangers."

"They are not," Sam replied. "And moving some of them would be the final straw. We should talk to Bausse and her people about getting crew from *Truhto* onto the corvettes instead."

"I'll leave that up to you, then," Phil noted. "We've done everything we could at this point, and as Bausse points out, far more than she expected."

"She saw the guns and expected the worst, Phil," Sam said. "I remember thinking the same thing, when Trinidad first came aboard and played an exceptional game of bad cop on my operations crew."

Phil grinned. That was putting it mildly, since *Stunt Dude* had offered to chuck the lot of them into escape pods and be done with them, though only a handful had ended up needing to be jettisoned.

"Everyone always assumes the worst, Sam," he nodded. "They look in the mirror rather than seeing us for who we are. That's usually the most telling indictment you can ever encounter."

"Understood, Phil," she sighed. "I knew what I was signing up for, and it hasn't been anywhere close to as bad as I feared at any point. Can *Zerzan* be stopped?"

"I doubt it," he said. "At least in the short term. Their entire culture has been built on the concept of hunting down what turned out to be *Yaumgan* and punishing them for slights centuries old at this point. All I can do is hold the line and force them back. Whether I am Canute and the tide or Horatius at the bridge remains to be seen. In my perfect world, Bausse Aublahzieu could convince them otherwise, but she'll be one voice against multitudes, and one that is assumed compromised because she was our prisoner and comes back so radically different from the woman she likely was."

"What about her crew?" Sam asked.

"*Truhto* is capable of flight, however slow they would be through JumpSpace," he replied. "I've considered loading all her people up and sailing everyone close, then pulling Dar and the last group off via shuttle and turning Bausse loose to return to her folks."

"Could she forestall a battle?" Sam pressed.

Phil shrugged.

"Not my call," he replied. "Canute or Horatius, but the

enemy First Centurion has to decide. And the *Unification* itself might go into convulsions at the prospect."

"Would that be good or bad, in the long term?" she leaned forward to study him. "I've been in the middle of a revolution that resulted when the single defining characteristic of your culture failed. A lot of people come apart, but the Holding of Man stopped being a threat to *Fribourg* at that point. Or anybody else. And, in the last few years, has started to turn into something more like a place folks might want to live, instead of a social experiment in authoritarian governance."

"If Bausse Aublahzieu hadn't already come around, I'd have you talk to her," Phil said. "As is, I think she's convinced. And will carry home her stories. Plus, her crew will vouch for a lot of it, which is why I want them free as well. Nobody will be able to accuse us of seducing all of them, unless the *Unification* wants to deify us as terrible space wizards who can twist minds, at which point they might destroy themselves. Or turn this into a religious crusade so terrible that all of the *RAN* and maybe most of our allies back home have to come to our rescue."

"Would they?" she asked.

"*Fribourg* would," Phil said. "If only because I asked. It would take Casey a while to get us help, but they would come. The First Lord has said she has things ready. *Corynthe* might even pitch in, though I think *Lincolnshire* would tell us to get stuffed. At least the first time we asked. And not without reason."

"Not without reason, no," Sam agreed. "So in my lifetime I might be witness to *Götterdämmerung* twice?"

"I've already been there three times, Sam," Phil reminded her. "The war with *Fribourg*. Then *Buran*. Then the Horvat Affair. *Zerzan* would unfortunately be only a fourth in that list. And only fourth for importance, because we can win. Our tech is better, and we're in a build and upgrade mode already, so we can push harder and farther. Maybe build a superfleet of old, small cutter boats like Kigali had when he first met Keller, but running the leading edge of pulse tech for those damned mechs. It can be done."

"But you'd rather not," she nodded.

"Always," Phil agreed. "The philosophers tell us that war is *diplomacy by other means*, but I prefer to think of it as diplomacy that has failed. It might yet fail with *Zerzan*. Until then, I will do everything I can to push forward towards peace."

"And I believe in you, Phil," Sam smiled. "And I believe in Trinidad and Heather and everyone else. Let me talk to Bausse and her people on *Truhto* and see what I can do. We might be able to shift some of the terminal cases over, as well as everyone who is doing better. That would leave about a half dozen on the corvettes that I need to keep under better care, so I might need about thirty or so *Zerzan* sailors to keep them company."

"Let Harinder know," Phil said. "That's why I hired you, because you have a better understanding of that than anybody else I could find."

She nodded and departed, leaving him alone with his dark thoughts.

Any number of things could happen at this point, almost none of which were in his control.

FORTY-EIGHT

Heather was in her day office, reviewing the never-ending mountain of paperwork that came with a ship this big and a crew this complex. The room was generally blank, mostly because she didn't want the addition of sensory distractions around her. A picture behind her that she never saw. A fern plant that was the responsibility of one of Sergey's people to keep alive.

Otherwise, bland walls in a soft green and a dark blue floor. Calming. Soothing.

She needed that today as her paperwork load had gone up. Reports from *Yaumgan* captains as their escorts and Skycruisers got repaired and ready for the next battle.

She hated to think of it as the final battle, because it wouldn't be. Win or lose, the *Zerzan Unification* could only be shoved back for a time. They would likely come back.

At that point, was she on the hook to remain behind and command *Yaumgan* fleets? Or maybe return later?

Heather had no way of knowing. And the current selection of ships wasn't enough to turn the tide. Maybe fight those two supercarriers to the death and win, but the costs would be stupidly enormous, on both sides.

Today was one of those days when that fourth stripe,

however imaginary it was on her arm, weighed more than the rest. As Phil had occasionally warned her.

"Boss, you need to see this," Leyla's voice suddenly emerged from the overhead speakers.

"Ship on alert?" Heather asked automatically as she rose, saving all her files and sliding the tablet into the docking slot.

"Negative," Leyla replied. "Better than that."

Shit, she hated it when her Science Officer got that practical joke tone to her voice. Still, she was four steps and onto the bridge, even as bodies came piling in from elsewhere.

Iveta had the bridge at this moment, but waved with a smile as Heather got to her station.

Then Heather looked at the main screen Leyla had been projecting.

"Oh, shit," Heather muttered.

"Told you so," Leyla laughed.

The screen showed a small mob of ships, running six different color transponder codes.

Six?

RAN Hollywood was obvious. *Dalou* was next. *Ewin. Aditi. Gloran.*

Fribourg? What the hell?

"Is Phil awake?" she asked.

"He was in the shower," Leyla laughed. "Frantically drying off and getting dressed now. I wanted to see the look on your face. Oh, hey, we're finally being hailed. Stand by for main screen."

Heather more or less fell into her chair and automatically buckled herself in, still counting and goggling at the results.

Then he was there, projected giant, because that was the way everybody saw him, even in the flesh.

Makara Omarov.

Morninghawk.

"Greetings, *Urumchi*," he said with about a three-second delay. "I happened to have a number of folks visiting *Urwel* when the message came. I hope it was okay to invite everyone to the party. Including *IFV Skuodas*."

Imperial Fighting Vessel *Skuodas*. An Expeditionary-class in a style known as a Longbow. Front-line combat.

Morninghawk's smile could have lit up any room Heather had ever been in.

"Welcome and thank you, Lord Morninghawk," she replied. "For now, everyone in your force should transfer to *RAN* transponder codes. We'll transmit orbital instructions, so expect a few hours of maneuvering, and then an event, either here or on the main station nearby. Details to follow."

She leaned back and swore under her breath.

Phil finally came on a private line, still a bit breathless.

"Am I really seeing this, Heather?" he asked.

"So it seems," she replied. "But I think at this moment I do get to tell you I told you so."

"You do," he agreed instantly. "Now, the fun part, *Supreme Yaumgan Commander*. You need to call your other bosses and make arrangements for them not to freak completely out at this moment. I'll take the flag on this side, but you'll need to metaphorically change uniforms."

Heather nodded. And sighed.

This much force meant that Phil could walk right over there and indelibly stomp a size twelve boot into somebody's ass, instead of just trying to hold *Zerzan* off for a time.

Would they listen?

FORTY-NINE

KYULLE STATION ONE, KYULLE ORBITAL SPACE

Yating had been asleep when the alarms rang. He stumbled to his feet and ignored boots for pants and a shirt and a dead run out of his sleeping chambers into the main room. One of his aides was already there, the young man flustered but attempting calm.

"Yan Hee Shoi, what is going on?" Yating demanded, tucking in his shirt and looking for a tunic or jacket that he could wear.

What did one wear to the apocalypse, if this was *Zerzan* returned to finish them off?

"A new fleet of warships has just emerged from Jump, Scholar Hu," Hee replied. "They appear friendly and are talking to *Urumchi*, but station authorities are in something of a panic. The First Speaker has called a meeting."

"Good," Yating said, turning for the door.

"Sir, are you going like that?" Hee asked, horrified.

"It was the middle of the night," Yating replied. "Is the middle of my night. I'll go. You see if you can find something in my closet that will keep me warm and make me somewhat presentable, but I need to be in the Chambers immediately."

He didn't bother looking back. Or walking with anything approximating dignity. Instead, he jogged as quickly as sixty-year-old legs and feet in socks on metal decks would allow. Guards saw him coming and opened hatches for him to move through without pausing. Or asking.

He got there faster than Wen, but it did involve both of them racing each other like children down that last corridor. And laughing.

The old man wasn't nearly as slowed down and retired as he liked to tell everyone, but Yating beat him by a step.

One.

Old man was tough.

They collapsed into seats and looked around, gasping and laughing entirely inappropriately. The rest were mostly here, missing only a few Yating knew were on the surface or elsewhere on missions, such as retrieving ships for Command Centurion Lau.

"This is a quorum," Chang announced, looking around and counting noses. "As you know, Kosnett sent one of his ships off with a message for the *Dalou* lord Morninghawk to return with whomever he could recruit to come to our aid in this time of existential crisis."

Yating was still catching his breath, but he heard the note of disbelief in the woman's voice. Not fear, but wonder.

"*Morninghawk* has indeed come, fellow Scholars," Chang continued. "In that, we have an even greater problem, perhaps, than we might have had if they turned their noses up at us."

"First Speaker?" Yating asked, because it was obvious as he looked around that nobody else would speak up.

"Those of you who have kept up on the various reports from Xue Dao Zhiou will recognize many of the ships that have come," Chang said. "*Morninghawk* itself is here, on the very ship that bears his name and legend. Other *Dalou* ships accompanied him. The *Aditi* Ship-of-the-Line *Khandoba* comes, with a small squadron of escorts. The *Ewin* Battleship *Utron Heavy*, flagship of Prince Kalidoona of their Eastern Squadron, as well as the Hunter *Freewind* who some of you might know. Kalidoona also brings a squadron of escorts. *Gloran* sent a trio of ships bearing Penal Squadron markings, but I suspect that to be a holdover from their time, rather than a statement of insult from the Emperor, as *Arteshbo* leads them, commanded yet by his own cousin, Kira Zaman. Ladies and gentlemen, those of you who doubted Kosnett owe that man an apology. He asked the entire Balhee Cluster to come. And they did."

Something in her voice still sounded wrong. It was there in her eyes, when the two of them locked across the short distance.

"And?" he asked, looking for the other shoe.

"And the Imperial Fighting Vessel *Skuodas*," she replied. "A *Fribourg* Expeditionary Cruiser of a model remarkably similar to *RAN Viking*."

"Kosnett has said more than once that he remains penpals with the Emperor of *Fribourg*," Yating noted. "That he sends her letters when he ships updates home to his own superiors. Obviously, one of them made it far enough, and she chose to see what was happening here. Why do you express doubt, First Speaker?"

She nodded. But then, Li Chang Ling was one of the smartest people Yating knew. She had seen something not obvious on the first handful of layers. Something hidden by the logic of the situation, and the response by so many others.

"Because *Yaumgan* must be destroyed," Chang said simply. Flatly. Unequivocally.

Yating nodded.

Around them, the shouts of anger and denial overwhelmed everything, until Wen stood up, walked over, and slammed his steel-toed boot into a metal wall loud enough that whoever was in the next chamber might have pissed themselves in surprise. Yating almost did.

Silence did come quickly, though.

Yating rose and laughed when the hatch opened and Hee literally balled up a tunic and threw it across the room, not allowed to set foot in these spaces while the Scholars met.

Yating caught it and bowed to the man. The rest of the room fell into sullenness or brittle laughter, as was their usual bent.

"She's right, you know," he addressed the mob as he pulled the tunic over his head, focused on many who might be usually counted as allies. All of whom scowled at him now. A few hurled insults that slipped off his back like water on a duck.

Instead, he walked a few steps to glare brightly back at everyone, threatening them with his cheerfulness as a deadly weapon.

"You all claim to be *scholars*," Yating continued sarcastically, turning from face to face until each looked away. Only Qing did not, but the old man was meaner than the rest of them put together. "What does it say that six other nations—seven as we should count *Meerut* as a true neutral in this—chose to join us?"

"Do they see a future we cannot?" Qing asked brightly, obviously relishing any role that would allow him to ask annoying questions of this room. He still lived for that.

Growls met that question, so Yating marked that as the first of the man's bullseyes. He suspected that there would be many ere the day was done.

"What future can you *Scholars* see?" Yating asked, dripping the word with sarcasm as he swept an arm. Like sweeping all the plates and stemware off a table. "Chang is right. *Yaumgan* must be destroyed."

"And why is that?" Qing pressed, happiness itself from his tones.

"Because *Yaumgan* is the past," Yating replied, watching Chang move to where he had been sitting on the couch, as though she was ceding him the death ground for this battle.

Perhaps she was. Or had seen that he would draw all the fire to himself, leaving her free to referee if things got heated.

Yating was counting on Qing's wit and savage tongue in that case.

"The past?" the resident Socrates asked with a savage grin.

"It was the thing we built when we were no longer *Zerzan*," Yating reminded everyone. "That land of scholars, rather than inherited aristocrats that we had been, once upon a time before the *Monarchy* was judged a poor political outcome for too many."

"What made it poor?" Qing grinned now, like this was some comedy routine the two of them had worked up, instead of merely three decades of verbal fencing alloyed to pure intellectual respect.

"The fact that the people our ancestors ruled chose to rise up and murder so many of our kin," Yating replied. "That they built the *Unification* in its place and have apparently maintained that for a long stretch of time. One presumes that a wider base of support upholds that government and thus does not face revolution from within."

"Why can *Yaumgan* no longer hold?" a woman asked from the corner, several of them huddled and often speaking with similar voices.

"Because without Kosnett and *Aquitaine*, we would already be prisoners of *Zerzan*," Yating turned to her. "They would have scoured our skies clear of ships. Even if we could have gotten messages out to the other worlds, would they have been able to form up a fleet capable of driving *Zerzan* away? Or would they have been destroyed in turn, taking the rest of the *Domain* with it? *Without Kosnett,* Yaumgan *is already fallen.*"

Qing rescued her by shifting noisily on those heavy boots and drawing eyes to him.

"Without Kosnett, *Zerzan* never learns we had hidden in Balhee," Qing pointed out, less emotion and more logic. "Does he bear the guilt for our losses?"

"Was the civilization of the Cluster a better place when pirates ran rampant?" Yating volleyed back at him. "When we paid *Nagi Syndicate* to savage *Ewin* and *Gloran* for us, so that we had clean hands? Apparently clean, I might add, because we ordered it and financed it, even if someone else held the blade. We still bear ultimate responsibility. As do all the other nations who did the same. Kosnett's responsibility is ending that as a way of life. Our failure was not understanding the implications."

"What does a future without piracy imply?" Qing asked, eyes big and filled with humor.

"Trade, as Kosnett reminded us time and again," Yating nodded. "Diplomacy that was more than a hard line on a map and a willingness to open fire without any other provocation than presence. Treating our neighbors as something other than a pack of wild dogs that could be distracted with raw meat or intimidating stares. We failed to move beyond that."

"Why should we move?" Qing asked. "It has served us well for centuries."

"Because *Morninghawk* was right," Yating stated, his voice growing dark and heavy as he drew them all in. "He told *Dalou* that the future was at hand, and they could either embrace it, or be ground under the avalanche it brought. *Gloran* saw that and transformed themselves to the point that the woman Zaman is an acknowledged member of the Imperial House, and a possible heir to the throne. *Aditi* did not understand, so Kosnett made them change. *Made* them. *Ewin* was *Ewin*, and only learned after someone hit them on the nose with a rolled-up newspaper enough times. Who does that leave?"

He rotated in place, again looking at every face who would meet his eyes.

"Why must *Yaumgan* change?" Chang tossed out there, as if she hadn't been the one to start all this in the first place.

"*Yaumgan* has already changed," Yating countered. "Why should it not be destroyed?"

"What would you replace it with?" Qing grinned, having carefully helped him bring most of the rest of the room through an abbreviated and somewhat sanitized history lesson of the last year.

"What is *Yaumgan?*" Yating asked, flipping the tables now and forcing Socrates to perhaps turn into Plato. Or at least Aristotle.

"*Yaumgan* is a land of Scholars," Qing nodded. "A place where meritocratic virtues have replaced inheritance of blood. That so-called Magic Penis Theory of History, where a penis can convey its power and magic down the line of male descent, but only the male. Where only a male with a magic penis can rule."

"How could the *Zerzan Monarchy* be overthrown, if such penises were so magical?" Yating asked, laughing inside because just over half the room was female, including the First Speaker.

The sour looks Qing was getting were worth getting out of bed in the middle of the night for this comedy routine.

"Obviously, the magic failed," Qing said with such deadly seriousness that people laughed. As intended. "Whether other magical penises would have been better remains to be seen. They cast down the *Monarchy* and killed many. Our ancestors escaped. Fled in deadly terror, perhaps, as a better way to describe it. We settled on *Kyulle* and absorbed the native population. But the *Monarchy* had already fallen, and we chose to create *Yaumgan* instead, doing away with the theory of the magical penis as a source of governmental authority."

"Has *Yaumgan* failed?" Yating asked, circling long ways back to Chang's original posit that had started all this.

"Of course it has failed!" Qing roared. "The *Zerzan Unification* has arrived and we can do nothing but dither like a bunch of old housewives. But for Kosnett, we would already be prisoners, or more likely heads on stakes somewhere. Six nations answered Kosnett's call for aid, and yet we could not even decide how to react to *Zerzan*, let alone Balhee. We are fools!"

The roars answering him took a bit to fade to quiet.

Or rather, Chang stood up and her authority caused every mouth to slam shut. Yating nodded and stepped to his left as she approached. Qing moved to the right. It was like a boxing match where the referee has sent the fighters to neutral corners.

Except there were no neutrals here.

Chang took a moment and drew them all into her charisma, which was exactly why she was First Speaker. Then she smiled.

"*Yaumgan* must be destroyed," she said in a quiet voice brooking no arguments. "We as Scholars have been adjudicated by our fellows as the best equipped to guide *Yaumgan* as a society, as a culture, and as a civilization. Qing is correct that we have failed. We have grown insular just as the others did, excluding only patiently-expansionist *Aditi* from that classification. In any other situation, I would stand down as First Speaker for our collective failures, but there is no person in this room free of such taint, so nobody could replace me in the short term."

"Then who should lead?" Yating asked in a quiet, careful voice, uncertain as to what game Chang was playing with all their lives now.

"That has become a military question, so we have already answered that," Chang nodded. "*Aquitaine* Command Centurion Heather Lau has accepted my offer to take supreme command of our military forces as we attempt to resist the *Unification*. That buys us time to consider what must replace *Yaumgan*, because *Yaumgan* has already fallen. An outsider will lead us. Hopefully save us. Two such, with Kosnett. Never in our history has there ever been a reason for such a thing, so the *past-that-was* has failed to prepare us for the *present-that-is*. I charge all of you with determining what shape the *future-that-will-be* takes. For now, the three of us who have been representing failed *Yaumgan* will go to Kosnett and Lau and see what their orders are."

"Are we to assume *Yaumgan* must be tossed onto the scrap heap of history?" Yating asked, again because it was on so many faces right now, but few would speak.

"It already has been, my friend," she nodded. "Now, we seek the lifeboat that might—*MIGHT*—see us to shore."

Yating nodded. The First Speaker had perfectly encapsulated their quandary.

She was like that.

How did they survive?

FIFTY

HEAVY ESCORT MORNINGHAWK

Makara would have liked to stand off to one side as the group exited the shuttle. Be like a bodyguard or a mere escort today, as had been his wont for so long.

Alas, that was not possible. Instead, he led the others.

Herald, with all that implied, even when two of the people following his standard today were his own older brothers, Darra and Pich.

But he was Lord Morninghawk.

At least Lady Morninghawk refused to be any farther away than holding his hand as he walked.

With her strength, he could move mountains. Kingdoms.

History itself.

Had he not already proven that?

Iveta met him and his party beyond the airlock. Tradition demanded that Heather at a minimum would be the one to greet him. Possibly Kosnett himself.

Iveta's smile told Makara that she had put her foot down and demanded this. Hadn't she been the one to proclaim him to the rest of the squadron, back before he had done the same with all of civilized space?

Her smile transformed the woman as he drew close.

Samnang got a hug before anyone could speak. He suffered the same. Even Kira Zaman, the *Gloran* Imperial Cousin, joined in, though most of the men held themselves aloof and uncertain.

Which was, again, why he was needed.

"Iveta, Prince Kalidoona," Makara gestured the man close so as to be *hugged*.

Each of them, even a stuffy Captain from the *Fribourg Empire* who was operating nearly a year behind current events, in light of the orders he had been given by the woman Kosnett occasionally called *Casey* when he wasn't paying attention.

All of them got hugged eventually.

He was Lord Morninghawk. He could throw out traditions and invent new ones on the fly. And have people accept them.

That power frightened him more than any battle—any foe— he had ever faced.

"Phil is looking forward to seeing you all again," Iveta finally said as the group's formality had dissolved entirely. "*Yaumgan* is hosting a reception for him, but I wanted to greet you first. And say thank you myself for everything that you have done ere today. And everything that I might call upon you to do later."

"There are more ships coming, I hope," Makara explained. "This group were all the friends present at *Urwel* when *Hollywood* arrived, and time seemed more important than collected numbers."

"You have already altered the balance of power, perhaps the course of history itself in *Yaumgan, Morninghawk*," she smiled up at him. "More will hopefully convince our new foes to withdraw and bother others."

Makara nodded. Samnang took his hand again and they let Iveta draw them through the next set of doors and down a corridor to a raw chamber filled with faces he knew.

Kosnett was here. Lau as well. A few others in green he recognized as aides and bodyguards. All the others were here to support those two. Including him.

He stepped close to the two and bowed formally. All of this, most of it wildly good beyond imagination, he could honestly lay at their feet. Iveta had spoken the words, but Kosnett and Lau had created the avalanche.

Both smiled at him now.

"You are a sight for sore eyes, Lord Morninghawk," Kosnett returned the bow. "And all your friends, some of whom I do not yet know."

Considering the group, that only stretched to two people, so Makara picked out Director Joshi, sailing in command of *Khandoba* rather than the man who had been there at *Vilahana*.

Tall, stout, and much less of an arrogant punk than Director Narang had been. *Aditi* was turning over new leaves, and a lot of cockroaches had chosen to retire rather than be called to account for things they might and might not be proud of later.

Makara had no complaints about Joshi, save that the man was occasionally too eager to please, which suggested that he had orders from home to make sure *Urwel* and *Morninghawk* were *Aditi* allies against an uncertain future. Certainly, the man had brought a Ship-of-the-Line and four Moat escorts along on Makara's invitation.

It was the other man that Makara stepped to now.

Imperial Captain Horst Friedemann Steinmann, commanding *IFV Skuodas*, which was apparently something of a special name to *Fribourg* for reasons Makara hadn't bothered pursuing. The man commanded an Expeditionary-class vessel closely reminiscent of *Viking*, though Makara now understood just how dangerous the warlike side of *Aquitaine* could have been, having seen the infamous Bubble Gun test fired at an asteroid.

Steinmann bowed deeply as they approached, crisply perfect in gray that was so much blander than everyone else.

"Captain," Kosnett said. "Welcome to the Balhee Cluster and the *Yaumgan Domain*. What were your orders from the Grand Admiral?"

Steinmann grinned now.

"***Centurion* zu *Weigand*** instructed me to put my ship at your disposal, First Centurion," he emphasized. "The Grand Admiral expresses his profound regret that she would not allow him to accompany *Skuodas* on this adventure."

Kosnett grunted but smiled, so Makara assumed all that was good news. Some of the names made a little bit of sense, but *Aquitaine* and *Fribourg* had an intertwined history that was too opaque for most outsiders to understand.

He made a note to travel to *Ladaux* himself someday. And to ask Kosnett and Lau to include historians in the group requested to train new officers and landholders on *Urwel*. People who knew all the players in the east and could help him later when he needed to negotiate trade linkages that went beyond *Vilahana*.

"We are facing a new foe, Captain," Kosnett said, stepping back and turning some so that everyone was included in this conversation. "They attacked *Kyulle* without warning or mercy. We drove them back, but I cannot tell you how quickly they will return. Interestingly, the smallest ships you brought with you will be the most effective, because they have one-man snubfighters in the humanoid shape that *Yaumgan* does, but much smaller. We have captured a few and my engineers have torn them apart. Technical specs will be distributed to everyone shortly. For now, however, *Yaumgan* has asked for our help defending their borders, and in doing so protecting the entire Cluster. Come, let us step through and introduce you to the Philosophers of *Yaumgan*. The people who are the Domain itself."

Kosnett turned and started across the chamber to a door on the far side. Makara paused, but Darra stepped right up to him and smiled.

Darra, the eldest brother. First-born. The next Lord Omarov, when Father finally retired or passed. His senior in every way for all of Makara's life.

Until recently.

Darra gestured.

"*Morninghawk* leads," he said simply, as if that summed it all up.

Except that the others repeated it like a quiet mantra. Even Iveta and Samnang.

He squared his shoulders and took up the van.

As always.

FIFTY-ONE

Heather slipped ahead of Phil. Or he slowed down enough for her to take the lead. Then they were through into the larger space that her new bosses, the First Speaker and her Scholars, had set up.

At least Hu had finally listened about how Phil wanted to do things. It had helped when he had whispered to her at one point how informal that group got when they were alone to make policy.

Finger foods, either on trays being carried around or on tables for folks to graze. Wine and softer things as one needed, with a small team of *RAN* marines guarding one cache of cans and bottles that she could draw from without needing to keep track of Markus and his backpack.

All of the Scholars currently in system, from the First Speaker to Qing, the old man in the working boots who always looked like he had snuck in a side door when nobody was looking. At least he had shaved off that wispy beard, so he didn't look like a hermit living in a cave tonight. Hair was still too long and pulled back in a manner similar to hers.

First Speaker Li was standing between Qing and Yating Hu as she approached. The rest of the Scholars were in something of a hemisphere beyond, but all the command centurions and captains and such had intermingled and were breaking down any formality that might have accompanied the *Yaumgan* contingent into the chamber.

Heather came to rest in front of the First Speaker. Heather's new title, like everything else about this, was informal. Supreme Commander. *Warlord of Yaumgan.* Hey, you.

"Heather," Chang Li nodded, eyes twinkling as the mob coasted to a halt around her.

"First Speaker, this is Lord Morninghawk," Heather pulled him close. "Lord Morninghawk, First Speaker Li Chang Ling of the *Yaumgan Domain.*"

They were almost the same height, those two. Chang Li outweighed him, but she was a former athlete specializing in throwing heavy things great distances, and Omarov had been skinny since she'd met him a year ago.

"Lord Morninghawk," the First Speaker said. "Welcome. And thank you for coming."

"There was need, First Speaker," he said simply. "Balhee as it was must give way to Balhee as it will become."

Heather heard the collective gasps from the Scholars in front of her, including these three, so she assumed one hell of an interesting *discussion* behind closed doors on a similar topic.

After all, Lord Morninghawk had moved more than one nation by his example. *Yaumgan* might only be the latest. Probably not the last.

"What friends answered your call?" Chang Li asked now in a formal cant, as if they were old acquaintances.

"*Dalou,*" he said. "*Ewin. Gloran. Aditi. Aquitaine.* And *Fribourg.*"

More gasps. Like *Aquitaine* had been before Phil arrived, the *Fribourg Empire* was more legend than reality, its closest border even farther away as you headed towards the center of the galaxy up the eastern arm.

Heather gestured Captain Steinmann to step up. Tall, blond, and rugged-looking in a handsome way.

Recruiting poster kind of sailor, save that both Karl VIII and the old Red Admiral had trusted him with this mission, which spoke volumes about his competence, open-mindedness, and probably ruthlessness, as the timing to sail between worlds suggested that he should have come expecting to hunt pirates.

The man carried himself in that formal way that *Fribourg* senior officers did. Rigid spine, shoulders back, head up.

"*Fribourg* answers the First Centurion's call?" the First Speaker asked the man as he came to rest between her and Phil.

"*Aquitaine* saved *Fribourg*, First Speaker," he said, summing up all of Jessica Keller's entire legend in the fewest words Heather thought she might have ever heard to do so. "We can do no less."

Again, gasps.

Lots of folks in front of her were apparently having multiple shocks about how the rest of the Cluster had changed while they'd been hiding back in his corner thinking deep and contemplative thoughts.

Frankly, she was a bit appalled at how close-minded that suggested those folks had gotten.

But that was why they needed her to save their asses today.

Tomorrow, they would have to find a way to do it themselves.

Or hire someone permanently, which wasn't about to be her.

The First Speaker turned to Phil again, which was good. She was just here to handle military things.

"Your treaties with everyone," the woman began. "*Aquitaine's…*"

"All of them presume that *Fribourg* could sign something identical, once an ambassador of sufficient rank was involved on both sides," Phil replied. "I doubt that Captain Steinmann has such authority, but remember that my messages to *St. Legier* require a much longer transit time, because they have to first get to *Ladaux* before being forwarded. It is likely that the Emperor had heard hardly anything beyond that first call for the Five Nations when she responded. And even then, much time had passed."

Steinmann nodded but didn't speak. Possibly in awe of the situation. And his orders.

Not the first time an *RAN* officer had been put in charge of *Fribourg* ships without any restrictions being placed on the orders given.

Still, Chang Li turned to Heather now, possibly a little lost.

Suddenly stepping onto a stage of that size could do that.

"It is enough that he is here," Heather offered. "That his orders would normally attach him to the *Aquitaine* squadron in a manner similar to *Li Jing* or any of the others. When we go to confront *Zerzan*, my suggestion will be that every ship present fly its own national flag as a transponder code, simply so that the *Unification* can come to understand that *Yaumgan* is not alone."

First Speaker Li nodded. She had hired Heather for her expertise. *Yaumgan* was going to get that.

The crisis, if you wanted to call it that, passed as she watched, like a fog burning off.

Heather turned to Steinmann and nodded.

"Come, Captain," she said informally. "Let's introduce you to some of the folks I have been sailing with for the past year, so you can make even more friends."

Because that was what they were at this point. Sailing mates she had trusted with her life more times than she cared to count, regardless of how strange and formal they had all been at the beginning.

That was how far Phil's mission had come.

FIFTY-TWO

Phil had summoned all the command centurions, tactical officers, and important players for a meeting, once Barnaby had given him a quick briefing that detailed how badly damaged the *Zerzan Unification* force had been when *Viking* had peeked in the window.

The crew had needed to strip one of the dining halls of tables and drag in chairs from elsewhere to seat everyone. But then, Morninghawk had brought twenty-one ships including his own. Heather had command of another thirty-odd Skycruisers and the *Zhōng* medium escorts.

Plus the piracy hunting squadron that had formed over *Aditi*, once upon a forever ago.

Worse, *Morninghawk* was expecting more ships, once the messages got to *Meerut*, *Derragon*, and a few other places, but those would likely dribble in a few at a time.

Right now, Philip S. Kosnett, First Centurion, had a striking force at his command sufficient to alter the course of empires. Of *History* itself.

Phil stood and looked out over the group, suddenly back on the deck of *Cyrus* at *Hemera*, watching the sudden emergence of that impossibly-vast Imperial fleet under the command of the

RAN's own Denis Jež and bearing the future Imperial Consort *zu* Arlo home to *St. Legier*.

A sea of ships poised to unleash any destruction their commander called for, when Phil had a pitiful squadron that would have gotten stomped into the mud before they even knew what had happened, had that been what it would take to assuage *zu* Arlo's rage.

Phil drew a breath and smiled. Everyone here were friends, whether they understood that or not. Even the strangers, like Captain Steinmann or the six men from Kalidoona's missile frigates.

"Two years ago, as I was completing the planning and training for this mission, nobody could have imagined this day," he said, pitching his voice to carry but holding it warm. Students up too early after being up all night studying or partying. "I brought nine ships and crews with me. Today, we are over sixty vessels, all joined in a single task, that of protecting *Yaumgan* from being destroyed by the *Zerzan Unification*."

He paused, pacing laterally like he often had when he'd had a stage in front of an auditorium full of students. All that was missing were the projectors to put up diagrams and notes on the wall behind him, but this was not a test.

Not even a class.

Everyone here had long since proven themselves worthy of the uniforms that they wore and their place in this room.

He paused and picked out Chevalier Aublahzieu, escorted by *Stunt Dude* on one side and Ambassador Hu on the other, with several *Yaumgan* Scholars present, including the First Speaker and Old Man Wen, as he liked to be called these days.

"*RAN Viking* has just returned from scanning the moorage at *Loong*," Phil continued, including her in his words, because she would be such a pivotal player going forward.

Not his *fetial*, but his javelin.

The others all perked up now, leaning forward as he knew they would.

"The *Unification* Overlord Carrier *Rauda* was badly damaged," Phil said. "Barnaby's people think that it might take them time yet before they are ready to make the long sail back to *Kohri*, but it is also possible that the time elapsed from him scanning them and when we could arrive might give them the time they need. Therefore, time is our enemy. The sailing distance is short, so we are going to move quickly."

"Are we attacking their moorage?" Lord Morninghawk asked.

He could do that, speaking for so many others.

He was *Morninghawk*.

"Auke Alma tells me that we could descend from the heavens and possibly wipe their entire force from existence if we chose," Phil replied. "They are sitting in deep space rather than within the gravity well of a friendly planet. Some of you will remember the methods that Keller's people in the *First Expeditionary Fleet* used, swooping in and unleashing heavy weapons with surprise. Such a thing would be child's play at *Loong*."

He paused, watching all the blood drain out of Bausse Aublahzieu's normally pale face.

"But it would not solve my greater issue," Phil interrupted the growls and sounds emerging from that crowd like a mob forming. "Destroying this first invasion force would just guarantee a second one that would be even larger. Or a third if *Yaumgan* defeated that second. A fourth. The *Zerzan Unification* represents hundreds and possibly thousands of worlds that might supply ships and warriors, and their entire civilization is geared towards the destruction of the folks they believe are today known as the *Yaumgan Domain*."

The warriors in the crowd saw the immense battles. The historians saw the greater problem.

When would it end?

How?

"All of you are prepared," Phil said, gesturing to the room. "The distance is short enough that we will drop out once, form up, and then sail directly into their harbor, but we will not arrive firing."

Cries of surprise, but mostly from the newcomers. The ones that had not been at *Second Ewinhome* at that, as Kalidoona and his people all nodded crisply.

"Instead, we will attempt to speak to them of peace," Phil continued, still watching Bausse's face as she processed what he was saying.

Her words would be necessary for the *Unification* to understand.

If they would listen to her.

Phil rated that almost dead-even odds. Much would rest on his shoulders. And others, which was why he had Heather and Iveta. Harinder and Fleet Ambassador Aliza Babatunde.

Kaur Singh. Xue Dao Zhiou. Gotzon Solo. Adham Khan. *Hollywood* Ward.

And Makara Omarov.

Morninghawk.

"We will be prepared, if they choose battle instead of diplomacy." Phil turned his eyes back to the commanders he would rely on, old friends and new strangers. "You will have the technical specifications of the thing they call aeromechia. There will be close to two thousand such craft available, if the entire force remains present when we arrive. Battle will be brutal and bloody if we are left no other choice. However, we have advantages there that *Zerzan* has not taken into consideration. Some of you remember *Buran*. Those terrible sharks that could bounce around gravity wells on their Capriole drives, alighting and savaging a squadron before vanishing again. The aeromechia are not jump-equipped. We are. *Urumchi*'s Tactical Officer will supply you with her planning dossiers detailing various maneuvers she may call upon you to execute. If we must fight, you will treat orders from her or Heather Lau as commands on your very souls. Anything less and we might none of us survive such a battle. Together, we are stronger than the *Zerzan*

Unification. You being here tells me that you understand that the union of the Five Nations and their allies is necessary. I hope it is sufficient. Questions?"

Bausse rose now, awkward and nervous, still wearing her *Zerzan* uniform that marked her as an outsider in this space. An enemy in their midst, but only until everyone chose otherwise.

"Can there be peace, First Centurion?" she asked.

"That is up to Chevalier Fortier and *Unification* Commissioner Abaroa, Bausse," he said. "They will listen to me. Whether they choose to understand is not something I can state for certain. Perhaps they will flee. Perhaps they will attack. The former guarantees that the war will be long, bloody, and destructive to all sides. The latter promises that it will be short, because I honestly believe that the force around you has the training, temperament, and equipment to annihilate *Bertev*, *Rauda*, and everyone that traveled with them, leaving no survivors. That is not necessary. Not today. Ask me again when the first shot is fired."

"Me?" she asked.

"You," Phil said. "Centurion Dar assures me that *Truhto* is ready for flight, at least over this short of a distance. You will return to your command and bring that ship and crew with you to the waypoint, at which time I will remove all of my people and ask that you accompany us to *Loong* to talk to Chevalier Fortier and Commissioner Abaroa."

Her mouth fell open. It wasn't the only one, either.

Phil smiled. *Stunt Dude* and Iveta shared it.

"We promised that we would get your people home, Bausse," Phil said. "That is on the honor of the *Republic of Aquitaine* Navy. *We will see it done.* If Fortier attacks us, you might end up being the only survivor capable of carrying the message to *Kohri* afterwards, but *we will see you home.*"

He scanned the room. Shock on some faces. Anger on others. Deadly firm commitment on the right ones.

"People, Chief Bottenberg has worked their ass off today to

prepare us a meal, so we will move now to the forward wardroom and break bread as friends," he continued, still staring at Bausse. "All of us, regardless of uniform or flag. In six hours, we will depart. Join me."

Phil turned and headed towards the side door. There was no better way to alloy all these metals than dining as one people. If nothing else, he had given the Balhee Cluster that option.

Now, he needed to make sure that they remained free enough to enjoy it.

FIFTY-THREE

Iveta nodded to Command Machinist Rais Hosni El-Amin and indicated for him to join her at the table she was sharing with Kira Zaman and that woman's two Frigate-Captains, Nadim Tikka and Zeenat Vaishya. He scowled, but sat, placing his tray with the sorts of exact precision of movement that marked the man when he got serious about things.

The food was fantastic, as though Rei had risen to a whole new layer of ascension tonight in their kitchen. Iveta understood. She went there occasionally when she turned into the *Junkyard Bitch*. Heather did it as *Ground Control*.

She watched the man eat for clues. Mainly, his body language was good. Nervous, but that was the fact that she had three outsiders with her. If you could call them that. Technically, Kira was business partners with Heather, which more or less made her family around here, and her two sidekicks knew when to keep their mouths shut.

"Will it work?" Iveta asked.

Rais still scowled at the others.

"It will become public knowledge soon enough," Iveta said sharply. "It's been how many years since they did it at *Second Petron*, Rais?"

He sighed. Stuffed a bite of biscuit into his mouth and chewed to compose himself, based on the scowl in his eyes.

"Handing sharp knives to children," he finally growled.

"We broke the Syndicates, Rais," Iveta reminded him. "All of the nations of the Cluster are here, right now, to fight as a single entity. Anyone using such a weapon in the future guarantees an avalanche of ugly shit landing on their asses afterwards. Plus, it's defensive, so only a problem to people attacking."

He sighed a second time. A Command Machinist outranked her, at least most of the time. Not when she had Tactical. Not when she went *Junkyard*.

"Yes," he said. "It will work. I had to jury-rig shit because the original design in the computers involved a Primary shell, which I haven't touched in years. Instead, we'll overload a couple of extra batteries in the back of a shuttle with a spare, backup Jumpsail installed. Ugly as shit, but it will work. Dunklin did a lot of the welding."

"Markus?" Iveta asked.

He hadn't said anything to her about it, including a few nights he'd spent in her bunk since she had first broached the topic with Rais.

Rais smiled. Like maybe he owed her a few. Probably did, at the end of the day. She'd asked him to build something so advanced and experimental that it had only been used once.

Second Petron, during the Horvat Incident, when shit had gotten so hot and out of control that an *RAN* carrier fleet had attacked the capital world of *Corynthe* itself.

And gotten their asses handed to them so badly that Jessica had kept all of the surrendered *RAN* ships and inducted them into her own navy afterwards. With that old fleet carrier, *RAN Adamant*, requiring nearly a year in drydock after the surprise that Bedrov and Barrett had unleashed on them.

Iveta nodded now and turned to Kira.

"This will be a secret that you three need to keep quiet," she said simply.

Kira nodded. The two men paled more, but they were just Frigate-Captains who had had the extraordinarlyy good luck to be attached to *Arteshbo*'s squadron at the moment when Kerenski decided to grow up and bring his cousin in from the cold.

Minor players who would probably end up as nothing more than footnotes in the end, but didn't that describe most of them? It took a nerd like Iveta to know all the major players, once you got past Jessica Keller and Moirrey *zu* Kermode-Wolanski.

Folks would know Phil. Smart ones would know Heather.

The rest of them would be legends when it was done.

Iveta was okay with that. She'd be in line for her own cruiser after this mission.

"There was a battle," Iveta said quietly, falling into that same storytelling mode that Phil got when he wanted your attention. "Bad guys attacked the good guys, though the *RAN* were the bad guys in this one."

Gasps, but only from the two Frigate-Captains. Kira already understood that perspective was everything in war and diplomacy.

"*Corynthe* was, in those days, served well by three of the most dangerous design engineers I've ever *studied*, let alone met," Iveta continued. "*Pops* Nakamura, who was *Corynthe*'s Crown Designer. Yan Bedrov, who designed *Urumchi*, *Viking*, and the corvettes after he replaced *Pops*. And Lady Moirrey. She designed the weapon that killed the god *Buran*."

Wide-eyed surprise, but Iveta didn't suppose that those stories were even legends, this far west and rimward. Not yet.

"*Urumchi* mounts Type-4 beams," Iveta nodded. "Lady Moirrey designed a 6.5. The power curve is logarithmic in scale, so you can imagine what it did when they fired it."

More gasps this time. Three commanders who understood their engineering classes well enough to follow this conversation. Rais just nodded and kept shoveling food into his mouth so he didn't have to get involved.

"In the process, those same folks invented a type of mine," Iveta let her voice get dark and serious.

The Balhee Cluster understood mine warfare and used it defensively, like most folks.

"What does it do?" Kira asked quietly.

"Technically, it breaks JumpSpace," Rais said around a mouth of salad. "The math is crazy and stupid, but it works. I had all the right information handy to adapt something for Phil."

"Breaks?" Vaishya asked, turning to the Command Machinist.

Iveta nodded for Rais to continue.

"JumpSpace is stable, once you get beyond the gravity well of a planet or moon," Rais said in response. "That's why you have to come out a ways, because your matrix scrambles otherwise. Lady Moirrey's mine hops up into JumpSpace and detonates a type of warhead that causes waves of localized instabilities sufficient to prevent any ship from remaining in JumpSpace."

Iveta nodded.

Nobody else studied Keller's battles like she did. Jessica hadn't even been there, but had so many of the key players of that generation present. And in its own way, *Second Petron* had broken the back of Horvat's attempt to start a galaxy-wide war.

Because that fool had chosen Lady Moirrey as an enemy.

Iveta rated that idea a half-step *more* suicidal than Keller herself, which should have told the rest of civilization what a dumb idea that was.

"So what happens?" Kira asked, shifting her tones to a Tactical mode Iveta recognized from the mirror.

"So we come out of JumpSpace at *Loong*," Iveta replied. "And then we trap the entire *Zerzan* fleet in front of us. They don't have the opportunity to flee, so they either have to talk, or choose to fight us."

"Rats in a corner," Kira noted.

"Yes," Iveta replied with calm certainty. "Right up until I exterminate them."

She rose. The others looked at her expectantly.

"I need to go tell Phil," Iveta said.

LOONG

FIFTY-FOUR

Bausse was back aboard her ship. Her home. Most of her people were with her, minus the atrocious casualties from the battle. A handful remained on *Aquitaine* corvettes, with promises from the First Centurion and others that would see them home eventually as well. Or their bodies.

Should she have demanded that they be transferred to *Truhto*? Or was that an implicit acknowledgment that she expected them to die with her in the coming battle?

Bausse didn't know. None of this had happened in any form she could have predicted, at that moment when *Urumchi* and *Viking* suddenly opened fire on her from too damned far away.

Beside her, the main hatch opened and Centurion Dar emerged, trailed a step later by Trinidad Mildon. *Stunt Dude* himself.

Both came to rest and smiled. Around them, her new bridge, with folks promoted to fill holes, smiled back. Dar had worked like a mule to get things repaired. Her people had put in eighteen-hour days, fuming and cursing that they couldn't do more. Or do it faster.

Just to get *Truhto* ready to fly home.

Bausse bowed to the two of them. They had spoken at length

an hour ago, when Dar had seen all of her people into shuttles save the six of them that had boarded first, back in *Kyulle* orbit.

Before.

Now, they were running the film in reverse, where it would see *Aquitaine* gone and *Truhto* returning to the *Loong* base.

Bausse held out a hand. *Stunt Dude* took it and squeezed. He understood. Dar understood as well. She was beaming. The crew around them returned it tenfold.

Could they have all been friends? Bausse didn't know.

Could they yet become friends? Kosnett was about to lead a massive fleet to have that very discussion with Fortier and Abaroa. What would come of it?

"You went looking for Sam," Bausse said, voice heavy with emotion. "And found her."

Stunt Dude nodded.

"I would greatly appreciate the ability to host the two of you for dinner in my home someday," she managed before her voice cracked.

Home. She would actually be going home. Even if Kosnett was required to annihilate the rest of the *Zerzan* force, he had promised her that none of his ships would fire on her without provocation.

On his honor.

All of their honor.

"I'll talk to Sam about it," *Stunt Dude* said with a wry smile. "She's always up for travel, but it might take some time to arrange."

Bausse slammed her jaws shut so hard her teeth rattled. He was skirting around the fact that there might have to be an entire war fought between *Zerzan* and *Aquitaine* for that to happen.

A month ago, she would have been certain that the *Unification* was unbeatable in battle.

She would have been wrong.

When had the *Unification* gone wrong?

Bausse did not know, but she intended to find answers when she got home.

Home.

"Thank you," Bausse managed. "On behalf of my crew, they thank you as well. We have learned much in a brief time."

Stunt Dude bowed now. A formal thing echoing the *Unification*. Bausse wondered if *Yaumgan* did it, as she had seen something similar around the Scholars.

"It has been my great privilege to make your acquaintances," he said, turning to include the others in his words. "To get to know you as a people. As with Bausse, perhaps one day I can host you at *Ladaux*. When this is all over."

"When this is all over," she echoed.

Dar bowed and pivoted to the hatch. She and *Stunt Dude* withdrew. She watched them go with mixed feelings.

Kosnett was about to call down the wrath of the very gods on her people. Her friends.

Some of her friends.

She had made new ones in the most unexpected places.

FIFTY-FIVE

Phil looked around his flag bridge, wondering if this was indeed the culmination of everything that Pet had tasked him with, all those years ago. The years of planning. The design of a force intended to explore the west. The recruitment that allowed him to pretty much skim the cream off an entire generation of younger officers and teach them life beyond warfare.

He was *The Professor*, after all.

Phil Kosnett, Explorer Extraordinaire.

Harinder sat across from him, poised as always. Nam and Kohahu on each side, forming the compass rose in his head. First Speaker Li, Old Man Wen, and Ambassador Hu had joined them, because Phil was going to determine the future of their entire civilization shortly.

He hadn't asked if they trusted him. They had no choice.

Well, they had one, but it involved running for their lives on whatever ships they could scrounge up, and hoping they could find another world on which to settle someday.

Phil was playing for keeps.

He had considered using his usual tactics for this operation.

Drop everyone out a ways and send *Viking* in for one last look before arriving. Smart. Safe. Effective.

Without a defensive gravity well protecting the *Unification* ships, he could have also dropped out right on top them like a feeding frenzy of *Buran* sharks, blasting everything that moved as soon as the guns could clear. That wouldn't solve anything except add to his body count, making him the butcher that history might yet have to record him to be, in spite of all the times he *hadn't* done things that way.

Iveta and Rais, however, had given him perhaps the perfect tool for the situation. Iveta really had grown up over the last year, from perhaps the best of the Keller clones available on the market to a deadly, sneaky commander in her own right, worthy of her own piratical nickname.

Here, she'd guaranteed that *Zerzan* would have to listen to him. If they couldn't slip away into JumpSpace, they had no choice. Plus, he was planning to detonate the mine right on top of them. Perhaps a little beyond, so that his ships could withdraw, if the *Unification* had chosen to reinforce the moorage with any more of those monstrous supercarriers.

Two thousand aeromechia would be a mess, but one he could win. He had enough ships and people behind him for that.

Four thousand would be a statement of purpose that required Phil to get ugly. It meant that the *Unification* wasn't going to talk.

Only conquer.

And that, he would not allow.

Heather's voice came over the line from her bridge. He had offered her space on the flag bridge, but hadn't been surprised when she turned him down to command her wing from forward. Had the three representatives from *Yaumgan* not been here, she might have.

Their presence pushed her forward. Truth be told, she

commanded better from there anyway. Her next promotion would take her away from it soon enough.

"All hands to battle stations," Heather called. "We will emerge in ninety seconds. Iveta has Tactical. Flight deck, stand by to launch your bird."

Phil nodded. He had told the First Speaker and her people that he had a surprise planned, but not the shape it would take.

Breaking JumpSpace was the sort of thing that needed to be kept quiet as long as possible. Too many pirates would see it as a tool, which would cause planetary defense systems to need it to trap said pirates from fleeing.

At least until someone like Kermode found a way around it. And she, or someone like her, would.

Mischief was like life.

Emergence.

Scanners came live, filling in details as Leyla and her various people on all the ships scanned with everything they had.

"Flight Deck, launch and engage," Heather said.

Phil took a breath and watched all those stars appear on the screen around *Urumchi*, with nobody closer to the enemy right now than the *Unification* Assault Carrier *Truhto*, the escort *Forktail*, and leading them all in, the Heavy Escort *Morninghawk*.

"All ships, this is Kosnett, aboard *Urumchi*. I have the flag," he called the old cadence. "All vessels stand by for combat operations, but nobody will fire until our foe starts it. We have the firepower to hold them at bay, and the ability to withdraw and return later."

One more breath as everything crystallized.

"Escort *Morninghawk*," Phil said. "As you bear."

FIFTY-SIX

Donatien was in a meeting with the *Unification* Commissioner, aboard her ship, when the intruder alarms sounded.

Of course it would happen when he was away from his own bridge and his people.

He found the controller for the local comm and located the setting he needed.

"Bridge," the woman on the other end replied.

"This is Chevalier Fortier," Donatien said. "What is the situation?"

"We have an enemy fleet that has just come out of Jump, Chevalier," she said. "We appear to be in range of the heavy beam weapons on *Urumchi* and *Viking*, as well as a third ship of identical lines to *Viking* that appears to be flying a transponder code identifying itself as the *Fribourg Empire*."

The what?

"How many ships?" he demanded, rising as the Commissioner did the same, in preparation for running to the bridge.

If there was a fleet out there, trying to get back to *Bertev* in a shuttle might be suicide.

"Over sixty, Chevalier," came the reply, stopping him in his tracks.

"Repeat that," he said, shocked almost out of his wits.

"We are scanning over sixty vessels now, Chevalier. One of them is…"

"WHAT?" he screamed when the man fell silent.

"One of them is *Truhto*, sir," she said. "We're being hailed by both Chevalier Aublahzieu and a second vessel identifying itself as the *Dalou* Heavy Escort *Morninghawk*."

"Is anybody firing?" Donatien asked.

"Negative, sir," she replied with disbelief. "They are just watching us."

"I'll be right there."

FIFTY-SEVEN

HEAVY ESCORT MORNINGHAWK

Makara was back where he really belonged, even though he was adult enough to admit that this was probably one last hurrah. Still, it would enable him to shape the future of the Balhee Cluster and points beyond.

He was *The Herald*, after all.

"Status?" he asked, turning his attention to Keo, commanding the guns and sensors today while Bulat handled piloting.

They still traded off regularly.

"Same group *Viking* identified earlier," Keo nodded, serious for once. "Station is the same basic hull configuration as *Truhto*, and identifies as *Hrafsto*. Stand by, I'm getting a reply to our hail."

"Keep all the weapons hot," Makara said. "We're closest to that shitshow if things go bad. The corvettes will help, but we'll be the breakwater against which *Zerzan* loses their teeth. At least for as long as we survive."

Keo nodded again. Makara turned to Samnang and caught her smile.

"Hell of a second honeymoon, huh?" he grinned.

"Fourth," she grinned without missing a beat. "I knew you were trouble when I let you seduce me."

He wasn't the only one who laughed, but everyone had adopted Samnang as one of them.

"Okay," Keo said now. "*Hrafsto* is asking us to stand by for their Chevalier. I assume they are also talking to *Truhto* right now and asking for guidance."

"Good luck with that," Makara grinned. "Emperor Osamu didn't get run over as hard by Kosnett as *Truhto*'s captain did. Still, let Kosnett know we're standing by. And keep watch for the first ship attempting to slip away into JumpSpace. That realization will be when they get desperate."

"No doubt," Keo nodded.

Makara leaned back and sucked a breath to the bottom of his soul. He was back at *Ellariel-jo*, waiting for the Emperor and Crown Prince to dock, when nobody had the slightest clue what to do next.

At least Makara was prepared today.

FIFTY-EIGHT

MISSION BRIEF: ASSAULT CARRIER TRUHTO.
OPERATIONS BASE LOONG

Bausse watched the main screen light up from *Hrafsto*, showing Donatien Fortier's face, with *Unification* Commissioner Abaroa next to him. His surprise was probably greater than hers.

"How?" he demanded.

"It is a long story, Donatien," Bausse replied. "Kosnett's people made it a point of honor that my ship and my crew would make it home. And they did. Right now, he wants to talk, and brought as many allies as were immediately available to assure that you would listen."

"Can we fight that force?" he asked simply.

"Kosnett believes that he has enough ships and friends to stop the *Unification* invasion," Bausse said. "He also made it clear to me and his commanders that he was choosing not to come out of Jump directly on top of *Bertev* and *Rauda*, where he could immediately destroy all of you at short range. Instead, he says you are trapped here, though I do not know what makes him believe that."

Donatien's face turned hard and angry, but she was merely the messenger here. Kosnett had been true to his word. All of them had been. She had only her own people aboard, minus a few who had volunteered to stay behind to be with wounded comrades who could not be moved.

"All *Unification* vessels, this is Chevalier Fortier, commanding from *Hrafsto*," he said, obviously pushing the signal to include her. "Everyone immediately transition to JumpSpace and rendezvous at station-keeping position six."

Bausse turned to her own transport officer and nodded when the woman looked up. Kosnett had said that they were free to go. That none of his ships would fire on her as long as she didn't make any hostile moves.

Running for her life didn't count as hostile.

The JumpSails engaged. Then the entire vessel lurched like it had lost gravity again.

Lights flickered everywhere before they stabilized. Metal seemed to warp and knock.

A bang somewhere as something newly repaired and fragile shorted out within earshot. Smoke.

Stars on her screen, where there should have been only the gray shadows of JumpSpace.

"What happened?" she asked, not surprised but concerned.

Kosnett had warned her.

Truhto had been facing *Bertev* on beam. Now her ship had turned more than one hundred and twenty degrees to starboard, down nearly thirty, and rolled perhaps fifteen.

"We're not in JumpSpace," the woman flying said in disbelief. "Engineering, what happened?"

"We just lost the entire, damned Jump matrix," someone yelled over the line, with pops and minor explosions audible in the background. "I'm not sure how long until we can rebuild it. I've got fires and secondary explosion risks going on."

Bausse nodded sagely when her officers looked at her.

Kosnett had said he could do a thing. He was not a man who had struck her as one to bluff. Not at that scale.

"Optics," Bausse said. "What about the rest of the *Unification* force?"

"Everyone is present," the man said. "As with us, all ships seem to have been bodily cast out of JumpSpace and have lost their previous formation and headings. *What did Kosnett do?*"

Bausse smiled sadly. The man had merely trapped the entire *Unification* invasion force in a small space where he believed he had the firepower to annihilate them. And might be about to.

She turned back to the main screen and saw the horror dawn on Donatien's face. On all the faces she could see, on either bridge.

"Kosnett has said he would like to talk, Chevalier," Bausse offered simply. "He sent a Herald. I suggest you speak with the one named *Morninghawk*, as that man seems to be considered little short of a demigod by more than one culture in this Cluster."

Rather than say more, Bausse reached down and cut the line herself. Donatien would have questions, but she had nothing useful for him at this point.

No, she did have one thing.

"Transport, plot and initiate a sailing course that gets *Truhto* out of the way if we are going to witness a battle of the gods," she ordered. "There is nothing we can do at that point except get hurt, and I would still rather make it home to *Kohri* when this is all done."

FIFTY-NINE

HEAVY ESCORT MORNINGHAWK

Makara had settled his scowl in place as he waited for someone on the other side to call.

Kosnett had warned him what was going to happen, or Makara might have pissed himself when it did. His crew were barely holding it together in spite of knowing.

"How?" Keo asked, white. What they already knew.

"*Junkyard*," Makara replied, as if that covered it.

It might. Iveta Beridze scared all of them in deeply visceral ways.

Makara at least was still reasonably certain that she was human, and not some vengeful ghost come for all of their souls.

Reasonably certain.

The *Zerzan Unification* was about to meet the woman though, if they weren't careful. They might have to decide for themselves.

The screen came live.

Male, wearing a uniform identical to the captain of *Truhto*. Chevalier. Weird.

He gave the impression of being tall, but Makara was tall. Muscular, which Makara generally wasn't. Grim.

Makara understood that in his bones.

"This is Chevalier Donatien Fortier," he said in accented Hindi. "To whom am I speaking?"

"I am *Morninghawk*," Makara said, leaving off titles or anything fancy. If it was who he was, that was the legend as he had intentionally formed it. "I speak for First Centurion Kosnett of the *Republic of Aquitaine*. He offers diplomacy instead of violence, if you are willing to meet and talk as equals. You are currently trapped here, and he could have just as easily emerged and opened fire on your ships. He refrains, for now, but if you launch any of your aeromechia, we will assume that you have chosen war and intend to die fighting today, so there will be no mercy offered later. Do I make myself clear?"

All in all, not a bad first impression to make. Kosnett could always charm the man later, after being set up by the *Morninghawk*.

That was what heralds did.

The distance wasn't all that great. Farther than Makara could threaten the man with the falcon firebird on his bow. Presumably optimum for *Junkyard* and her two cohorts. Plus, Makara had two of his three brothers present, the crown prince of *Dalou*, the next Shogun, and *Forktail* if things got ugly.

Kosnett would be protected. *Zerzan* would have to fight their way through *Morninghawk* and *his entire civilization* to threaten the rest of Makara's friends.

Makara let that scowl fill the air.

"Diplomacy?" Fortier asked now, slowly recovering from the horribly bad tactical situation some fool had put himself into by not having a gravity well to hide inside. Or sufficient firepower to keep Kosnett from crushing him like a bug.

"*Aquitaine* stands by its honor, Chevalier," Makara answered. "That brought *Truhto* here, and they will be free to depart later, regardless of what happens to you in the meantime. The First Centurion offers you safe passage aboard a shuttle to land on *Truhto*'s deck that you can meet with him to discuss the future of the Balhee Cluster."

"We are here for only *Yaumgan*," the man sneered.

As if it mattered.

"You threaten all of us with *Unification*, Chevalier," Makara snarled back angrily. "Whether we choose it or not. In that, you have done the unthinkable and unified the nations of the cluster into a single voice, a thing never before witnessed in our history. *You will face us all.*"

He didn't look away from the screen, but he could feel love and strength radiating from Samnang right now. And the rest of these goofballs who had originally chosen to fly with a Fourth Son.

Unlucky. Death-bringer.

Herald of Destruction bearing Kosnett's flag into battle.

Which will it be?

The line froze at their end, so Makara did the same here. He presumed that the Chevalier was currently arguing with the *Unification* Commissioner. And perhaps others. The carrier *Bertev* was dead-centered in Iveta's range, because she had been expecting to find him there. *Hrafsto* was almost an afterthought, but still close enough to be hit by a falcon if Makara needed to.

They were carriers, not warships. Makara didn't think that they could launch enough of those damnable aeromechia fast enough to stop a falcon from slamming home. Not if everyone else opened up at the same time.

"Still no launches from the *Zerzan* ships," Keo said into the silence that had fallen. "*Truhto* is maneuvering off enough that nobody shoots them by mistake, but largely maintaining their distance from *Bertev* and *Rauda*."

Makara nodded. He and Kosnett and Lau had spoken at length about how this was likely to go down. Shortly, either that Chevalier was going to accept *force majeur*, or *Zerzan* was about to commend their souls to Iveta Beridze's wrath.

Makara still wasn't sure which outcome he would find more interesting.

SIXTY

MISSION BRIEF: OPERATIONS BASE LOONG

"All ships," Donatien ordered over the general line. "Do not launch any aeromechia at this time. Repeat, arm and hold, but do not launch."

That much he could do while he sorted all of this out.

Donatien turned to Commissioner Abaroa. Standing, they were almost the same height.

"You must do something!" she demanded.

Donatien gestured vaguely in the direction his doom would take.

"They brought sufficient forces to destroy us, Commissioner," he replied, holding his tongue from blistering her hide.

She was still a Commissioner. One of the leaders of the *Unification* itself. She could have his hide any time she chose. That would at least remove the weight of the decision from his shoulders.

"What can you do?" she asked, modulating her emotion—fear or rage—into something more professional.

"We can launch every aeromechia currently ready," he said. "That amounts to probably about fifty, though I have no doubts that our pilots are powering things up as quickly as they can.

Doing so presumably provokes this Kosnett to unleash everything and everyone he brought with him. And *Morninghawk* said that doing so means we intend to die in battle, so they will not offer us the chance to surrender later. *Truhto* did surrender. Bausse was apparently well enough treated to fly with Kosnett today. Looking at her bow, it is obvious that she attempted to go to Jump when we did, with equal failure. I have two choices, Commissioner. We can go talk to them, hopefully buying time for the aeromechia to prepare and maybe figure out how they broke all of our Jump matrices. Or we can die right now in glorious battle. Kosnett knows where I am, so I can promise you that the first salvo is no longer aimed at *Bertev*. What are your orders?"

Rather than do anything else, he fell to parade rest. Feet shoulder-width apart. Hands crossed behind his back holding each other so he didn't shake an angry fist in her face. His own mien was as calm and composed as he could manage, given the beartrap that had just slammed shut around his leg.

At least that got through to the woman. Truthfully, she had been the aggressive one, demanding the *Kyulle* raid that Donatien had planned. They could share that failure.

He owned this one, right up until she ordered him to do something.

"Nothing?" she asked quietly.

"Talk or die," he nodded. "We don't seem to have other options."

"*Yaumgan* must be destroyed," she hissed.

"That, madam, is not happening today," he rebuked her in a hard tone. "I am trying to save this squadron from being annihilated. Do I have your permission to go aboard *Truhto*? If nothing else, whatever they did has to wear off at some point. Or has an edge that we can sail beyond and eventually escape. I cannot see all those other ships choosing to commit a glorious suicide by starvation, just so they can watch us go first. *There must be a way.*"

Her eyes unfocused and flickered back and forth as he watched. Calculating the odds, the options, the corners. As he was, but she wasn't seeing his face right now.

Donatien supposed that she had never tasted defeat before. The *Unification* was a brutal, ruthless place on the political side. At least the armed forces understood that sometimes you were simply unlucky. That was when a bigger fleet would come back later to finish the job.

Would it matter? Two Overlord Carriers and four Assault should have been sufficient to conquer *Yaumgan*, based on the records of the pirate spy.

But that was just *Yaumgan*. From the transponder codes in front of him, he was also facing the *Republic of Aquitaine*, the *Ewin Principalities*, the *Gloran Empire*, the *Aditi Consensus*, the *Fribourg Empire*, and the *Hegemony of Dalou*, represented by a diamond of similar ships at the tip of Kosnett's formation, ahead of even those damnable escorts with the rapid-firing beams that had so savaged his own pulse torpedo waves before.

This *Morninghawk* had summed it up nicely. *Zerzan* had unified the Balhee Cluster into a single defensive entity. Could the *Unification* overwhelm that?

Possibly. All of the *Unification*. What would *Aquitaine* and *Fribourg* do in response, as that one, lone *Fribourg* ship seemed to be a sister of *Viking* in lines, with even more power available on the scan they had?

His gaze settled on *Unification* Commissioner Murielle Abaroa as she came to some internal conclusion.

"We must meet Kosnett," she said firmly.

"We?" he asked.

"Indeed, Chevalier," she nodded crisply, however fragile she seemed when he looked deep in her eyes. "This has become a contest of nations. I would know all of my foes before I return home and gather up enough ships to unify the entire Balhee Cluster."

He held his tongue rather than respond. Abaroa hadn't

understood the implications of seven nations sailing in a single war formation. The *Unification* had never faced something like that, preferring to bite off small chunks and chew them up.

The entire Cluster would be like a snake eating a water buffalo.

Still, she gave orders when it suited her.

Donatien turned to *Hrafsto's* Chevalier, Elisa Hammerstein, and nodded. He hadn't worked with the woman much, as *Hrafsto* wasn't a carrier built for combat, instead being a mobile base kept in reserve.

But the woman was professional.

"We'll need a shuttle to transport us and a few aides to *Truhto*," Donatien said simply. "Clear it with *Morninghawk* before launch, so they do not think we are starting that battle they have been prepared for."

Hammerstein nodded and went to work. Donatien gestured the Commissioner to follow him and headed aft to the small flight deck that had been left when most of the ship's interior had been given over to base operations.

He had no idea how he would thread this needle.

Heather stepped through the hatch into the lounge where Phil and the others were waiting for her. Through the window behind them, she could see Phil's usual GunShip being readied to carry everyone over to *Truhto*.

He stared at her in surprise, but then nodded. Heather scowled back at the others as her chin came up, daring them to make any comment.

Trust Markus to wolf-whistle at her. He could get away with it. Nobody else.

She had changed uniforms for this meeting. Ambassador Hu had supplied it, and it was a perfect fit, unsurprisingly.

The soft, cotton fabric was in a color the package called strawberry, which turned out to be a soft pink verging over into orange. Knee-length tunic that was unbelted, closed up the front with simple cloth knots instead of buttons, done in white cotton. Two patch pockets on the front for her hands on a cold day, she supposed. The sleeves came just past her wrists but not to her knuckles, and the sides were slit clear to her hip bones so she could sit easily. Matching pants that were baggier than she preferred but not hideous and tucked into knee-high riding boots in black leather with a brushed finish instead of a polish.

She'd even had the barber French braid her hair quickly for this, so that she looked like the *Warlord of Yaumgan*, rather than Command Centurion Lau of the *RAN*.

The First Speaker was remaining aboard *Urumchi*. Phil had turned her down flat when Chang Li asked. Yating Hu and Old Man Wen were accompanying them instead, but *Yaumgan* needed their leader safe in case something happened today and Iveta had to end the current *Zerzan* threat in fire and a graveyard of shattered ships.

And the *Junkyard Bitch* would.

Heather moved to stand next to Old Man Wen and dared him to wolf-whistle at her. That one might, but he held his manners and bowed deeply to her instead, however bright the smile in his eyes.

Hu simply nodded and sighed, but they had offered her this role and that included shutting up and letting her command things. Wen and Hu were her aides today, not the other way around.

Her and Phil, against the universe.

Again.

Markus and *Stunt Dude*, too, with only Sam not joining them for this from the original band of pirates.

Xochitl Dar grinned as she rose and gestured her various marines to the hatch. Today, that included four men in the stylized-though-perfectly-effective combat armor of *Dalou*.

Samurai. With actual swords over one grim shoulder.

They emerged, roughly twenty folks, and boarded the Gunship, with almost no conversation. Everyone was deep in their own heads right now, and Heather didn't feel like breaking the silence just to have noise.

She never wanted noise.

Instead, she sat and meditated as the GunShip crossed over to *Truhto*, coming to rest next to two others, one of which was from *Morninghawk*, having borne the man himself.

A docking hallway extended from the side and covered the GunShip's hatch, providing a soft seal sufficient for now.

Dar lead half of her killers up the hallway and into the lounge at the far end, while Heather and Phil walked side by side and everyone else was behind them.

Harinder was back on the flag bridge, with both Nam and Kohahu, because the last thing the Cluster needed today was to lose the next generation of leaders. *Storm Petrel* was right next to *Urumchi* at the center of the formation for the same reason.

That fool Chevalier could kill her and Phil, but that would put Iveta in command.

Phil's orders at that point would let her go Mongol on them, leaving no two bricks left stacked and heads impaled on sticks, before she salted the earth itself and left this place as a warning to all eternity.

Heather found herself smiling at that image.

Sixty ships back there, all prepared to do exactly that, including thirty-six that answered to the *Warlord of Yaumgan.*

Truhto had unarmed marines meet them, plus Bausse, who did a triple-take when she realized who was walking next to Phil.

Nobody else had seen this uniform before today. Heather hadn't even planned to wear it, until the very last moment when she realized that she had to represent all of *Yaumgan,* just as Morninghawk heralded for the rest of the Cluster while Phil…

Heather supposed that Phil spoke for all of Civilization at this point, if she could say that without sounding like an arrogant git.

Aquitaine had stood up to *Buran* and killed that son of a bitch. First Lord Kasum had retired, then taken up a *Fribourg* position as Admiral of the Blue so he could command their fleets operating in the former *Holding of Man* as that nation slowly disintegrated.

Now, Phil Kosnett was at the wall in Balhee, literally as well as metaphorically.

She nodded. It was right.

"Permission to come aboard?" Heather asked, stepping right up to Bausse and jarring the woman out of her frozen stasis.

Bausse blinked, studied them all, nodded.

"Welcome," she said in a husky voice, as if she didn't trust herself with more words.

Heather grinned. That seemed to help.

"This way," Bausse said, turning and gesturing her people ahead of her.

Dar fell in next with her four samurai, but that was just showing off.

At least Heather hoped so.

The walk wasn't long. *Truhto* had been repaired as well as it could be in the short time available, but Heather could see where new panels had been welded in and left unpainted. The steel they'd used was two different tones, representing all the metal *Urumchi* had supplied from stores, over and above everything *Truhto* had.

The room looked like one of those spaces for officers to plan a campaign, with a big, rectangular table higher than something you comfortably ate off of. Chairs had been brought in, but then stacked in a corner, because sitting would be awkward.

Zerzan had two key players present, with a handful of folks along the far wall behind them. Nobody but Phil's people were armed, and Dar walked slowly around the room, scanning everyone with a handheld unit right now that pinged loudly. Making her point.

Heather came to rest across from the woman on the far side, with those two meters of table separating them. Phil was next to her, facing Chevalier Donatien.

Bausse moved to the top of the table, midway between the two sides and not in the way of words flying back and forth. Or anything else. *Morninghawk* moved opposite Bausse at the bottom of the table, dominating that end of the room with his solid presence.

Phil spoke first.

"I am *Republic of Aquitaine* First Centurion Philip S. Kosnett," he said simply. "Governor Plenipotentiary of *Aquitaine*-aligned forces in this theater of operations. This is Heather Lau, commanding *Yaumgan* forces currently attached to my fleet."

"Chevalier Donatien Fortier," the man replied with a nod, otherwise standing parade rest and grim. "With me is *Unification* Commissioner Murielle Abaroa, representing the *Zerzan Unification* itself."

Phil was obviously feeling feisty. Heather watched him take another step, right up to the edge of the table.

"You attacked *Senza* without warning," he said distinctly. "You attacked *Kyulle* without even a declaration of war beforehand. Depending on legal interpretations, that makes you pirates in some jurisdictions. Did your prisoner tell you my opinion on pirates?"

"We declared war on the *Zerzan Monarchy* five hundred years ago, Kosnett," Abaroa growled back now. "That has not changed since. *Yaumgan* is the successor to the Monarchy, so they remain our enemies."

Rather than rise to the bait, she watched Phil nod knowingly.

"Just so we understand each other, Commissioner," he said. "I could have come out of Jump and blown all of your ships to scrap. Killed every single person in your fleet without a trace of mercy, then had *Truhto* carry my message back to *Kohri* for me. I chose to speak with you today instead, because there must be conversation. War can wait until tomorrow. Or never, if you are willing to listen to reason. Or I can order you all destroyed where your ships stand. Do I make myself clear?"

"What are your demands?" Fortier asked in that brief moment when the Commissioner drew a breath to potentially say something ugly and stupid, given the power imbalance in the room.

"My demands are peace between *Zerzan* and *Yaumgan*," Phil

said, waving a hand as those two started to speak. "I will make my case. You will hear it, understand it, and think on it. Then you can decide what you want to do about it. Are you listening?"

"Go ahead," Fortier spoke, eyes dark with some emotion that never made it to his face as Heather watched.

"I am reasonably certain that the *Zerzan Monarchy* was composed of some seriously shitty people," Phil said firmly, nodding. "I've had to deal with some of the more backward elements of places like *Fribourg*, but that nation has since emerged from a social revolution caused by several ugly wars and are looking forward to a better future. In that, I happily grant that your ancestors were correct to rise up and overthrow the *Monarchy*. Probably even to execute those mostly responsible for things. However, that was five centuries ago."

Heather noted the way the two strangers absorbed Phil's compact history lesson. She'd spoken at length with Hu and Wen before this and Phil was heavily glossing over certain bits.

However, everyone involved at the time was long since dead and presumably burning in whatever hell those various cultures had ascribed to at the time.

Deservedly.

Phil had paused, but Fortier and Abaroa didn't take his bait. Probably a smart move on their part.

"I have an entirely different problem today," Phil continued after holding for three beats. "*Yaumgan* is not the *Zerzan Monarchy*. It represents a handful of clans, from two minor planets, that managed to escape whatever justice was coming for them on that date. They fled the *Unification*. And continued to flee ahead of you, moving inward for most of a century, before they came to hide here for four more."

He paused, then leaned forward and tapped a single finger on the table for emphasis.

"Nobody alive today is guilty of any of the crimes you wish to punish them for," he said in a hard, deadly voice. "Everyone on your proscription lists died more than four hundred years ago. Everyone. You are dealing with the twelfth or more generations of descendants here. What have they done to warrant your attacks?"

He leaned back. Stepped back now, standing shoulder to shoulder with her. Heather had fallen into a parade rest similar to Fortier's.

"The *Unification* will not rest until they are all punished," Abaroa growled.

"Who?" Heather snapped angrily at the woman, unable to hold her tongue anymore. "Who are you going to punish? Random strangers on the street who might happen to be related to someone who one of your distant ancestors hated? Any planet that might have a drop of blood from anybody who was ever part of the *Zerzan Monarchy*? Or are you just going to attack and destroy *Yaumgan* because that's all that the *Unification* really is? Predators? Then what? You move on to the rest of the Cluster?"

She stopped there, feeling her heart pounding with rage. It was probably a really good idea that a high table kept her from climbing over there and strangling those people with her bare hands.

Heather could still taste it.

Fortier's face didn't have the pure rage that Abaroa's did, but he was a sailor, not a politician. In that, Heather felt the faintest hint of camaraderie. Barely.

Bausse spoke, shattering the brittle silence like the bell tolling the apocalypse.

"When did the *Unification* go wrong?" she asked in a quiet voice that still seemed to echo off all the walls like an alert siren.

Everyone turned to the woman.

"Wrong?" Abaroa demanded.

"Yes, wrong," Bausse said, her chin coming up in exactly the same way Heather's would have. "We have been seeking the *Monarchy* for centuries. Along the way, we have conquered and unified how many other civilizations that committed no crime beyond possibly being a place those ancestors passed while fleeing us? To what purpose?"

"Empire," Phil said.

Bausse nodded grimly, then turned back to her superiors. At least superiors on paper.

"Kosnett and Lau have spoken with me about the arc of empires, Commissioner," she said. "I have given much thought to the *Unification*. It started out as a way to rebuild the *Zerzan Monarchy* into a new things, representing all those people who had not been born aristocrats. Commoners and slaves alike. That took a generation to build and two more to secure. Call it a century. Then what?"

"What do you mean, Bausse?" Fortier asked tentatively.

"We spent a century building the *Unification*," the woman replied, her voice finding strength now. "Then we went on to spend the next four expanding it to unify anybody who stood in our way. What was the justification? Or was there any beyond conquering the galaxy? As Kosnett notes, everybody our ancestors wanted dead is dead, either punished or of old age while hiding light-centuries from home as fugitives. What is the purpose of the *Unification* at that point? What is the justification? Why are we here?"

"The *Monarchy* must be punished!" Abaroa raged.

Fortier remained silent.

"The *Monarchy* is gone," Heather interjected tartly. "How many people did you execute? How many served life sentences? How many were cast down from their pretty mansions to live out their days in proscribed squalor? Who is left on your list? Or are we back at the top, with you demanding to punish every other planet in the galaxy for not immediately asking to join the *Unification*? Which brings up an interesting question. If the *Unification* is such a great and grand thing, how many worlds demanded to join you, instead of doing so at *gunpoint*?"

Abaroa might have been struck mute. Fortier rocked back on

his heels as though Heather had slapped him across the face with an open palm.

I'd use a closed fist, bucko. Followed up by several kicks to the ribs.

She smiled harshly at the two. Let it smolder angrily, like a lit fuse.

"I'm here because if we cannot come to understand one another, then *Aquitaine* and *Fribourg* will have no choice but to declare war on the *Unification*," Phil barked sharply at them. "I'd much rather fight over your worlds today than wait for you to come to mine in a decade. We've already defeated *Fribourg* and made them an ally. *Buran*, the so-called *Holding of Man*, was destroyed next. I came to Balhee as an explorer, but I have also fought many wars in my time. I know how to annihilate your aeromechia swarms. If there cannot be peace between *Zerzan* and my ally in *Yaumgan, and* the entire Balhee Cluster, there will be war. We killed a god, after all. A mere *Unification* will not tax the *RAN*."

Heather watched the knowledge dawn in Fortier's eyes first. That cold dread that none of his ships could escape Phil's wrath if he unleashed Iveta right now.

She flashed back to a conversation with Bausse, on *Urumchi*, where that woman had expressed her terrible shock at what the *Aquitaine* ships had been able to do, compounded later by the knowledge that *Urumchi* was a Survey Dreadnought and *Viking* a Survey Cruiser, rather than being front-line warships. *Skuodas* was even more dangerous, because they still had a Bubble Gun on the bow, where Phil had his arboretum.

That war would be ugly and one-sided, just as quickly as *Aquitaine* could build out a string of forward operating bases to supply the fleets that could hop from world to world, blowing up carriers and their aeromechia.

Ending the *Unification*. Just as they had ended the *Holding of Man.*

Again, Commissioner Abaroa started to speak. To rage

perhaps, as her right hand came up to point an angry finger at Phil.

Bausse interrupted her.

"No," Bausse said sharply. "You have not answered my question, Commissioner."

Again, every head turned to Bausse Aublahzieu.

"When did the *Unification* go wrong?" Bausse asked forcefully. Angrily.

"You will be removed from command, Chevalier," Abaroa snarled. "Insubordination. Possibly treason, if you have been conspiring with these enemy agents."

"You have not answered my question," Bausse repeated. "Can you? Can you even admit that we might have made a mistake, anywhere, at any point? Or will you Court Martial me and demand my head for asking questions you cannot answer? I will be happy to repeat this conversation. It is being recorded. Answer me!"

Fortier's mouth opened to speak, but nothing came out. Abaroa's simply fell open and hung there like a corpse on a gibbet, slowly swinging on an invisible breeze.

Bausse turned this way now and nodded.

"First Centurion, at first I was furious with you for your words," she said. "For what you and Heather asked of me, because I had no ready answers. You offered your honor to me and to *Truhto*, then went above and beyond that to make sure that as many of my crew as could be here were in a position to go home, rather than to die on some foreign world. I have given your words much thought. The Chevalier and the Commissioner have not had the time to stop and ponder those underlying assumptions that have shaped us as a people."

"What would you suggest?" Heather stepped in and asked, calm and contained, in spite of all the emotions swirling like tides around her feet.

She was the *Warlord of Yaumgan* today. Phil was an outsider, even now, but Heather wore a strawberry tunic with white lacing.

"*Truhto* should return to *Kyulle*, Heather," Bausse said. "Carrying with me the Commissioner and Chevalier Fortier. The rest of the fleet can return to base back home while *Yaumgan* and *Zerzan* come to some understanding of one another. Hopefully, it will not require a war to the death between our cultures. As *Morninghawk* has noted, *Yaumgan* is not alone, but stands with all of their neighbors to resist a *Unification* that may not be necessary."

Fortier surprised Heather by stepping to the edge of the table on his side.

"Bausse is correct," he said. "I ask for your pledge of honor that we will all be allowed to return home after such discussions, regardless of the outcome."

"Granted easily, Chevalier," Heather spoke. "Bausse can speak of the meaning of honor to the *Republic*. We promised to see her home. We will see you home as well if you would rather depart than fight. In my best outcome, you would also carry an ambassador from *Aquitaine* as well as representatives of the Five Nations of the Cluster. We did not come here for war and conquest, but to trade. To meet our distant neighbors to the west. You are even farther than that, but we have spent the last year turning strangers into friends in the Cluster. There is no reason that the *Unification* and the *Republic* must be enemies, but Phil's point stands. Your behavior demands that the sins of the fathers, however many generations removed from the present, be borne by the sons and daughters. We will not accept that logic. Period. Phil has taught Command Ethics to cadets and senior officers alike, because he is among the best there is at such a thing. Your behavior is *unethical*, Chevalier and Commissioner, however *moral* you might think it. We ask that you reconsider. That you carry such thoughts home and ask yourselves what the *Unification* truly stands for in the modern age."

Heather wondered, as she fell silent, if the Commissioner had suffered some sudden medical event that had struck her mute. Or paralyzed her. The rage was there, but held in check.

That was good, because the only weapons in the room were with Dar and her people.

And Dar would not hesitate if provoked.

Fortier turned to the Commissioner. Paused, as if looking for the words.

"They could have destroyed us, Commissioner," he said.

Heather nodded as those two fought a silent battle of wills.

Could have? Still could.

Do you have the courage to change, sirrah?

SIXTY-TWO

MISSION BRIEF: OPERATIONS BASE LOONG

Donatien thought about what he would do when his career was over. When Abaroa had him cashiered in disgrace when they got home. For the crime of…what?

Asking questions? Listening? Wondering if Bausse and the woman across the table from him were right?

Kosnett could have landed and opened fire so quickly that all of his ships would have been destroyed. Annihilated to the last escape pod had he wished.

And had chosen not to. Had bent over backwards to offer Donatien and his entire command the option of returning home alive.

All they had to do was talk to the strangers.

Looking at Abaroa's face, that seemed to be one of the highest crimes possible.

When had the *Unification* gone wrong? Wasn't that what Bausse had asked?

And she had spent weeks with the outsiders, apparently being treated well enough that her and her crew were being sent home, even if Donatien had to die in battle today.

Sometimes, that was part of the oath you took. And

repeated, every time you were promoted to greater responsibility. That it might be necessary to die in battle today.

This wasn't even battle. It would be the chicken resisting the farmer. Donatien had read the grimness in Kosnett's voice. The rage in Lau's.

He focused on Abaroa now.

"We can return to *Hrafsto* and fight, if those are your orders, Commissioner," he said in front of all these witnesses. "Or we can accept their hospitality and fly with Bausse to *Kyulle* and at least listen to what they have to say. Kosnett has promised to return us home later, regardless. Which will it be?"

He didn't lay out any other options. There were none. Dying was implicit in fighting.

Dying for your honor was one thing. Throwing your life away stupidly was something entirely else.

Her mouth opened, then closed with no words emerging.

Donatien nodded and took a step back. She needed time to process things. He understood that. Seeing *Truhto* with Bausse Aublahzieu in command had been the point when he began to question certain assumptions, so he had been granted a few hours head start on the Commissioner.

Instead, he pivoted and took a step closer to Bausse, not ignoring the Commissioner, but giving her space.

"How are you?" he asked Bausse. Not a friend, but perhaps his closest Chevalier. And best.

"Better than expected," she said quietly. "*Truhto* is repaired enough to return to the yard for formal repairs. Crew casualties were far less than initially predicted, because Kosnett sent every medic he had, then evacuated all who needed it to his ships, while delivering engineers to repair things. At present, fourteen crew remain with Kosnett, seven too injured to move and seven more who volunteered to stay with them so they weren't alone. All the rest flew with me today, alive or dead."

"And guards?" he asked, glancing over at Kosnett and Lau in surprise.

"They departed at the one stop we made to organize for this attack," she nodded. "I could have sailed directly home, but Kosnett asked me to be here, that perhaps I could help smooth things with your force."

Donatien blinked and felt all his processing start over again. Would the *Unification* have done such a thing? Would he?

Then he hung his head because Donatien understood that he would not have. That he would have rounded up all the crew of a captured ship and put them in a reeducation camp to be taught where they had gone wrong.

Even if wrong could be summed up in *Resisting Unification*.

What was the word both Bausse and Kosnett had used? Empire.

The *Unification* was an empire, in everything but name, wasn't it? Was that where they'd gone wrong? Power?

It did corrupt. Everything, eventually.

And he wouldn't have treated *Aquitaine* prisoners well at all, to say nothing of *Yaumgan* citizens who fell into his hands.

He pivoted again to face the two strangers. Kosnett looked like an angry patriarch from some religious text, missing only the beard and wild hair, but possessed of the lightning bolts in his eyes.

Lau...

Her scowl was rage itself, where Abaroa's anger was a pissy squirrel chittering in a tree. Lau's eyes promised that nobody in his fleet save Bausse would ever return home. Ever.

Because he had started this. And she would finish it.

Donatien turned back to the Commissioner, seeing the woman in entirely different eyes than even five minutes ago.

Petty. That was her anger. Juvenile, in the context of things that could only exist in black and white, with no shading allowed.

Good and evil.

When had the *Unification* gone wrong?

He stepped closer to the woman, drawing her eyes back from

wherever they had gone, until they locked on his. He came to rest and waited.

Abaroa turned to Kosnett and Lau.

"We would prefer peace," *Morninghawk* spoke abruptly from the end of the table before she could, his voice deep and heavy. "All intelligent, right-thinking people do. I have given much thought over the last year to the way of life that existed before Kosnett showed us a better way to build our civilization. The piracy and crime that was accepted, because nobody knew any better. The loss of life and wealth cast away frivolously because we had not matured as a people to demand better of ourselves. Kosnett demanded better of us. When victorious, he was magnanimous. When threatened, we went for our enemy's throats. I am *Morninghawk*, and I can speak of such things. You have only heard the words of a fool pirate who never matured past those teenage rebellions. Balhee is not far past them, but we move. And we will unify in our own way, because Kosnett demanded that we grow up and become responsible citizens of the galaxy. That is the challenge I will lay before you, my friends. Are you capable of growing up?"

Donatien had turned to the man, so he was facing the correct direction to see the Commissioner sag. He caught her arm, but she did not collapse. The sound that emerged from her seemed to come from the depths of the woman's soul.

Raw pain.

She straightened a moment later, though he remained close. Abaroa looked over at him and blinked.

Bausse stepped around the table now, coming to rest on Abaroa's far side.

"Commissioner, are you well?" she asked in a careful voice. "Should I summon a medic?"

Abaroa drew a breath.

"I will live," she said in a shaky voice.

Donatien heard the hope in her tones that such would last longer than the next hour.

Longer than it took to order *Bertev* and *Rauda* to launch everything in order to die gloriously in battle.

Movement across the way caused them to turn. The older of Lau's two aides had stepped up next to her. He wore formal robes similar to hers, but still gave off a hint of grunginess in spite of being cleanshaven.

"*Yaumgan* is destroyed," he announced, surprising most of the room, save Lau's other aide and the one known as *Morninghawk*, to look at the surprised faces across the table. "Just as the *Zerzan Monarchy* fell when our ancestors flew into darkness, the *Yaumgan Domain* could not survive meeting Kosnett. Already, the Scholars argue with great energy—and some pretty good profanities—about the thing that will replace *Yaumgan*, because our entire civilization was already wrong before you arrived, cousin. We will have to build a new thing to replace it. This is the invitation to join us in considering how to best serve Humanity."

"Cousin?" Commissioner Abaroa spoke now. "Did you call me *cousin*?"

"You are," the old man nodded serenely. "Once, we were all part of the *Zerzan Monarchy*, same as you were. Then you became the *Unification* and we transformed ourselves into the *Domain of Yaumgan*. We are still cousins, however many generations removed. Just as we are cousins with *Morninghawk* and Lau. Galactic civilization will make many demands upon us, demands that *Yaumgan* was not prepared to address. Ergo, we must throw down *Yaumgan* and build something new, something better to replace it. What will *Zerzan* do to make the galaxy a better place tomorrow?"

Donatien blinked, walloped yet again by philosophical inquiries he did not feel adequate to face.

But face them he must. Kosnett had understood the black and white nature of *Zerzan* logic, and forced them into a hard, binary choice. Donatien Fortier had been unprepared to face it.

Kosnett nodded and stepped back up to the edge of the table.

"I do not care what form all of your futures take," he said grimly. Evenly. "I care that everyone has the right to choose for themselves, rather than having it forced upon them by conquest. The *Unification* will behave, or I will bring it down myself. You can be cousins at family reunions. You can ignore each other until hell freezes over. But you will not launch attacks against Balhee Cluster worlds if you wish to survive my wrath. Those are my words, Commissioner. You have heard them. You have heard Lau and *Morninghawk*. Scholar Wen speaks for the philosophers who lead *Yaumgan* today, but do not order her or me. I am done speaking. What will it be?"

Donatien felt the floor threaten to open beneath his feet and cast both him and Abaroa into hell.

The Commissioner drew a heavy breath and straightened out her jacket. She turned to Bausse, on her far side, and saw something. It was there when she turned back and looked into Donatien's eyes.

She nodded to herself. Perhaps to eternity.

The woman squared herself up to Kosnett, and Donatien wondered how much longer he had to live.

"We will travel to *Kyulle*," Commissioner Abaroa said in a firm, if ragged voice. "We will meet with the former *Yaumgan* and try to understand each other, five centuries removed from the revolution that defined both of our families. I make no promises as to the rest of the *Unification*, but I will listen with an open mind."

"That, Commissioner, is all anybody can ask," Kosnett replied with a matching nod.

EPILOGUES

EPILOGUE: THE PHILOSOPHERS

Heather wouldn't say that she was excited about the strawberry tunic that had become her uniform recently, but she had grown comfortable in it. Didn't twitch too hard when she looked down and realized that she wasn't wearing the black and green uniform that had been her life for more than twenty years.

Yaumgan had still needed her as the terrible Warlord, but a month of talking with Commissioner Abaroa and Donatien Fortier had shown considerable progress.

Honestly, though, it was probably the arrival of full fleets from *Aditi*, *Dalou*, and *Gloran* that had gotten their attention. Even King Doysan IV had sent a force from *Ewinhome* to supplement Prince Kalidoona, but Heather was willing to bet that there had been some level of blackmail involved first.

All one had to do was look out a porthole and count all the new hulls orbiting close by and ready to go *Junkyard* on the next fool who attacked *Kyulle*.

Or anywhere in the Cluster.

She found herself in front of such a porthole now, gazing off into space. *Urumchi* was barely close enough to be a longsword hanging nearby like Damocles. The others were there as well.

She caught her reflection in the glass and nodded. Her hair was coming in gray underneath now, but she was forty-three, and her hair had stayed black longer than her mother's or either grandmother. She had lines in her face that hadn't been there two years ago, that moment when all this had really transitioned from being theoretical to practical.

To sailing into the darkness.

A chime at her hatch. Heather shook her head and moved to it. Time was growing short. The party would be starting soon. Thank all the gods who might listen that it wasn't for her.

All she had to do was show up and smile at everyone.

Heather opened the hatch and got her first shock, although in retrospect she probably should have expected those two troublemakers to find each other eventually.

"May we enter?" Old Man Wen asked with a smile wide enough to fill the night.

Heather stepped back and gestured him and *Stunt Dude* into her quarters. Unlike Phil, she had put her foot down and demanded a small space for herself on the station. Sleeping chamber in back with an en-suite head, plus a small chamber in front for hosting quiet conversations. Such as this.

She moved to the only chair and pointed them to the only couch.

"Technically," Old Man Wen began, "I suppose that I should ask Phil, but *Stunt Dude* and I both agreed that we should speak with you and get your opinion on a few topics, in your various roles here in the Cluster."

Heather couldn't help but roll her eyes at these two goofballs, but she'd known *Stunt Dude* for more than a decade at this point. And they were right.

Command Centurion. Businesswoman. War Goddess. Warlord.

Both men laughed like juvenile delinquents.

"Heather, they have offered me a most interesting position,

here at *Kyulle*," *Stunt Dude* spoke, but she interrupted before he could say anymore.

"You deal with Sam directly," she said sternly. "I refuse to intercede there."

From the looks the two men shared, and the laughter, somebody was paying off on a bet when this was done.

"Already done," *Stunt Dude* laughed. "As with other things, she is generally in favor. However, I have a more complicated question for you, in your guise as Phil's Right Hand and Soothsayer."

"Go on," she prodded.

"I would like to stay," he nodded. "Having spent more than a year on *Li Jing*, I probably know *Yaumgan* culture better than anybody in the *Republic* right now. And I had a long head start on *Zerzan*, being assigned to work with Bausse up front. The problem is that I'm pretty sure Phil wants me back at *Ladaux*, at least long enough to tell a bunch of ambassadors and bureaucrats everything I know. How do I square that circle without pissing everybody off?"

She considered the implications. She was probably next on that list behind him, having taken a foreign posting, however odd and part-time it was, as Warlord of *Yaumgan*.

"Sam's willing to be separated from you for a whole year?" she asked.

"I'm not sure I'd go that far, Heather," he shrugged. "But she understands that it might be the cost we have to pay."

"I'll do you one better, then," Heather grinned. She turned to Old Man Wen and watched his face suddenly grow guarded. He'd learned to watch himself around her, though she'd never had a reason to snap at the man. "Offer Phil a replacement for his current Chief Medical Officer and hire Sam for something around here."

Useful, watching the man's eyes blink too rapidly as he digested that concept. *Stunt Dude*'s smile suggested another bet paying off. She wondered who was going to get rich off this conversation.

"That way," Heather continued, "we can train someone on all our medical technology, so that they know what parts they want to buy or trade for later. And vice versa. I'm certain you have all manner of interesting kit that we might want to acquire. The two lovebirds get to stay together, and whoever you send home with Phil gets to be the victim when everyone wants to pump them for information. I suggest you add a couple of historians, in addition to your ambassador and Phil's doc."

"Would he go for it?" Wen asked carefully.

"The worst that can happen is that he says no on Sam," Heather replied. "*Stunt Dude* is technically a civilian with a high security clearance, so Phil can't really say much there. Sam's got a contract with the *RAN*, but this would fall well under diplomatic exchange, since she was originally born and trained in the *Holding of Man*. That would eventually make her one of the best trained doctors out there, having seen the inner workings of three different stellar civilizations. Hell, maybe you eventually convince *Zerzan* to play nice and she could go there as well. Weirder things have happened."

"I will inquire," Wen nodded soberly. "Which brings me to my next question, one that *Stunt Dude* informs me should be asked in an informal setting, and private, so that you can chew my ass out without everyone else having to watch and listen."

Heather stirred. Suppressed the growl that wanted to emerge, but only barely.

"Go on," she said.

Wen straightened his shoulders.

"The First Speaker has asked me to inquire if you yourself would be interested in a position with our government. Continuing to wear that uniform and training our people in…*Stunt Dude*, what was the term?"

"Fleet Strategic Operations," *Stunt Dude* said precisely.

Both men recoiled at her scowl, but Heather couldn't help

that. She wanted to go home. *Ladaux*. A fourth stripe, as Phil generally contended she was overdue for. Possibly a fifth, one of these days. Depending on who was the next First Lord of the Fleet.

At the same time, wasn't that what they were offering her right now? A fifth stripe, in strawberry and white? Possibly a sixth, equivalently, as what these two were suggesting would probably look more like First Lord of their entire Fleet.

Warlord of Yaumgan. Or something like that.

Heather leaned forward and focused on Wen.

"You do understand the implications, yes?" she asked. "Fleet *Tactical* Operations is maneuver and combat. Training teams to work together against enemy ships and forces. Dao Zhiou would be excellent at that."

"And *Strategic* Operations is the person deciding how to build out our defensive forces, Heather," Wen nodded. "What choices to make about the next generation of ships that we very obviously need to build, not just to replace the massive casualties that the *Unification* inflicted, but how we incorporate new tech that *Aquitaine* has developed. Hell, if I thought we could hire the man, I'd offer Bedrov a job. From everything that Phil and *Stunt Dude* have told me, he might be the most dangerous starship architect in the universe currently."

"You would not be wrong with that assumption, Wen," she replied.

Then she stopped and considered things. Bedrov should be in his early fifties now. Crown Naval Designer to *Corynthe*, but he maintained an office in Penmerth on *Ladaux*, as well as a second one he had had to rebuild from scratch on *St. Legier* after the planet was nearly destroyed.

But nobody over there worked with giant fighting robots that flew through space, from those aeromechia that Fortier had sent home up to *Zhang Gualao*, nearby in orbit.

"He might actually do it, if approached correctly," Heather said. "Your stuff would intrigue the hell out of the man, and I could see him mounting something like a Type-3-Pulse as a fist on an escort, with Pulse-Twos for eyes."

"Thus, do you make my case for me, Heather," Wen said. "We would not know to even consider such things, because we have lived too isolated an existence here."

"Still planning to seal off the passage at *Loong*?" she asked.

"Quietly, we have located a ship mounting a tractor beam," he nodded. "We will study the technology and I presume that we will be able to improve it significantly enough to move several such small moons as you faced at *Vilahana*, down into the narrowest part of the gullet. As with the lagoon at *Meerut*, so *Stunt Dude* has explained, we can build a platform designed to engage ships forced out of Jump."

"Talk to Iveta about how to defend it," Heather said. "She'll have plans from *Meerut* that can be adapted quite easily."

"Again, you know things, Warlord," he smiled. "We would like to take advantage of that expertise. Of our friends, and all they bring to the table, now that *Yaumgan* has been destroyed and a new thing is busy being born. *Aditi* has their *Consensus*. We do not feel that we should join it, but perhaps the two can negotiate a third thing that will subsequently draw in the other three."

Heather nodded. She did know things. And could fill in holes while she was here, but she also knew that Phil was ready to go home. They had stretched their orders significantly in remaining this long, but the First Lord would also understand the good that Phil was doing.

The future he was making possible by traveling to each of the five capitals. Six, with *Meerut* having become the prototype of a neutral open port to trade with all sides. As it might yet be, if *Hollywood* and the others managed to get everything lined up right.

She turned to *Stunt Dude* and noted how calm he was. The man had grown comfortable with himself over the years, from the young, almost-frenetic Dragoon she first met on *CS-405*.

He had become a philosopher, and thus fit in well with these folks.

Heather didn't know where she belonged, save on the bridge of a starship in command.

At least today. Eventually, she would be on a flag bridge instead. Or teaching. Or retired somewhere, trying to reinvent herself after a life in uniform, like so many of them did.

She took a breath and turned back to Wen.

"I am not saying no immediately," she offered. "I am not saying yes, either, but I will not immediately, categorically reject the offer. I'm not done with Phil, and I will see *Urumchi* and my people home. After that, I do not know."

Both men nodded.

"And your current uniform?" Wen asked, gesturing to the strawberry and white that had grown comfortable.

"I will wear it tonight for the party," she said. "Tomorrow, I will put it away in my closet. At least for now."

They nodded again and stood, accepting that for the dismissal it was. She saw them to the hatch and out, closing it and locking it behind them so she could return to her chair and think.

What did she want next?

EPILOGUE: THE BIRTHDAY PARTY

Phil nodded to Dar and followed the woman out of the quarters he had been assigned here on the station. Markus followed, having held up both hands to confirm ten fingers when he entered. That the man had made it through all this with both of his hands intact was a testimony to how little he ever wanted to return to engineering, though Phil wasn't sure what would happen next.

That would be retirement for Phil, when *Urumchi* made it home to *Ladaux*. To at least a few weeks of sitting on his back porch or in the living room, looking out over the hills and forests spread out below the hillside that was his backyard. Maybe he'd get himself a puppy.

Tomorrow's issues.

He followed Dar.

The walk was short. A couple of corridors and a quick elevator ride that deposited him at the entrance to one of the largest public spaces available on the station. Previously, it had held small sporting events and temporary markets.

Today it was filled with people. Lots of them.

Almost, but not quite all of them, because Iveta had put her foot down and kept her A-team on the bridge and flag bridge of

Urumchi, having learned the lessons of Baron Russand's attack on *Meerut*.

Iveta had the flag tonight. Everyone else was here.

Some fool had even hung a hand-painted sign from two pillars, a meter tall and several wide, black letters on a green background.

Happy Birthday, Phil!

Not the way he had envisioned his forty-seventh birthday unfolding, but it would do. He should have already been home by now, save for things outside of his control.

But not outside his ability.

First Speaker Li—Chang—walked up to greet him, with Ambassador Hu on one side and *Morninghawk* on her other.

It made an appropriate tableau. Hu had been the one they sent to *Aditi*, when it became obvious that a stranger had come to town. They had feared *Zerzan*, and found *Aquitaine* instead.

Morninghawk, because he was *Morninghawk*.

All three bowed warmly as they came to rest. Phil returned it. He had made many friends here, even in the short time he had known this former jock who used to grip a big, steel ball on the end of a chain and throw the damned thing competitively. Extremely competitively.

"How go things?" Phil asked loosely.

He'd avoided most of the negotiations with Abaroa and Fortier, other than being a menacing presence in the background to remind them to behave. Remarkably, everyone generally had, save for occasional screaming matches of the type that resulted when highly committed people ran into their peers and had to carve out a new space in which to work.

Again, *Morninghawk* had been the most useful person in the room, because he could speak of *Dalou That Was*, as well as support Kohahu Kugosu—as little as she needed it—when that youngster spoke of *Dalou That Would Be*.

It was too soon to know if the *Unification* would fully behave, but *Yaumgan* had put a squadron of ships at the *Loong* entrance as they worked to seal it off, with runners specifically tasked to bring the message if a new *Unification* fleet arrived.

By now, the rest of the *Unification* Commission knew of Phil's ultimatum. And the mass of firepower that had been assembled over *Kyulle* if they chose to ignore it.

From never having been visited by outsider vessels to hosting a remarkable fraction of the combined firepower in the entire Cluster, it had been an interesting six months.

Chang Li smiled at Phil's question and turned to look over her left shoulder.

Phil could see Kira Zaman and Kohahu talking to Bausse. That ought to be interesting, especially as those first two had gone into private business on the side and would bring *Dalou* and *Gloran* along with them in time.

"Well, so far," Chang Li noted, turning back. "It helps that they have only memories and tales of the *Monarchy*, while we have evolved so far as a civilization that we've had to take Bausse and the others to museums so they could see those things they had been expecting when walking down any street."

Phil noted that he called her Bausse, instead of Chevalier Aublahzieu. That was good. It suggested a breaking down of the old barriers that kept people at a fussy distance. Relaxing.

Speaking of…

He turned to Markus and noted that the man already had a can of juice in his hand, cracking it and handing it to Phil.

He hoped that he wasn't getting predictable, but Markus had been with him for a very long time, and ought to be able to get that much ahead of him. Just as Harinder did, even as she looked up from some conversation across the way and caught his eye with a grin.

"However," *Morninghawk* spoke up now. "It is your party, Phil. Your birthday. Heather has told me of the events at *Ladaux* before you left, so we have made arrangements to have every command centurion and their equivalent present for a picture that you can take to the First Lord as a book end. That's first.

Then you will cut the cake, several of us will drink wine and tell extravagant lies, and eventually, return to our various duties."

Phil nodded, suddenly overcome with emotion. It had been one hell of a two-year stretch, topping even *CS-405* in that way. He smiled and let *Morninghawk* lead him inward to where a photographer had his equipment already on a tripod. *Morninghawk* and others began to yell, and the crowd sorted itself into two large groups.

"No!" Phil yelled, gesturing to the folks moving away to come back. "All of you in the picture. I could not have done this without every single one of you, command centurion or not. First Lord Naoumov had just the command centurions because of the space, and because it was a way of saying goodbye before I left. I want all of you in this picture for her, because this is us— all of us—saying hello to the rest of the galaxy. Bausse, that includes you, Donatien, and Murielle, just as Kira, Kohahu, Nam, and everyone else. You are my friends, and I want the folks back home to know that. More of them will come later. Think of this as that first family reunion, because I want there to be others."

Surprise on many faces, but fewer than he'd expected. People had wanted to be part of this. To be able to point to the picture and tell their grandkids that they'd been here today, when that sort of thing would matter later. That should be their right.

He ended up standing between Heather in her strawberry uniform and *Morninghawk*, with Chang Li and Bausse both standing close by. All the people he was on first name basis with squished in close, even though the photographer worked her way backwards until a wall intruded.

She took several pictures, then proclaimed herself happy.

"What's next?" she called.

"Now, I want one with my squadron," Phil replied. "*Hollywood*, that includes you, even though you claim to be a civilian here. Esser Jones, wherever you are, you, too, because *Varmint* was the first one to fly an *RAN* flag here."

People shuffled around, with a lot of good-natured ribbing and laughter that warmed his soul.

Heather. Barnaby. All the corvette commanders: Galia Abbasi, Erle Kuiper, Radoslava Dobrev, Kotone Uehara, Mitre Saitou, Nanami Satou, and Isabèl Pan.

Kaur Singh. Makara Omarov who would be forever known to history as *Morninghawk*. Gotzon Solo. Adham Khan. Xue Dao Zhiou.

Hollywood Ward and Esser Jones. Lin Na Tai.

Even Bausse Aublahzieu, Donatien Fortier, and Murielle Abaroa suffered to stand next to him and be immortalized, in descending increments of warmth that he had expected. Abaroa would have to stand before the rest of the *Unification* and make whatever case she intended, but Fortier had moved to Phil's side of neutral and he could truly count Bausse as a friend and comrade after everything.

Finally, one picture that was insisted upon by Kaur and others who knew the story.

Phil, Heather, *Stunt Dude*, Sam, and Markus.

The Pirates.

"Enough, damn it," Phil roared. "I want some cake."

He'd done formal. They could relax now. Talk. Plan. Scheme to get rich or travel the entire galaxy.

Phil had won.

The folks of the Balhee Cluster were finally talking.

EPILOGUE: MORNINGHAWK
MOUNT PENMERTH, DALOU COLONY URWEL

Makara Omarov, Lord Morninghawk, sat on the overlook at the corner of his hilltop, looking down on the river below and the forest that he had designated as a game preserve park so that the city on his left expanded all other directions and this particular view was never spoiled.

Behind him, a palace castle in stone was taking shape, but it would be years being born and completed. Next to it, the wooden house where he and Samnang lived for now as rulers of the several thousand folks that had come to live on *Urwel*. Or remained when he'd chased out most of that last group of squatters.

He sipped some tea and smiled at Samnang, before turning to look at Phil and Iveta also seated up here and enjoying the view. Heather had the flag, up on *Urumchi*, and had insisted that the *Junkyard Bitch* be the one to make this final port call after all the parties and events celebrating around here were done.

She had been the first to notice him, after Phil.

The two outsiders smiled back at him and sipped their tea. The late afternoon sun was still warm and night wouldn't fall for another few hours, but he could smell the finality in the air.

"We really did it, didn't we?" he asked Phil, including

Samnang and Iveta in the question, but addressing himself to the man who had driven it all.

How might the Cluster have turned out if he hadn't met Phil at *Vilahana*? Or if the Shogun had chosen to send one of his favored captains to *Aditi* in response to the call to hunt pirates? Or if Makara had been required to go through with his sacrifice at *Meerut*, when *Wulfa* set course to ram *Urumchi* and *Morninghawk* had plotted an intercept course to ram the pirate instead?

"We did," Phil nodded.

From the look in his eyes, Phil was having those same thoughts.

"I know we've talked about it, but you've never really answered the question directly, Phil," Makara said. "What happens when you get home? Where does Balhee fit into the scheme of things?"

Phil watched him for a long moment, then turned to Iveta and nodded to the woman, some unspoken message passing. She nodded back.

"I will share a secret with you, *Lord Morninghawk*," Phil began, but Makara interrupted him.

"Here, please, I would like to be Makara," he said. "*Morninghawk* is that dire legend that will be deified next to you in another century, Phil, when we are all gone. Let us today just be friends."

"Makara," Phil nodded. "This is one of those secrets that you two might need to take to your graves, but at the same time, it will help you frame out the rest of your lives in ways that I think will be beneficial."

Makara recoiled in shock at Phil's words. At the openness in the man's face right now.

What terrible burden would Phil place upon his shoulders?

Makara would bear it. He was *The Morninghawk*. An escort's duty was to carry such loads. In that, nothing would change, save that Phil would return home and no longer need *Morninghawk* on his bow.

Instead, Makara would protect his flank from *Urwel* as much as possible.

He was also *The Herald*.

He nodded to Phil to continue.

"One of my orders from the First Lord of the *Aquitaine* Fleet was extremely secret, Makara," Phil informed them. "Such that the number of people who know can be counted on both hands, including you and Samnang. I was tasked by the First Lord with certain operational parameters before we left, but the two of us had both been in contact with the man who was Jessica Keller's right hand, before he retired to take up a position as an advisor and something of an adopted uncle to Emperor Karl VIII of *Fribourg*."

"Your old squadron mate, Casey *zu* Weigand," Makara nodded.

Makara had asked Iveta for a history of the east that he could read to better understand, and had ended up with electronic copies of *Jessica Keller, Volumes One* and *Two*, written by the man who at some time had been her greatest enemy, and perhaps only peer, in the galaxy, Emmerich *zu* Wachturm. Before becoming a friend.

One of these days, Makara intended to find printed editions for his shelf. So that they were never lost. Perhaps find a way to get them signed by Wachturm as well. So much had Makara learned.

"Casey, yes," Phil said. "Denis Jež has a theory that changes to how the *Republic of Aquitaine* Navy operated, instituted twenty years ago by then First Lord Nils Kasum, would eventually—possibly—lead to a thing Denis called *Imperial Aquitaine*."

"Empires," Makara echoed the old conversations that had consumed so many bottles of wine by so many people over the last several months.

"Worse, one grown powerful with trade and technology far in advance of many of our neighbors," Phil nodded.

"Like Balhee," Makara replied.

"Exactly like Balhee," Phil nodded. "Or even *Zerzan*, because they are not our peers right now. *Yaumgan's* certainly, but not *Aquitaine's*. So far advanced that we would become an even greater threat to the galaxy than the *Zerzan Unification*, because we could come to combine that level of militant culture with better ships, able to conquer and even hold places like the *Unification*. We could do it now, but our culture lacks that aggressiveness."

"But your grandchildren?" Makara asked.

"That's the theory as Denis proposes it," Phil agreed. "Our grandchildren will be different people. So the First Lord sent me here with a secondary, ultra-secret mission, Makara. To ensure that the Balhee Cluster was strong enough, integrated enough to resist such potential aggression from the east. From an *Aquitaine* grown terrible and imperial in their foolishness. I had not expected my work to bear fruit so quickly, but I suppose that *Zerzan* can be seen thus as the thing that caused your crystallization. You will be squeezed between the two sides, but that is the natural outcome of being the largest single group of inhabitable stars between the two galactic arms. And you will be better prepared to hold your lines. In that, I have succeeded, but the rest of the Cluster must not be told. Instead, I would ask you to whisper certain things in the right ears occasionally, when fools introduce divisiveness that might allow east or west to spall off chunks of the Cluster for short-term gain."

"Should there be a Balhee Empire?" Makara asked, intrigued. "Already, you have three of the five nations primed to some level of aristocratic government that might make such a fusion easier."

"No," Phil shook his head. "*Yaumgan* was correct in overthrowing the *Monarchy* and replacing it with a society where meritocratic elements hold favor over the randomness of birth or wealth. *Aquitaine* has long had a tension between the old Fifty Families that helped found the *Republic* and everyone else. The aristocrats of blood and marriage are currently in disarray, perhaps for another generation, as Keller's legend continues to inspire us. But Empires and aristocracies are inherently conservative, in bad ways."

"Old Man Wen has mentioned his magic penis theory of governance," Samnang pointed out to general laughter.

"Just so," Phil agreed. "*Aditi* and *Yaumgan* have the better idea, plus what *Dalou* and *Gloran* bring to the table with their eyes always decades and generations out, but never losing sight of the current issues. You must build trade and expand to fill more worlds. *Urwel* is just the start, but what Kohahu and Kira are doing near *Vilahana* will be important and useful as well. They are teaching the people of the Cluster a better way to run a civilization. Without the piracy, people can build themselves up. Knowing that you have rivalries on both sides means that you have a reason to look beyond your own world or nation."

"Is war inevitable, Phil?" Samnang asked now, having previously largely only watched.

But she was at least as smart—as canny—as Makara was. Maybe in Phil's league.

"Until people learn to live with one another, I fear so," Phil replied, nodding to her. "In the end, we as a galactic civilization are still just beginning to flower, having emerged from the darkness that the ancient *Concordancy War* collapsed us all into. My dream—my job—is to make sure that we don't fall back. Your jobs are the same."

"Do you think it will be possible?" Makara asked.

"You are *Morninghawk*," Iveta spoke up suddenly, after having been silent for so long that he thought she had nothing to add. Of course, he would be wrong. "All things are possible."

EPILOGUE: KAUR SINGH
ADCON CRUISER ARANYANI

Kaur Singh looked forward to that next challenge. That long-promised promotion, finally, to Director, where she might be able to shape the future. Not just of the Consensus, but of the entire Balhee Cluster.

Who could have imagined what would happen, on that fateful day when Phil and Heather came out of Jump at *Vilahana*, looking for trade? More importantly, looking for friends.

The chime on her hatch announced a visitor, so she rose from her chair and opened it, grinning like a fiend at Sub-Commander Arya Chaudhari, shortly to be promoted to Commander of *Aranyani*, and Nam Nagarkar, no longer a mere Senior Officer, as her promotion to Sub-Commander had already come through. Past due, in Kaur's eyes, but she understood that many things had needed to wait until *Aranyani* returned to proper *Consensus* service, rather than being on a diplomatic mission to help Phil.

She gestured them in and sat them on the couch, while she took the chair.

"Not used to the old uniform?" she teased Nam as the woman tugged at things.

"*Aquitaine's* uniforms are a much tighter fit, but also stretchier," Nam shrugged.

"And they make your ass look nicer than ours do," Arya laughed.

Kaur watched the look of utter mortification come over the woman's face for a moment before she relaxed.

"There is that," Nam nodded.

"That was not, however, why I asked you two to join me tonight," Kaur chuckled.

"So what terrible thing will we be called upon to do next?" Arya laughed.

Kaur shared her smile.

"Hopefully, nothing more taxing than perhaps you sailing to *Ladaux* or someplace to show our flag, as they had done here," Kaur replied. "No, I wanted a chance to talk, one last time, before the ceremony tomorrow, when you get promoted in rank and given command of this ship, finally."

"Finally!" Arya grinned. "I had begun to wonder if I was going to have to ask for a transfer somewhere else if I ever wanted my own bridge."

"Is she always like this?" Nam asked. "I feel like I missed something when I was here, and you two sound more like Phil and Heather and the rest."

"There is something to that, Nam," Kaur agreed. "We have all changed, but I supposed your delta has been the greatest, because you have become, in many ways, one of them."

"Is that why I'm being transferred to the Command Staff on *Aditi*?" Nam pressed.

"Partly," Kaur nodded. "They will need your insights into *Aquitaine* from the inside. Partly, to make sure you haven't been utterly corrupted by the outsiders."

She paused there, as Arya was doubled over, howling with laughter.

"Okay, poor choice of vocabulary on my part," Kaur offered

once Arya got control again, which just set her off a second time. "Are you done?"

Arya pressed her lips together in a huge grin.

"Them, corrupting us," Arya laughed.

Kaur and Nam shared her smile. Kaur shrugged. They were in her suite. She could do that.

"We've always known that the *Consensus* tended to fall a hair short of their ideals," she said next, just to make both women laugh again. "However, Roshni Mishra is in charge now, and she won a historic landslide by promising to clean up the government and start actually enforcing all those laws we've passed over the last generation. Do not underestimate that woman. Phil warned me that she's playing a much deeper game than even he originally expected."

That sobered both of them right up.

"Phil said that?" Nam asked, a little frightened.

"He did indeed, Nam," Kaur nodded. "That she sees a way for her and her party to stay in power for a significant amount of time, based on being on Phil's good side from day one and throwing down the government they had allied themselves to when it became clear what we'd done at *Carinae II*. Thus, I intend to make sure she likes me. Both of you are hereby ordered to do the same. Okay?"

"Got it," Arya replied. "You think we can convince her to send us to *Ladaux*?"

"I expect you will need a good rest and refurb now that we're home," Kaur nodded. "And some time off for your crew, after the operational tempo I've held everyone at for so long. Even with breaks at *Meerut*, everyone will want to relax."

"Then what?" Arya asked, her eyes noticing something.

"I may not be assigned *Khandoba* specifically," Kaur grinned. "That's still up in the air because my mission with Phil was so open-ended."

"But?" Nam asked, relaxing herself. Again, Phil's influence. Or maybe Heather's.

"But when I do, obviously whichever Ship-of-the-Line I take command of will need a full echelon when it sails to *Aquitaine*. My goal is that one of my cruisers is *Aranyani*. Nam, you might make it a point to brain-dump everything you know as quickly as you can, in case they need to send some even-more-senior Directors with me. Or perhaps you can get yourself assigned to whatever Embassy Mishra finally assembles. I'd like both of you to be there with me, as you were at the beginning here."

"Is that the next adventure you wanted to warn me about?" Arya asked.

"Yes, but you also both need to make a point of getting on good terms with the *Gloran* and *Dalou* embassies," Kaur said, sobering herself. "Kira Zaman and Kohahu Kugosu will be people you have both met. Nam, you'll actually be able to say you trained with Kohahu. Considering what those two women are planning around *Vilahana*, I'd like to see how we can be on point when it comes time for *Aditi* to join them."

"You think they will?" Nam asked.

"That is your mission, newly promoted Sub-Commander," Kaur smiled. "Find out. And find out how both the *Consensus* and the three of us can get a share of that, because I think that will eventually be so much money that we can't imagine it right now. I'm happy being famous, but rich would be even nicer. And not just from giving speeches about *Aquitaine* when I retire."

"Understood, sir," she said.

Arya nodded as well.

"Is that all?" Arya asked.

"No," Kaur said.

Quickly, she retrieved a bottle and three glasses from deeper in her cabin, then poured.

"To the future," she toasted.

Both women smiled and joined her.

What would that future bring them?

EPILOGUE: HEATHER LAU

DATE OF THE REPUBLIC NOVEMBER 16, 412
RAN URUMCHI, VILAHANA ORBIT

Heather studied the standard plot as *Urumchi* came out of Jump. As was normal these days, the squadron came out long and high, instead of close into the edge of the gravity well like an attacking force.

"Everyone still with us?" she asked Leyla, glancing over to see what her Science Officer was up to now.

The woman loved her practical jokes.

"Everyone," Leyla grinned. "And then some. And some more."

Heather rolled her eyes.

The mission had technically been completed at *Aditi*, coming full circle from that first call for ships to go hunt pirates with. Everyone had returned for a grand, formal ceremony.

And then every damned one of them had announced that they were sailing to *Vilahana* with Phil.

One last mission, as it were.

At least she was back in black and green today, though that strawberry tunic haunted her from time to time, tucked in the back of her closet and vac-sealed against time and entropy.

Urumchi's mission—Heather's mission—was not complete. Not yet.

The plot started showing more ships than expected, even accounting for *Vilahana's* growth in trade over the last twenty-one months. And those stupid junkyards in space that used to be so valuable.

Before everyone realized that they could find better junk in *Aquitaine's* leftovers than most of these planets could build new.

Hopefully, this place wasn't about to turn into some bizarre cargo cult. More likely, folks would build cargo carriers, sail them to *Aquitaine*, then trade up for better ships to sail home. That would necessitate new factories making replacement parts, which required investment here.

Thus, Phil would establish the links that connected across the darkness to *Ladaux*.

"All friendly ships, this is Kosnett, aboard *Urumchi*," Phil's voice came over the main line now. "I have the flag. Heather, hail all those folks and confirm who I'm seeing, please?"

"Stand by," Heather said, nodding to Leyla to get off her ass.

Leyla just grinned and pushed a button on her console that made a low-pitched bell sound. Forward sensor array. On a Survey Dreadnought. Big scanners going *ping*.

"Confirmed," Leyla said unnecessarily. "*RAN Kongō* and *RAN Warspite*, plus sixteen of the old 400-series corvettes. We're being hailed. Lag is two and a half seconds."

"Greetings, *Urumchi*," Fleet Centurion Raizō Tanaka said as the line came live. "Welcome to *Vilahana*."

Heather snorted.

"A little late to the party, *Kongō*, but they can use you at *Kyulle*," she replied, waiting for the delay.

Tanaka was an old friend of Phil's, but Heather had only met Tanaka in passing a few times. Asian ethnotype, but different than hers. Her height, give or take. Smart as a whip, and another one of the First Lord's projects, along with Phil.

As was Heather Lau, she supposed.

"Those were our orders, but I have a little slippage built in to my schedule, and figured I'd miss you at *Aditi*," Tanaka nodded.

"Plus, I have mail and updates from Fleet Headquarters for you folks. Permission to come alongside?"

"You missed my birthday, buddy," Phil said in a laughing growl.

"I did remember a card," Tanaka laughed back. "Got a few folks to sign it before I left. And a few birthday presents that had been forwarded on to *Ladaux*. Pet figured you'd appreciate them."

"Permission granted," Heather said formally, just so those two would shut up.

Otherwise, she might be here all day.

She cut the line and turned to Iveta.

"You have the bridge," Heather said simply. "I'm going to keep those two from getting into trouble."

A lot of laughter followed her out the hatch.

<hr>

Heather stood next to Phil in the forward landing bay. Since the shuttle coming over was *RAN*, it would fit in here and could dock right up to the airlock without needing to pressurize the space. Faster.

The tiny craft docked and locked. Heather glanced around to see Dar at attention and Markus sitting in a corner reading, his backpack of supplies and goodies leaned against his foot.

The inner hatch of the airlock opened and Fleet Centurion Tanaka stood there, escorting a pair of sailors with a rolling pallet holding a big box.

Urumchi would lay in supplies here. Phil's people had negotiated a treaty with Governor Annen Patte, who had managed to survive all the changes to local society that resulted from no longer being a chop shop. The *RAN* even maintained a normal squadron of ships here as of about three months ago, more of the old 400-series boats used mostly for defending the orbital platform and being available in a pinch.

If Phil had really needed every single ship he could have laid his hands on to deal with *Zerzan*.

"Conference room or office?" Phil asked as Heather judged the two men.

Senior officers weren't supposed to hug, but the two had known each other for a long time, so Heather supposed decorum was less necessary.

"Most of this can wait," Tanaka said with a wave. "Things that I wanted to deliver personally, just so I could say hello. Since the war with *Zerzan* seems to be on hold, I didn't need to race over to *Kyulle* to bash heads. At least not without showing the flag here. And get whatever last minute briefings you thought I needed before I walked into that mess."

Heather grinned. Mess was the one word she would not have used, but Fleet Centurion Tanaka wouldn't understand what Phil had really accomplished. And her, she supposed she should add. At least if she was going to be honest.

"Conference room, then," Phil said, nodding to Dar.

They all traipsed across the hallway, while Markus peeled off to get the two sailors and their box moved.

Even Dar waited outside, leaving just the three of them.

Tanaka turned to smile at her.

"*Warlord of Yaumgan*, huh?" he asked. "How good are they?"

"They are us, right before Bedrov designed the Expeditionary ships," Heather replied. "And poised on that same fork in the road."

"Oh?" the man pressed.

"They've asked Heather if she wants to be their equivalent to First Lord of the Fleet, so she can help them integrate all the new tech we're likely to sell folks," Phil inserted.

Tanaka whistled.

"Gonna take it?" he asked in a much more interested voice.

If she did, she might become this man's superior in some ways. Especially if *Kongō* and *Warspite* were assigned to the *Kyulle* frontier as defenders.

"Going home right now," she replied evenly.

Tanaka nodded, taking the deflection for what it was worth.

"What should I be prepared for when I get there?" Tanaka asked, looking back and forth between her and Phil.

"At present, I think peace," Phil replied. "They originally attacked because they thought that they could overwhelm *Yaumgan* and conquer the place. And that nobody else would care because *Yaumgan* had always stayed back in their corner."

"But for you," Tanaka said.

"Heather and I might have caused a few changes around here," Phil nodded with a chuckle. "Not the least of which was everybody else sending ships. When you get there, Karl VIII has even sent the cruiser *Skuodas* to help out. Right now, they are at *Kyulle*, anchoring the defensive formation, but Captain Steinmann is easy to work with, as are the rest. I'm guessing that your job will be to stand around looking tough, while the Five Nations figure out how to become one larger place that can resist the *Zerzan Unification*. Meanwhile, the *Unification* is going to have to decide how badly it wants to fight us. Your 400s will be murder on their pulse torpedoes if they try, plus everyone is now building new ships with Type-1-Pulse mounts."

"Is that good, or bad?" Tanaka asked.

"You have a time window of risk, Fleet Centurion," Heather said.

"Call me Raizō," he said.

"Raizō," Heather nodded. "If *Zerzan* is serious and crazy, they need to launch and attack in the next three to five years, while nobody but Expeditionary ships can handle them. After that, they risk getting their asses handed to them because I suspect a lot of folks will build small escort frigates with good shields and a crap-load of short-range firepower, specifically to stand up to *aeromechia*. They can do that cheap and fast."

"So I need to hold the wall for a few years, while the others build new fleets?" Raizō asked.

"You and whoever replaces you," Phil agreed. "That's

basically my message to Pet when I get home. If we can do that, then everything I've tried to talk them into gets baked into the DNA of the Cluster itself. One big central council, however the nations themselves remain organized. Hopefully, one big fleet to defend against *Zerzan* and anybody else who wants to try to conquer this region. Peace."

"Can they do it?" the man asked.

"We've given them the opportunity, Raizō," Heather said. "They have to take it. All we have to do is hold the wall. That's on you after we leave. But there is someone you should talk to. And he's here, so Phil can introduce you to him and he can escort you back to *Kyulle* before he goes home."

"Won't that be out of his way, if he's not from *Yaumgan*?" the man asked, confused.

"He sees that sort of thing as his duty," Phil spoke up, already knowing who she was talking about.

"Really?" Raizō asked. "Who?"

"*Morninghawk*," Heather said with a smile.

She could leave it in his hands. They would be capable.

Heather rose at that point and nodded to both men.

"Remember, you are supposed to head out in less than two hours, Raizō," she said. "You were the one that told me to remind you, but I'll leave you two to chat for now, then ping you again."

"Thank you," he said. "Maybe I'll see you again at *Kyulle*."

"Maybe," Heather said ambivalently.

She exited, nodding to Dar as the hatch closed.

"Got an alarm set?" she asked.

"Already on it," Dar nodded back.

Heather headed to her cabin instead of returning to the bridge. She needed time to process, because Raizō Tanaka had asked a question, and Heather really didn't have an answer, though she felt like she should.

Warlord of *Yaumgan*? That sounded like a lot of peopling. A lot of work, around folks that didn't know her or understand her.

At the same time, it might be the greatest adventure ever, especially if she could convince that pirate Bedrov to get involved.

For now, however, she just wanted to go home.

EPILOGUE: PHIL KOSNETT, EXPLORER EXTRAORDINAIRE

DATE OF THE REPUBLIC NOVEMBER 17, 412
RAN URUMCHI, JUMPSPACE

Phil settled in his office. Ship time was late in the day. Markus had gotten him some decaf, then probably settled in the chair outside and was napping. And would ignore an order to turn in, at least while Phil was in his flag bridge office, rather than his quarters.

Raizō and *Kongō* were both behind him, no doubt arranging a meeting with Makara that would see the Heavy Escort *Morninghawk* again leading an *Aquitaine* flagship, though hopefully not into any sort of battle.

With any luck, the wars of the Balhee Cluster were done, at least for now. Later, it would be somebody else's fault. He'd done everything he could.

But Markus had opened the shipping crate Raizō had brought and put everything in here. A stack of cards from folks, with Raizō's on top, then Pet's.

Two boxes, both flat rectangles like a nice shirt might be packed in. He recognized his wife's handwriting on a card attached to the outside of one, so he set it to the side to look at the other.

Casey's handwriting, once he stopped and looked at it for a moment.

He opened the box and saw an envelope filled with printed pictures. Casey. Vo. All four kids, from five-year-old Jessica to little Tomas who would be two in February. Several others he knew, including Denis and Anna-Katherine. Emmerich Wachturm and Freya. Even Tomas Provst and his extended family.

He tore open the letter.

<hr>

"P*hil,*

For your birthday, I wanted to include reminders of all the good things that have come out of all the generations of war that had consumed Fribourg *and* Aquitaine. *Pictures of happy families, in case you ever forget why it was that you flew into the darkness to explore. I also employ exceptionally good spies, so I have heard about the events at* Ewinhome *and how you resolved them. Hopefully, your trips to* Derragon *and* Kyulle *will have been completed successfully by the time this letter finds you.*

Also, by now you should have met Captain Steinmann. At Em's insistence, I agreed to send a warship rather than a scout, but overruled him on anything like your force. As you have said in your letters, it will be better for everyone if their neighbors to the east are seen as friendly. IFV Skuodas *will place in your hands sufficient firepower to convince people to behave, while not overbalancing all the delicate things you have accomplished.*

When the First Lord is finally done with you, please consider this to be your formal invitation to travel to St. Legier, *where you can be celebrated as one of the great explorers of our age and tell everyone here about your adventures. I have several little ones who will be rapt to know, because they constantly badger anyone they can to talk about flying in space.*

Additionally, I am enclosing a new recording for you. The premier of a symphony I wrote in response to the many letters that you have sent. Thank you for thinking of me and recording such sights and memories. At some point, with your permission, I would like to include excerpts from them with the sheet music, so that future generations can see how things were, as well as how they will become.

Finally, thank you for being you. Only a handful of people will truly understand what that means, but you are one of them. Jessica will overshadow all of us, as she should, but it is our duty to live up to her standards in making the galaxy a better place. I am trapped here in imperial robes that limit my reach as much as they extend it, so I frequently have to cheer from the sidelines, rather than being in the heart of things on some flag bridge, which I miss.

You will go. You will do things. You will uphold her vision, as well as that of all those people who she has touched.

I look forward to hearing your adventures in person.

Your shipmate eternal,

Casey zu *Weigand*

Republic of Aquitaine *Navy, Retired.*"

Phil was glad that he was alone in his office, so that nobody was here to watch him cry. Pet had offered him the chance to be one of the greatest explorers of the age, and he had succeeded. That Casey understood just reinforced his view that what he'd done had been right.

That he was going to leave this galaxy better than he found it.

Phil took a moment and got control of his emotions.

The second package opened to reveal two pictures. His wife, daughter, and son. From the background, it had been taken on the back porch, overlooking those mountains he was looking forward to.

The second picture set him to crying even worse than Casey's letter.

It had been taken at night. From that same back porch, but

looking inwards this time to the breakfast nook attached to the kitchen. The house was dark in the background, with a single, lit candle sitting on the sill inside providing the only light.

Guiding him home.

READ MORE

To read more of my fiction, sign up for my newsletter. You'll also get a free book!

http://www.blazeward.com/newsletter/

ABOUT THE AUTHOR

Blaze Ward writes science fiction in the Alexandria Station universe (Jessica Keller, The Science Officer, The Story Road, etc.) as well as several other science fiction universes, such as Star Dragon, the Dominion, and more. He also writes odd bits of high fantasy with swords and orcs. In addition, he is the Editor and Publisher of *Boundary Shock Quarterly Magazine*. You can find out more at his website www.blazeward.com, as well as Facebook, Goodreads, and other places.

Blaze's works are available as ebooks, paper, and audio, and can be found at a variety of online vendors. His newsletter comes out regularly, and you can also follow his blog on his website. He really enjoys interacting with fans, and looks forward to any and all questions—even ones about his books!

Never miss a release!
If you'd like to be notified of new releases, sign up for my newsletter.

http://www.blazeward.com/newsletter/

Buy More!
Did you know that you can buy directly from my website?

https://www.blazeward.com/shop/

Connect with Blaze!

Web: www.blazeward.com
Boundary Shock Quarterly (BSQ):
https://www.boundaryshockquarterly.com/

ABOUT KNOTTED ROAD PRESS

Knotted Road Press fiction specializes in dynamic writing set in mysterious, exotic locations.

Knotted Road Press non–fiction publishes autobiographies, business books, cookbooks, and how–to books with unique voices.

Knotted Road Press creates DRM–free ebooks as well as high–quality print books for readers around the world.

With authors in a variety of genres including literary, poetry, mystery, fantasy, and science fiction, Knotted Road Press has something for everyone.

Knotted Road Press
www.KnottedRoadPress.com